Books by Mark Cheverton

The Gameknight999 Series
Invasion of the Overworld
Battle for the Nether
Confronting the Dragon

The Mystery of Herobrine Series: A Gameknight999 Adventure
Trouble in Zombie-town
The Jungle Temple Oracle
Last Stand on the Ocean Shore

Herobrine Reborn Series: A Gameknight999 Adventure
Saving Crafter
Destruction of the Overworld
Gameknight999 vs. Herobrine

Herobrine's Revenge Series: A Gameknight999 Adventure
The Phantom Virus
Overworld in Flames
System Overload

The Birth of Herobrine: A Gameknight999 Adventure
The Great Zombie Invasion
Attack of the Shadow-Crafters
Herobrine's War

The Mystery of Entity303: A Gameknight999 Adventure
Terrors of the Forest
Monsters in the Mist
Mission to the Moon

The Gameknight999 Box Set
The Gameknight999 vs. Herobrine Box Set
The Gameknight999 Adventures Through Time Box Set

The Rise of the Warlords: A Far Lands Adventure
Zombies Attack!
The Bones of Doom
Into the Spiders' Lair

Wither War: A Far Lands Adventure
The Wither King
The Withers Awaken
The Wither Invasion

THE WITHER INVASION

WITHER WAR BOOK THREE: A FAR LANDS ADVENTURE

AN UNOFFICIAL MINECRAFTER'S ADVENTURE

MARK CHEVERTON

SKY PONY PRESS
NEW YORK

Sky Pony Press books may be purchased in bulk at special discounts for sales promotion, corporate gifts, fund-raising, or educational purposes. Special editions can also be created to specifications. For details, contact the Special Sales Department, Sky Pony Press, 307 West 36th Street, 11th Floor, New York, NY 10018 or info@ skyhorsepublishing.com.

Sky Pony® is a registered trademark of Skyhorse Publishing, Inc.®, a Delaware corporation.

Visit our website at www.skyponypress.com.

10 9 8 7 6 5 4 3 2 1

Library of Congress Cataloging-in-Publication Data is available on file.

Cover design by Brian Peterson
Cover artwork by Vilandas Sukutis (www.veloscraft.com)
Technical consultant: Gameknight999

Print ISBN: 978-1-5107-3490-6
Ebook ISBN: 978-1-5107-3493-7

Printed in the United States of America

ACKNOWLEDGMENTS

As always, I must thank my family for their continued support of my obsessive writing habits. Without them listening to new ideas or reading chapters, these stories would likely never get finished.

I also want to thank the great people at Skyhorse Publishing. They've been incredibly supportive through this adventure, and I appreciate all the effort the different editors and sales people and marketing experts put into my books.

Lastly, I'd like to thank my agent, Holly Root. Without her, I'd have never made it here. Thanks, Holly!

NOTE FROM THE AUTHOR

Wow . . . this is my twenty-fourth novel. I can remember writing my first novel late at night and early in the mornings, thinking it wasn't gonna go anywhere, but I kept at it. Like Crafter is fond of saying, "If you give up, you guarantee the outcome."

I didn't give up, even after writing my first four novels, each of which were spectacular failures in their own way. But I learned a lot from those failures, and they helped me write *Invasion of the Overworld,* my first Minecraft-inspired novel. Now, after four years of tireless writing, look what I have to show for my efforts:

I could have never made it through all the agonizing late-night writing sessions over the years without all of you—the readers. When my writing was stinking up my computer, and I couldn't think of anything interesting to say, I'd turn to the many emails you've sent me over the years and read through them. I'd look at the countless stories I've received from you, all of which are posted on my website, www.markcheverton.com, and I'd marvel at your creativity. I enjoy reading your stories and am always amazed at the positive comments being posted on my site. I also love receiving email from all of you at MarkTheMinecraftAuthor@gmail.com, and I answer every one personally. This has become a great community of readers and writers, and I'm honored to be a part of it, so please keep sending me your emails and stories; they are the highlight of my day!

Be sure to also check out www.gameknight999.com. There are many new things coming to the Gameknight999 Minecraft server (ip: mc.gameknight999.com); maybe we can play a game of paintball together, or even try to battle the monsters in the Zombies Attack! RPG game.

I really hope you enjoy *The Wither Invasion.* I gave this story a lot of thought while I was crafting the Rise of the Warlords series as well as the other books in the Wither War series. I hope all the little hints put in the other books will come together and that you'll find a few unexpected twists at the end.

Keep reading, and watch out for creepers.

Mark Cheverton (Monkeypants_271)

You must never fear failure. Our failures have a way of shaping who we are and can be great, yet sometimes painful, teachers. If you shy away from challenges in your life, then you'll never truly know what you can do, and who you can become.

Accept your strengths, learn from your weaknesses, and refuse to give in just because things get difficult. Be the best *you* possible and you'll achieve great things!

CHAPTER 1

The dark wither's six eyes glared down at the monsters and villagers with vicious contempt, their willingness to live in peace offending every inch of his black, skeletal body. Krael, the wither king, was still furious about being bested by that pathetic boy-wizard, Watcher, who had stopped Krael's army from leaving this world so they could invade the Far Lands and exact some revenge on all the NPCs (non-playable characters) there.

"That idiotic wizard probably thinks he defeated us," Krael's left skull said, its voice scratchy and filled with perpetual rage.

The center and right skulls nodded.

"He will soon learn his mistake." Center glanced at the left, then right skulls, his eyes glowing with rage. All that skinny little wizard had done was delay his plans . . . but not stopped them. "But first we'll practice some tactics."

Kracl glanced at one of his nearby generals and nodded his three skulls. Moving silently, the thrcc squads of withers floated toward the cluster of wooden buildings, descending behind the boxy oak and birch trees that covered this section of Minecraft, hiding their approach.

His ground forces beneath him held their position; this was a test of his air force. The army's test would come soon enough.

"Come here, by my side, Kora." Krael glanced at his wife. "Let us watch our troops execute a three-pronged attack."

"Yes, husband." The wither floated to her husband and hovered next to him. "Will the villagers be able to see us?"

Krael shook his skulls. "The moon has not risen yet. Our black bodies will blend in with the night sky and—" He stopped speaking as the attack commenced.

One group of withers moved into the village from the east, launching flaming skulls at the pathetic NPCs and monsters, their detonations punctuating the silent night like rapid-fire thunder. The NPCs quickly pulled out bows and opened fire, shooting at the dark creatures. As instructed, the withers fell back as if startled by their resistance, allowing their enemies to move forward, confident of their victory.

But then another group of withers advanced from the west, these monsters hovering high in the air, using their presence to terrify those below. When the NPCs and monsters on the ground saw the new group of withers, they clustered together in a small group, standing back to back, ready to fight in both directions. The two groups of floating terrors slowly moved around their enemy, coming together south of the village, all eyes focused on them. The monsters and NPCs never saw the third squad of withers sneaking up behind them from the north. When the withers from the north attacked, so did the rest of the flying monsters; they bombarded the group of pathetic NPCs and traitorous monsters, each wither sending their flaming skulls down at the creatures. A massive explosion occurred in the middle of the village, carving a deep crater where the NPCs and monsters had stood, sending up a huge cloud of smoke and ash and debris. When the air finally cleared, none were left standing, only glowing balls of XP (experience points) and items from their inventory littering the ground, marking their graves.

"Well done!" Krael shouted. "Destroy the rest of the village in case any are hiding in the buildings. Leave nothing standing."

The floating monsters bombarded the village, crushing homes and buildings until only smoking ruins remained.

"They did well?" Kora asked.

"They followed the battle plan exactly as I instructed." Krael smiled. "That will be the tactic we use on that annoying boy-wizard and his friends. We'll lure them out, distract them with a second group, then smash them from both sides, as if they were in a vise; it'll be glorious." Krael laughed with vicious glee. "The wizards during the Great War, centuries ago, tried to exterminate us, but they failed. This time, we won't give the NPCs the same opportunity; the villagers, led by that runt, Watcher, will never get the opportunity to raise an army and try to destroy us again. We'll squash them all, then destroy the Far Lands, just for good measure. Destroying all villagers is the only way to guarantee our safety."

"But husband, how will we leave this world and get back to the Far Lands?" Kora sounded confused. "That scrawny wizard, Watcher, destroyed the portal that would have allowed us to leave. We're stuck here."

Krael gave his wife a knowing smile. "While all of you were imprisoned in the Cave of Slumber, I read many books and learned the secrets the arrogant wizards tried to hide. Their egotism caused them to write much of what they did in books, explaining their tricks and traps for future generations, hoping for fame." Krael smiled with pride. "But I found their books and read their secrets."

He laughed. "The great wizard, Tharus, the most powerful of wizards, didn't trust his companions. He wanted a way to escape from this world in case the monster armies came looking for him, so he built his own portal leading to the Far Lands and hid it somewhere in Wizard City. We'll find that portal and use it to sneak into the Far Lands, and once we're there, we'll hunt the boy-wizard and destroy him. After Watcher's destruction, the Far Lands will be ours, and all the villagers will be our prey."

Many of the withers shouted with excitement, some launching flaming skulls into the air.

"Follow me, brothers and sisters. We head to Wizard City, to fulfill our destiny!"

Krael smiled at his wife, then floated off to the west, a huge army of withers in the sky behind him and an even larger army of distorted and disfigured monsters on the ground. The creatures glanced up at the wither king and growled excitedly, then followed, moving quickly across the landscape.

Scanning the skies and glancing down at the ground, Krael smiled with pride at the size of his army. "Those pathetic idiots in the Far Lands will cower in fear when they see my army, then beg for mercy . . . but they'll receive none."

"Good!" Left added, his voice scratchy and filled with anger, as always.

"We must be cautious," Right warned, her lyrical voice soothing Left's rage a bit. "There is more than one wizard for us to face. Watcher is one, but there are the girl and the old woman as well."

"I agree, my husband," Kora added.

"Have no fear, Right." The center skull's voice boomed with confidence. "By the time we reach the Far Lands, we'll have even more monsters in our army. I also have a little surprise to add to our air force; something I read about many years ago." He glanced at the magical crowns glowing on Left and Right's skulls. Center wore one as well. "Once we are in the Far Lands, the Crowns of Skulls on our three heads will give us more power than anyone has ever seen. With that and my little surprise, those three wizards won't stand a chance."

Left and Right both laughed with Center as Kora smiled at her husband, pride filling her eyes.

"Let's get moving!" Krael shouted at the monsters around him. "The last one to Wizard City will be destroyed!"

Hearing this, the monsters on the ground and in the air all moved as fast as they could, each knowing Krael, the king of the withers, would make good on that promise.

"I'm looking forward to seeing Watcher again . . . we have a debt to settle." Krael glared at the distant horizon as he sped toward their goal: Wizard City.

CHAPTER 2

Watcher moved through the eerily quiet forest, expecting zombies with skeleton heads or spider-slimes or any possible mishmash of horrific monster body parts to come charging out from behind the trees. They'd all just narrowly escaped a Minecraft world filled with distorted creatures of every kind, trapping the wither king and his army of withers there. Krael had been leading an army of the terrifyingly misshapen monsters, each as unnatural and twisted as the world itself, with the goal of destroying the Far Lands, but Watcher and his friends had stopped them.

The iridescent purple glow from the magical power coursing through his veins wrapped around his body and lit the shadows with a lavender hue. Watcher glanced over his glowing shoulder toward his former girlfriend, Planter, and the ancient wizard Mirthrandos. Both gave off a similar glow, for both had magic just like Watcher, but Mirthrandos was the strongest. The old woman had more power and experience with magic than either Watcher or Planter.

"Woof!"

Watcher glanced down. Next to him loped a wolf made of iron, a tiny mechanical creature no bigger than an NPC (non-playable character) child, known as a mechite, riding on the animal's silver-furred back.

"Fixit . . . you okay?" Watcher reached down and stroked the mechite's soft silver hair.

Fixit glanced up and smiled, then made a series of whistles and squeaks; it was how the mechanical creature communicated.

"Fixit says it is nice to be in a normal forest without any scars from the Great War marring the landscape."

Watcher turned and found the zombie, Er-Lan, walking on his left.

"You can understand him?" Watcher asked.

Er-Lan nodded. "Apparently." The zombie glanced around to see if anyone else was listening. "Er-Lan is sometimes able to communicate with animals. The mechite's sounds are like words to this zombie."

"Words?" a sarcastic voice said from behind. "It just sounded like a bunch of squeaks and chirps."

Watcher turned to the voice and found Blaster a step behind the zombie, Fencer following close behind him, as usual. Blaster glanced at the girl, causing a joyous smile to spread across her square face. Since Blaster had saved her from a zombie attack, Fencer's infatuation toward him had only grown. Previously, Watcher had been the target of Fencer's amorous attention, with Blaster enjoying his discomfort. Now, the tables had turned. Blaster hated it . . . and Watcher found it amusing.

"Animals speak in many different ways," the zombie explained. "The tone of the wolves' howls tells what is being said, the whistles and tones from the mechites are their words, even the iron and obsidian golems have something to say."

"How can you know what the golems are saying?" Blaster pulled his forest-green leather helmet off his head and ran his fingers through his dark curls. "They don't ever speak or even make any noise."

"The golems use facial expressions to communicate." Er-Lan turned and pointed to one of the metal giants. "The scowl on that golem with the unibrow raised on one side says he's tired of getting hit in the face by tree branches."

Blaster laughed. "That happens when you're so much taller than any villager. But if it's a problem for the golems, I have a solution in mind."

"Does it involve blowing things up?" Watcher asked with a smile, knowing how Blaster's "solutions" tended to go.

Blaster shook his head, grinning. "No, not this time." He glanced back to the zombie. "If the golems would be willing to hold an NPC in their hands, we could knock down some of the branches, making it easier for them to move through the biome. You think you could tell the golems that?"

Instantly, the scowl on the iron golem's face changed to a smile.

"Wow, that was fast." Blaster reached into his inventory and pulled out an iron axe. "How did you tell them so quickly?"

"The golems can hear, of course." Er-Lan sounded as if it was an obvious fact.

One of the metal giants reached down toward Blaster, extending his massive iron hand. Carefully, Blaster grabbed the creature's wrist and was lifted into the air.

"Fencer, pull your axe out and help," Blaster shouted.

The girl smiled and held an axe high over her head. An obsidian golem moved to her side and let her climb into its dark, stony hand, then raised her up so she could chop down the low-hanging branches. Other NPCs held axes above their heads, too, offering their service to the massive creatures.

Er-Lan put a hand on Watcher's shoulder. "Does Watcher still have the wizard's cape?"

Watcher nodded. "Yes, I do. Thank you for making sure I had it; that cape saved my life. Without it, I'm sure my Elytra wings would have snapped off after I fell from Krael's shoulders. I couldn't have survived that fall. You were right about me needing it."

"The need is not over." Er-Lan sounded serious.

Watcher pulled out the dark purple cape, its ornate gold stitching sparkling in the sunlight. "How can you tell?"

The zombie shrugged. "Er-Lan does not know; it is just a feeling, like visions of the future."

"Did you have a vision about Tharus's Cape?"

Er-Lan shook his green head. "No, just a feeling, but a strong one. Watcher must be careful with that cape and keep it safe, or . . ."

"Or what?"

"It is uncertain, but likely it would be bad if it were to become lost."

Watcher glanced down at the cloak and nodded, then stuffed it back into his inventory.

"It's good to see the golems bonding to the villagers," a scratchy voice said from behind. "They aren't used to being around other NPCs."

Watcher slowed his pace, allowing the golems to move to the head of the formation, then picked up the pace when he was near Planter and Mirthrandos.

Planter's mysterious midnight-blue armor sparkled with enchanted powers, tiny red embers dancing across its surface as if it were heated from within. She reached up and tugged at the helmet, hoping to pull it off, but she couldn't. In fact, since magically clamping around her body, the armor had remained stuck. Planter had tried many times to remove the glistening shell, but she'd been unsuccessful; it seemed unwilling to release the young girl, and that just added to Planter's hatred of magic.

"Weren't there villagers in Wizard City during the Great War between the NPC wizards and the monster warlocks?" Planter ran a finger under her helmet to scratch an annoying itch.

"Of course there were," the ancient wizard said. "But I made the golems after everyone had abandoned Wizard City."

"That must have been lonely for the golems, Mirthrandos." Watcher glanced at the old woman, a purple glow coiling around her body like an iridescent snake.

"You know, since I joined your little war here and let you borrow my wolves, mechites, and golems, you've all been so formal with me. The least you can do is relax a bit; call me Mira instead of Mirthrandos. I always feel like I'm in trouble whenever someone uses my full name."

Watcher glanced at Planter. They both smiled and nodded their heads.

"Okay then, Mira," Watcher said. "Are you planning on living with us? You, your wolves, mechites, and golems would be welcome."

Planter nodded. "That's right. We certainly have room in the Wizard's Tower for everyone. Our village is built within that ancient structure, to avoid being seen by any of the monster warlords, if there are any left out there."

"Yeah, we destroyed the skeleton, zombie, and spider warlords; who knows if there are more." Watcher scowled slightly. "The last thing we want to do is have more battles with monsters. It's better if they leave us alone and we leave them alone."

"That's always a good theory, Watcher." Mira gave him a faint nod. "But I've learned that keeping your eyes shut so you don't see bad things doesn't mean the bad things aren't coming."

"That's true," Watcher said. "But we aren't gonna go out looking for them. We figured staying hidden was a better choice."

Mira shrugged. "Perhaps." She closed her eyes as if reliving some distant memory. "I haven't been to the Wizard's Tower for many centuries."

"When was the last time you were there?" Planter asked.

The ancient wizard laughed. "The last time I was in the Wizard's Tower, our *great* leader, Tharus, punished me for helping out that wither back during the Great War, hundreds of years ago."

"You mean when he made it so you wouldn't age anymore?" someone said. Mapper moved to the old woman's side, his bald head reflecting the light from the high sun overhead, making his head and the ring of gray hair along its edges seem to glow.

"That's right, Mapper." Mira nodded. "Tharus used the magic woven into the Wizard's Tower to amplify his power. That let him cast the spell that sentenced me to this terrible eternal life." She grew quiet. "I swore I'd never care about anyone ever again. Watching all my loved ones grow old and die was heartbreaking."

"Then why did you help us?" Planter asked.

"Well, Fixit thought you were worth it." Mira reached out and ran her fingers through the tiny mechite's silver hair. The wolf on which Fixit rode gave her a playful bark. "I learned long ago that Fixit was a good judge of character, so if he thought you were worth helping, then who was I to disagree?"

Watcher smiled. "I'm glad you didn't disagree. Without your help, I don't think we would have been able to keep Krael and his army of monsters from flooding into the Far Lands and destroying everything."

"And though the Far Lands is millions of blocks from the center of the Overworld," Mapper added, "I think the wither king would have tried to destroy the rest of this world as well."

"No doubt." Mira nodded, her long gray hair swaying back and forth.

"You think we've seen the last of Krael?" Planter asked.

Mira shrugged. Watcher noticed a strange expression on the ancient wizard's face. *Is she hiding something from us?* he wondered.

Wizards always have secrets, a deep voice, not his own, echoed in Watcher's mind.

He reached into his inventory and pulled out the

Flail of Regrets. With a leather-wrapped wooden handle, length of stout chain, and a large spiked-ball at the end glowing with magical power, the Flail was a vicious weapon in battle. It was originally from the days of the Great War, centuries ago.

Like many of the weapons in his arsenal, this one had the mind of an ancient wizard within it. At the end of the Great War, the NPC wizards put their minds and power into weapons like the Flail, making it possible for a warrior without magical power to wield them and take advantage of the enchantments each held. The wizard trapped inside the Flail of Regrets was named Baltheron, and Watcher had learned to heed his advice.

What are you saying? Is Mira lying? Watcher was confused.

She isn't lying, but Mirthrandos certainly has secrets of her own. Be cautious. And then the deep voice in Watcher's mind grew silent.

"Are you planning on doing something with that flail?" Planter's brow creased with concern.

Watcher shook his head. He had two other weapons with wizards' minds trapped within them: his sword, Needle, and the Gauntlets of Life, one of which was clasped around each wrist. Planter, too, had such artifacts: her magical shield had likely saved their lives many times, though she hated using it. She also wore armor colored a deep blue, as if it had been made from rare lapis gems, with magical red embers sparkling at its edges. No wizard lived within the deep blue armor plates, as far as they knew, but they clearly had strong enchantments wrapped into their smooth surfaces.

"Are you listening to me?" Planter's face changed from concerned to annoyed.

"Ahh . . . sorry, I was just thinking." Watcher put the Flail of Regrets back into his inventory.

"Were you talking to that thing again?"

Watcher shrugged. He knew she hated all this magic and just wanted it to go away.

"No, I was thinking about Krael. I hope we don't ever see that monster again." Watcher felt bad about lying, but in this case, with Planter, it was better to lie; she didn't trust anything having to do with magic.

"I can see my spruce tree," Blaster shouted from atop the lead golem. "We're almost home."

"Spruce tree?" Mapper was clearly confused. "Why would there be a spruce tree in an oak and birch forest? Spruces are only found in Taiga biomes and—"

"That's the point, Mapper." Watcher nodded. "Blaster planted a spruce tree on the edge of a trail marking the path leading to the Wizard's Tower. With it being a spruce tree, it would stand out without being obvious."

"With the Wizard's Tower sunken into the ground, it's hard to find," Planter explained.

"Yes, of course." Mira glanced at Planter, then back to the ground.

"Do you know something about that, Mira?" Watcher moved a step closer to the ancient wizard. "How did the Tower sink into a huge hole?"

The ancient wizard shrugged. "Ahh . . . I don't know, sorry." Mira's words were rapid and rushed, as if she wanted the topic to end as quickly as possible.

Wizards always have secrets, indeed, Watcher thought, but he received no answer from Baltheron, Dalgaroth, or Taerian; none of the wizards inhabiting his weapons spoke up, but he sensed they knew something as well.

Watcher was about to ask Mira a more direct question when Blaster yelled again.

"I can see the Tower. Come on, everyone, let's get home. I need a rest, and I think my iron friend here needs one too." Blaster laughed as he patted the mega-giant on the arm, then chopped down another branch with his axe. As he did so, he lost his balance and nearly fell, but the golem reached out with his other hand and steadied the boy. Nearby, Fencer laughed at him as she chopped at a clump of branches.

"Come on, Planter. I think it best the first thing our friends see is us." Watcher cast her a smile. "An army of iron golems bearing down on them might cause a bit of panic."

"I think you're right," she replied. "Let's run."

Sprinting around trees and shrubs, Planter dashed ahead of the company, leaving Watcher three steps behind. Fixit squeaked excitedly as his wolf dashed forward, easily keeping pace with them, the metallic animal howling with joy.

CHAPTER 3

The forest suddenly opened onto an unnatural circular clearing, a huge, jagged hole torn into its grassy surface. Out of the massive hole protruded a cylindrical tower made of stone bricks and dark red nether bricks. Stained glass of various colors adorned the sides, allowing the afternoon rays to penetrate the structure, lighting it with colorful hues. The top of the tower, standing at a height that was just below the tops of the nearby trees, was covered by pristine white blocks of quartz with dark cubes of obsidian weaving geometric shapes across the roof.

Watcher moved to the edge of the gigantic hole and peered into its shadowy depths. Farther below, the tower connected to a gigantic palace-like structure entirely buried underground. Watcher knew the ancient construction stretched out in all directions, with passages and tunnels leading to more buildings, all of which were still buried beneath the forest.

This was the Wizard's Tower, built hundreds of years ago, before the Great War, and now home to Watcher and his friends.

Moving to the edge of the cavernous opening, Watcher stared down into the hole, always amazed at the building's construction. The tower itself was thirty to forty blocks high, but was barely visible within the oak forest since, at some point in the distant past, the tower and all the many structures connected to it fell into the massive hole here. Watcher figured the monster warlocks were responsible for this, but who knew? Maybe he could get Mira to tell him what had happened.

The sight of the Tower, their home, made Watcher smile. He glanced at Planter. "I have a feeling today's gonna be a good day."

She smiled. "It's good to be home." Planter stepped to the edge of the hole and stared down.

A wolf's howl pierced the afternoon air, followed by another and another.

"They can feel the magic woven into the Tower," Mirthrandos said. "I can feel it, too." She glanced at Watcher. "It reminds us all of Wizard City . . . of home."

Watcher nodded. "I know you gave up a lot to help us with Krael and his army of withers. We are forever grateful to you and your metallic friends."

He turned and gazed at the huge iron golems and the darker obsidian golems blending into the shadows of the forest. They stood at the edge of the clearing, some of them glancing at the forest, as if expecting to be attacked. The iron wolves spread out along the edge of the huge hole with the mechites still riding on their backs, each of the small metallic creatures holding on to the wolves' thick silver fur as they all gazed at the tower, the animals' tails wagging excitedly.

Fixit glanced at Watcher, then turned and whispered a series of squeaks into his wolf's ear. The animal nodded, then barked and howled. Instantly, a group of wolves with their mechite riders spread out, forming a large circle around the tower, then slowly moved under the trees, disappearing into the shadows. The golems, seeing the wolves go, moved deeper into the forest, their thunderous footsteps shaking the ground.

Suddenly, an NPC climbed out of the top of the tower,

his gray hair shining in the late afternoon sunlight. He wore a long white smock, the gray stripe running down the front matching his hair.

"Son, you're home, finally!" Cleric said. "I notice the terrible wither king isn't with you. Have we seen the last of him?"

Watcher smiled and nodded. "Yep, he won't be bothering us anymore."

"Great." Cleric gave his son a huge smile. "Come on in and let's talk." He pointed at the wolves, mechites, and golems. "Your friends are, of course, welcome in our village."

Before Watcher could respond, Cleric disappeared down the ladder that led to the top of the Wizard's Tower.

Squeak, squawk, hmmm came Fixit's tiny voice from beside Watcher.

Watcher turned toward Fixit, then glanced at Er-Lan.

"Fixit said, 'he looked like a nice villager.'" Er-Lan nodded, then looked down at Fixit. "The mechite is correct. Cleric is nice and wise . . . a true friend."

"Come on, everyone, let's go home." Watcher followed Planter into the hole.

They moved down a trail marked with redstone torches placed there by Blaster many years ago. Jumping from block to block, the villagers descended along the steep walls. The wolves with their mechite riders had no trouble keeping up, but the golems remained on guard duty in the forest . . . just in case.

Watcher followed Planter along the trail, her beautiful blond hair swinging back and forth from under her cerulean-blue helmet. He wanted to reach out and touch the golden strands, but he knew that wasn't their relationship anymore. Planter was still furious at Watcher; he'd forced her to use her magic with the enchanted shield in her inventory too many times, causing her to sever their relationship. Her angry words still echoed in the back of his mind: *"You and me . . . we're done. I can't trust you when all you care about is magic and power."*

A great sense of emptiness now consumed Watcher's soul.

Suddenly, a villager stepped out onto the roof of the underground structure that was still far below him, their body masked by shadows. Watcher glanced down from the trail at the person, unsure who they were, but as they stepped into the sunlight, her long brown hair and bright blue eyes instantly identified her; it was Winger, his sister.

"I hope you didn't break the Elytra wings I gave you when you left, brother." Winger smiled.

"Well . . . they were a little banged up, but that Mending enchantment you put on them helped out a lot." Watcher pulled them out of his inventory and quickly put them on, then ran toward the edge of the trail and jumped into the air. The wings snapped open and floated on the gentle air currents flowing through the gigantic hole. He turned in a smooth arc, smiling at Planter as he flew by; she gave him an angry scowl. Turning to the right, he descended, picking up speed, then pulled up at the last minute to slow himself as he gracefully landed next to Winger, who was smiling with pride.

"Here you go, sis." Watcher removed the wings and handed them back to her. "If I hadn't had these Elytra, I probably wouldn't be standing here right now."

She took the wings, then reached out and hugged him.

Watcher stood there for a moment, and, for the first time in a long time, he finally relaxed. "It's good to be home."

"I'm glad you're back, and everyone is safe."

Watcher released the hug and stepped back. "Not everyone." He gritted his teeth, trying to control his emotions. "Some of our friends didn't make the return trip."

"You mean they . . ."

Watcher nodded. "Krael and those ancient zombie warriors got many of them."

Planter jumped off the end of the path and landed on the colorful roof next to Winger.

"We saved a lot of people, but not everyone." Planter hugged Winger. "Everyone did their best, but some sacrifices were made." She grew quiet for a moment, then stepped away.

"You need to tell us all about it," Winger said. "But first, I have one question."

"What?" Watcher and Planter said at the same time.

Just then, an iron wolf stepped off the path and moved to Planter's side. Fixit, riding on the animal's back, looked up at Planter and smiled, giving off a series of squeaks and whistles.

"Did you meet anyone interesting or different?" Winger glanced down at the metallic animal and its rider, then looked up at an obsidian golem standing guard at the edge of the huge pit.

Planter glanced at Watcher, then smiled. "I don't think we met anyone interesting or different. What do you think, Watcher?"

"Nope, nothing unusual at all."

Mira stepped off the path and moved onto the roof of the structure, her metal-tipped staff clicking on the ancient structure with every step. She knelt and moved her hand across the surface of the Wizard's Tower as if she were caressing an old friend.

"Nothing out of the ordinary, huh? I see." Winger laughed. "Come on, the entire village has assembled below. They're anxious to hear if an army of withers is about to show up and destroy everything."

Watcher stood next to his sister on the roof of the ancient structure they called *home* with Planter and Mira on either side. The rest of the NPCs and the huge pack of wolves descended the steep staircase, each mechite smiling up at him as they passed. When the last had moved down the long staircase that penetrated the roof, Watcher sighed. "It's good to be home and safe again." He glanced over his shoulder at Planter. "I hope this is gonna be a really great day."

Watcher smiled and moved down the steps, but

suddenly stopped as a faint evil laugh echoed in the back of his mind. It wasn't laughter of joy or contentment; rather, the vile chuckle hurt, like a rusty nail poking him in the back of his head.

Baltheron, Taerian, Dalgaroth, is that one of you laughing? Watcher thought, sending his words to the enchanted weapons in his inventory.

The minds of the wizards trapped in the three ancient artifacts remained silent for a long minute, then replied with only a single word . . . but it made no sense. Watcher wanted to ask them again, but knew they would say no more; they told him only what he needed to know for now.

The three wizards had said in unison: *Danger.*

"So much for it being a great day." With chills running down his spine, Watcher continued down the steps toward his friends and home.

Watcher emerged from the long brick staircase to cheers and applause. The entire community was gathered at the foot of the stairs, many of them banging weapons against their chest plates or shields. Someone was shooting fireworks up into the air, the tiny rockets exploding against the high ceiling, showering everyone with sparkling colors. With a smile on his square face, Watcher jumped off the stairs as the village's celebration enveloped him with shouts and greetings and pats on the back.

The children gathered excitedly around the wolves and mechites, the animals licking their young faces as the mechites stood nose to nose with the kids, looks of astonishment on their metal faces; it was the first time any of the metal creatures had ever seen an NPC their size.

"Welcome home, friends." Cleric's voice boomed throughout the building, his words echoing off the cold brick walls. "We worried about your safety for many weeks. Your return has lightened many hearts." The old man moved to Watcher and just stared at him with his warm brown eyes. Reaching out, he pulled Watcher into an embrace and squeezed him tight. "I thought I'd lost you son," he whispered.

"Not yet." Watcher wiped tears from his eyes, some of them landing on his father's always-clean white smock.

Cleric glanced at Planter, admiring her sparkling blue armor for a moment, then reached out and pulled her into his embrace, too. When she hesitantly pulled back from the old man, Cleric glanced at Watcher, then back at Planter, confusion on his wrinkled face.

"That's a story for another time, Dad." Watcher wiped another tear from his cheek, but this one was there for another reason—for Planter.

Cleric nodded, then released his son and turned toward the old woman wearing the flowing burgundy smock, gold stitching along the hems, sleeves, and back.

"Who's your friend?" he asked.

"Oh, yeah." Watcher pulled his enchanted sword, Needle, from his inventory and banged it on his cracked-and-dented diamond armor, getting everyone's attention. Putting it back, he pulled out a block of dirt and placed it on the ground, then stood on top. "Everyone, quiet down." Watcher held his hands up in the air.

"Be quiet!" Cutter's thunderous voice instantly brought the room under control; everyone in the village had learned to do what the big warrior said. He never backed down.

"Thanks, Cutter." Watcher gave him a nod. "I'm sure you've all noticed we brought a few new friends."

"A few?" someone said. "It looks like you brought an army with you."

"Yeah," someone else added, "a metal army."

Watcher smiled and nodded. "Yes, we have many iron wolves here."

One of the wolves howled, causing the rest to add their voices. Many of the villagers laughed as Watcher tried to get the metallic animals under control.

"The small metal creatures who were riding on the wolves' backs are called mechites." Watcher glanced around at the crowd. "Where's Fixit?"

A quiet squeak drifted up from the crowd. Fencer

bent over and lifted the tiny creature, placing him on her shoulder.

"There he is." Watcher pointed at his new friend. "That's Fixit. He and all his friends helped us stop Krael and his army of withers. Also, we brought with us a wizard from the Great War." Watcher pointed. "This is Mirthrandos, and we wouldn't have survived if it weren't for her."

The NPCs clapped and cheered.

"She and the mechites and wolves are gonna be living with us now," Watcher said.

"Anyone have a problem with that?" Cutter's voice issued a challenge none dared take.

"Good, then we can—"

"Don't forget about the golems," Mira chimed in.

"That's right." Watcher nodded. "Mira also brought with her an army of iron and obsidian golems. They're up top, in the forest right now. We'll need to figure out a way for them to get down here that's a little easier than the redstone trail."

"I'm on it," Blaster said.

"I'll help you." Fencer smiled and moved to the boy's side.

Blaster grimaced while Watcher smiled.

Suddenly that strange, evil chill Watcher had felt at the top of the stairs spread across his body again. Instinctively, he gathered his magic, as if expecting some kind of attack; the iridescent glow coming from his body grew brighter, casting a purple hue on the surroundings. Instantly, the NPCs stepped back, all of them still afraid of his magical powers. He glanced at Planter and Mira; their magic was glowing as well.

Caution . . . something's happening, a deep voice echoed in his head.

Watcher instantly recognized the voice. "Baltheron, what is it?" He reached into his inventory and pulled out the Flail of Regrets; the leather-wrapped handle fit perfectly in his palm, as if the magical weapon had been made just for him.

"Son, is everything okay?" Cleric asked.

Watcher raised his hand, silencing both his father and many other questions being lobbed his way. Turning, Watcher glanced at Mirthrandos.

"Did you hear that?"

Mira and Planter both nodded.

"What's going on?" Watcher asked.

"We need to go to the Viewing Chamber." Mirthrandos pointed to a group of wolves and tapped the ground with her bent-and-crooked staff. Four of the creatures barked once, then filed in next to her as she pushed through the crowd. She glanced over her shoulder. "You two coming?"

"Ahh . . . yeah, sure," Watcher said, then glanced at Planter.

She nodded and followed the ancient wizard, Watcher right behind.

Footsteps echoed behind them, making a scratching sound with every step; Watcher turned and found Er-Lan following, an expression of concern on the zombie's face. Next to him ran Fixit, the mechite's little feet a silver blur.

"Er-Lan will keep Watcher safe in these passages," the zombie said.

Squeak, squeak, squawk, Fixit added.

"Ok, come on." Watcher ran after Planter and Mirthrandos.

The ancient wizard darted through the tunnels as if she still knew exactly where she was going, though she hadn't been here for a couple of hundred years.

"Where are you taking us, Mira?" Planter asked.

"Something's happened. Watcher's weapons felt it through the layer of magic that sits atop the Pyramid of Servers. Some event must have disturbed that layer; we need to go to the Viewing Chamber and see what's going on."

"Viewing Chamber?" Planter sounded confused. "What's that?"

"We never heard of the Viewing Chamber," Watcher explained.

"Wow . . . for a couple of wizards, you sure don't know very much." Mira glanced over her shoulder and smiled at her companions, then turned left at the next intersection. "The Viewing Chamber is a place where it's possible to see into the other planes of existence. I bet, if something strange has happened, the wither king is responsible, so we should look."

She skidded to a stop before a blank wall.

"Here it is." Mira tapped her staff on the floor, the various bands of metal wrapped around the magical weapon reflecting the scant few rays of light from a distant torch.

"We've been here a hundred times." Watcher moved to the wizard's side. "There's nothing here . . . it's just a stone wall."

Mira shook her head disapprovingly, then pulled out a torch. Instantly, the stone wall was bathed in light, the rays reflecting off the smooth surface and lighting the adjacent wall. "What do you see now?"

"It just looks like stone to me," Planter said.

Mira shook her head again. "Slide your hand across it and tell me what you feel."

Planter glanced at Watcher, confused. He shrugged and motioned to the wall.

"Go ahead, do what she says," Watcher said.

Planter reached out with a glowing hand and slid it across the surface, her eyes growing wide with surprise. "It's smooth."

"Of course it's smooth. This wall was constructed from polished andesite; that's not natural." Mira smiled, then put a hand on Planter's shoulder. "Use your magic and extend it into the wall."

Planter shook her head and stepped away from the wall, an angry scowl covering her face.

"You don't have to do it, Planter, I will." Watcher moved to her side and put a reassuring hand on her arm.

Instantly, she shrugged it off and moved back another step.

With a sigh, Watcher concentrated on his magic, then extended it into the wall. Instantly, he could sense other enchantments hidden within the stony surface; spells of protection, spells of concealment and . . . he found the trigger and pushed it with his magic. There was a click, followed by the sound of stone sliding against stone. A doorway opened in the wall before them.

"Well done, Watcher." Mira tapped her staff on the ground. "I might make a wizard out of you yet." She glanced at Planter, brows furrowed, then spotted Er-Lan and Fixit and smiled. "All of you, follow me."

She walked into the dark passage, the purple glow from her body lighting the way. Watcher paused for a moment, waiting for Planter, but she didn't move.

"Planter?"

She just shook her head.

"You can't run away from what you are." Watcher tried to keep his voice calm and reassuring, but it only made her more tense. "Planter, I think I'll need you in there with me."

"You mean you need my magic." Her voice had a sharp edge to it.

Watcher nodded. "I don't want to lie. Yeah, I need your magic. I wish I didn't, but I think something important is happening and we both need to be in there."

"Er-Lan and Fixit will be at Planter's side." The zombie's voice seemed to ease some of the tension in the air.

She glanced at the zombie, then down at the little mechite and sighed in resignation. "Okay, I'll try."

"Good," Watcher said, but cringed when Planter cast him an angry glare.

With a sigh, he waited as Planter, Er-Lan, and Fixit entered the passage, the zombie's clawed feet making a scratching sound with every step. Watcher followed the little mechite into the passage, the purple glow from his

arms and chest casting an iridescent hue on the polished walls and floors around them.

A dusty, stale smell assaulted his nose as he moved
through the narrow corridor. Likely, no one had been in
this tunnel for hundreds of years. Across the ground,
tiny clouds of dust billowed into the air as his companions' feet churned up the ancient layer of dirt, making
Watcher cough and sneeze.

As he moved through the andesite-lined corridor, that strange chill slithered down his spine again.
Watcher knew he'd felt it before, and he knew who was
responsible for the terrible feeling: Krael, the king of the
withers.

CHAPTER 5

Watcher glanced nervously about as he moved through the dusty passage. It felt as if someone or something was watching, waiting at the end of the tunnel; the creepy feeling caused tiny square goose bumps to form on his arms. Using his sensitive vision, something he was known for in his village, Watcher probed the darkness ahead, looking for threats, but saw none . . . for now.

The narrow passage led to a large chamber lit by a single redstone lantern embedded in the ceiling a dozen blocks overhead. The ground was curiously smooth—not like ice, but smoother than stone or brick. Watcher glanced around, trying to see any details; the lantern did little to reveal their surroundings, but by the sound of their echoing footsteps, he could tell the chamber was huge.

"This is the Viewing Chamber," Mira said. "It will allow us to use various charms or spells to see into the other planes of existence."

"A little more light would be appreciated." Planter's quiet voice was monotone and emotionless; she sounded defeated.

"More light?" Mira smiled, then banged her staff on

the smooth floor. Instantly, tiny glowing sparks shot out of the metal-banded end. The glowing embers circled the ancient wizard once, then sped outward to the distant walls. The orange sparks struck torches mounted on the walls, lighting the sticks until there were twenty of them flickering along the edge of the chamber, filling the room with light. "How's that?"

No one responded; they were all stunned at what they could now see beneath their feet. A solid layer of glass blocks covered the floor, allowing them to see what lay underneath: nothing. The ground beneath the glass floor was missing all the way down to the bedrock, but even the bedrock was gone. They could look down and see all the way to the Void, the black nothingness which was death to touch; nothing survived the Void.

The walls of the square abyss beneath them sparkled with an iridescent glow; clearly, there were some magic spells woven into the opening.

"It's kinda terrifying, being able to stare right down into nothingness . . . a deadly nothingness." Planter shuddered a bit.

"I never thought I'd ever see the Void," Watcher said. "Well . . . I guess I *hoped* I'd never see it. But having a strong floor underfoot makes it a bit easier to look at."

"Er-Lan has heard stories of zombies falling through portals in . . . the stronghold? Is that the correct name?" Er-Lan glanced at Watcher, a confused expression on his scarred face.

The young wizard nodded. "Yep, stronghold is the right name."

"The zombies fell into a strange island surrounded by the Void."

"That's The End," Planter said.

"The End?" Er-Lan nodded. "It is appropriately named, for the story says it was the end of Minecraft."

"What happened?" Planter moved to Er-Lan's side.

"The zombies saw the Void and just stood there in fear. One of the monsters spotted a strange portal in the ground with a black egg sitting atop a column of bedrock. The zombie jumped through the portal and reappeared in the Overworld. The other monsters were never heard from again." Er-Lan glanced at Planter. "The story was used to teach young zombies never to try new or unknown things, as the outcome might be bad."

"I don't understand. That's a strange lesson to teach children. New things can be good." Watcher sounded confused.

"Perhaps, but zombies are not known for being adventurous. Things that have been done before, that is what zombies like to do. Anything else, anything unknown or unpredictable; those things are not zombie things."

Planter and Watcher looked at their friend, contemplating his words.

I wonder if the zombie warlocks ever—Watcher thought, but was silenced by Mirthrandos.

"Enough of this." Her harsh voice echoed off the stone walls, surrounding them as if an army of ancient wizards was in the room. "We need to find out what's going on. I know a Seeing spell that will allow us to see into the other planes of existence, but it takes a lot of power. All three of us will have to work together and—"

"Don't worry, we know how to do this, right, Planter?" Watcher glanced at his friend.

She gave him a blank look, as if her emotions had all but disappeared.

"Just get some healing potions . . . please." He smiled at her.

Planter reached into her inventory and pulled out a splash potion of healing and held it at the ready.

"What are you gonna do with that?" Mira asked, narrowing her eyes.

Watcher reached into his inventory and withdrew the ancient artifact he'd taken from the spider warlord so many months ago—a glass lens with two long leather straps attached on opposite ends. He held it up for Mirthrandos to see.

The ancient wizard gasped. "Do you know what that is?"

"Of course we do." Watcher smiled. "It's the Eye of Searching."

"That artifact was lost centuries ago, during the Great War. It was thought the withers stole it when they switched sides and started fighting for the monster warlocks." She stared at Watcher, her old eyes burning with questions. "Where did you find it?"

"It was taken from the Spider Warlord." Er-Lan sounded proud.

Fixit gazed up at the sparkling item and whistled with excitement.

"With that thing, we can—"

Watcher interrupted Mirthrandos. "I know, I can use it to see anything I concentrate on." He smiled as if he'd just won some great victory.

"Not you, but us." Now it was Mira's turn to smile. "The magical powers in the Viewing Chamber will project the image for all of us to see." She backed up. "Move to the wall and put your backs to it."

They all moved to the edge of the room, standing next to each other.

Watcher held the lens up to his eye, then tied the leather straps around his square head. Instantly, pain surged through his body as the Eye of Searching used his health as its power source to fuel the magical enchantments that made it work. Closing his eyes, he concentrated on his enemy, the wither king, Krael. Instantly, the monster appeared in the middle of the room, each of his three heads wearing a Crown of Skulls.

Er-Lan hissed, his claws slowly extending from his fingers, ready for battle. Planter cried out in surprise, then pulled her enchanted shield from her inventory. Instantly, the edges of the shield ignited with magical purple flames.

Watcher opened his eyes at the sound and yanked his enchanted sword, Needle, from his inventory when he saw the wither king.

"Relax . . . it's just an image." Mirthrandos laughed. "A very realistic one, at that."

Fixit whistled his agreement but stayed back from the terrifying apparition.

"Where is our friend Krael going?" Mira glanced at Watcher. "Move back so you can see the surroundings."

Watcher focused his mind and imagined himself moving away from Krael. The wither in the center of the room shrunk in size, revealing his surroundings: he was floating over a birch forest with a smattering of oak trees here and there. Colorful splashes of color punctuated the scene, with flowers of red and blue and yellow mixed in with the green grass. Watcher pulled back even farther, making Krael appear as a minia-ture figurine in the middle of the Viewing Chamber. But now, the rest of the wither army was visible fly-ing a respectful distance behind their leader. On the ground, weaving between the trees, was a huge mob of distorted monsters: skeletons with zombie heads, slimes with spider legs, endermen with skeleton arms . . . every combination possible marched along beneath the wither air force.

"That's . . . a lot of monsters." Planter's voice cracked with fear.

Pain exploded again along every nerve in Watcher's body. He grunted as he clenched his teeth. Planter cracked the splash potion onto his shoulders, the cool liquid extinguishing most of the agony, but not all.

"Where are they heading?" Mira glanced at Watcher. "Change your view, so you're behind the army."

Watcher imagined himself drifting behind the terri-fying monsters, then looked up to see their destination. The scene shifted in the Viewing Chamber to show the monsters' backs. Far ahead in the distance, they could see a strange valley, with steep hills on either side.

Within the valley, tiny things zipped through the air, flying in all directions. '

"What is that?" Watcher was confused. "It looks like—"

"Oh no," Mirthrandos interrupted. "Do you know what that is?" She turned and faced Watcher and Planter.

They both nodded.

"The Valley of Arrows," Planter said.

"And behind that illusion is Wizard City." Watcher grunted again as agony ravaged his body.

Planter cracked another splash potion of healing on his back, easing the pain a bit.

Watcher made the scene zoom in on the valley. They could all see the stacks of dispensers piled up in the illusion, imaginary arrows streaking out of them and speeding in all directions through the valley.

"Why would the monsters want to go to Wizard City?" Er-Lan glanced at Mira. "This zombie does not understand."

The old woman sighed, shaking her head. "It was rumored during the Great War that Tharus had his own portal leading back to the Far Lands."

"Why would he have that?" Watcher asked.

The ancient wizard shrugged. "I think Tharus was a little paranoid; he didn't trust anyone. That's why he gave his cloak a spell of invisibility."

Watcher reached into his inventory and pulled out the wizard's cloak that had saved his life when he fell from Krael's shoulders during the last terrible battle. The gold stitching around its edges sparkled as if it were brand-new. "You mean this cloak?"

She nodded. "Yep. That's the one. Tharus used it to disappear when he wanted to move about without being detected. Many times, he'd reappear in the Far Lands, without going through the Hall of Planes. We figured he had his own portal, but no one ever found it."

"You mean he had a portal just to himself, and he

didn't let anyone else use it?" Planter scowled at the ancient wizard.

Mira nodded. "That's exactly right; Tharus didn't trust anyone. His suspicious nature matched his arrogance. I bet, to make himself feel famous, he wrote about his portal in some book, and likely the wither king found something, a book or scroll, maybe, that told about Tharus's portal. Now, Krael wants to find it."

"Great, so now Krael's trying to find another way to bring his entire army here to the Far Lands." Watcher sounded scared, as they all were.

"Don't you think you should have told us about this hidden portal when we were in Wizard City?" Planter asked.

"You didn't need to know about it." Mira didn't even bother looking at Planter, she just stared at the image floating in the center of the room.

"We didn't need to know?!" Planter was getting angrier. "You just decided, and that's it?"

"Pretty much."

"Just like you didn't bother telling us about this Viewing Chamber until you thought it was necessary." Planter scowled at the old woman.

Mira just nodded.

Planter turned to Watcher. "You see, wizards only do things for themselves."

Watcher didn't reply; he had learned sometimes it was best to stay silent.

Suddenly, an ice-cold chill slithered down his spine. Watcher turned his view toward the approaching army and found Krael staring straight at him.

"So, you're spying on me again, are you, boy?" Krael's three skulls glared at him.

The floating specter in the center of the Viewing Chamber drove icicles of fear straight into Watcher's spine. He felt as if he'd gone numb, his mind overwhelmed with panic.

"Ahh . . . I see you have the little girl with you." Krael

shifted his gaze to Planter, then to Mira. "And I see the old hag is still with you as well; excellent. I'm looking forward to meeting you again." The wither's three faces took on a confused look as he shifted his gaze from Mira to Er-Lan. "You have a zombie with you? Curious. Is he a pet?"

"That's our friend, Er-Lan," Planter shouted. "You stay away from him."

"Ha ha ha . . . the little girl is mad, how precious." The image of Krael moved closer in the Viewing Chamber, his entire body looming larger and larger. "Your little shield isn't gonna protect you when we next meet." He glared at them all. "If you think you're safe from me in the Far Lands, then you are tragically mistaken."

The wither king glanced over his shoulder at the illusion covering Wizard City, then turned back to his adversaries. "I'll be inside Wizard City soon, and I bet there's no one home to stop me. It's just a question of time before I find what I'm looking for. I'm sure the old hag knows what I'm talking about." He laughed. "Your days in the Far Lands are numbered. Prepare yourselves to meet your doom in the Great War; it'll be on your doorstep soon enough. But don't worry . . . I have a few surprises for you. I'm sure you won't be disappointed."

The Crowns of Skulls on his three heads started to glow brighter and brighter, the wither's eyes doing the same.

"Here's a little something to remember me by." The monster fired a magically charged flaming skull at them.

The image of the projectile slowly floated across the room, getting larger and larger. At the same time, the Eye of Searching grew hotter and hotter until it started to burn Watcher's skin. He reached up and pulled the scorching Eye off his head and threw it across the room. The artifact slid across the ground, glowing red with heat. Instantly, the image of the wither king disappeared from view. Watcher groaned, then collapsed to one knee, his health points (HP) dangerously low.

Reaching into his inventory, he pulled out an apple and ate it quickly, eliminating his hunger and allowing his health to replenish.

"He knows about the portal," Planter said. "We need to do something. If we find Tharus's portal in the Far Lands, can we destroy it and stop Krael?"

Mirthrandos nodded. "Yes, that would work with this kind of portal. The problem is, we don't know where it is in the Far Lands. Tharus never told anyone of its location; I'm sure it's well hidden or located someplace that's too dangerous to explore." She sighed. "We'll never find it in time."

Watcher stood after gobbling down a piece of chicken to further boost his health. "So you're saying there's no way to stop Krael from coming into the Far Lands?"

The old woman shook her head. "Eventually, after tearing apart Wizard City, he'll find the portal."

Planter glanced at Watcher, a terrified expression on her square face.

"Then it may be time to prepare," Er-Lan said.

"For what?" Watcher turned toward the zombie.

"For the Great War, of course." Er-Lan spoke as if it were no big deal. "War is coming to the Far Lands, whether it is welcome or not."

"Er-Lan is right." Planter put a hand on the zombie's shoulder. "Let's get out of here and tell the others."

Fixit squeaked, his scared metal face staring up at Watcher.

"Come on, let's get back to the Tower." Planter headed out of the room, Mira, Er-Lan, and Fixit fast on her heels.

Watcher stood there for a moment as the torches along the walls extinguished themselves somehow, bathing him in darkness. He stared down at the floor, the faint glow of the walls was barely visible all the way down to the Void.

"How am I going to battle Krael and his army again?" he whispered to himself. "We barely survived the last battle, and now it looks like he has even more creatures under his banner." He sighed. "This is impossible."

Hopelessness makes things impossible, Baltheron said in the back of Watcher's mind. *Where there is hope, there are possibilities, but if you give up, all are doomed.*

Watcher nodded but didn't reply; he had nothing to say. The thought of another war made him want to weep. Turning, the young wizard headed for the door, but gave the terrifying Void one last look. Something in the back of his mind told him it was important, but he had no idea why.

With a sigh, he headed out of the Viewing Chamber and toward a war that would likely consume them all.

CHAPTER 6

Krael turned in midair and stared down at the collection of distorted monsters weaving between the many birch trees in the forest, then glanced up at his wither army floating above the treetops and smiled.

"That foolish boy-wizard thinks this is the extent of my army and air force." The wither king laughed. "What a pathetic idiot."

"What was that, husband?" Kora floated up to Krael's side. "Who were you talking to a few minutes ago?"

"That stupid wizard, Watcher, was spying on us again," the left skull said, his voice scratchy and harsh, then laughed. "He won't be doing that again very soon."

"Did he see our army?" Kora asked.

All three of Krael's skulls nodded.

"The wizards likely know the size of our forces, for now, as well as our destination." Right's voice was smooth and melodic, as always.

"That's terrible!" Kora exclaimed. "He'll know what to expect."

"And that's exactly what I want." Krael's three skulls smiled. "The fool will think this is all we have . . . but he'll be wrong."

"What do you mean, husband?"

"The three Crowns of Skulls give me the ability to communicate with monsters on other planes of existence in the Pyramid of Servers. I've been whispering in the ears of hundreds of monsters in the Far Lands, slowly nourishing their anger and resentment toward the NPCs. Soon, they'll start their own revolution, and attack the villages, which will distract the three wizards and that zombie-pet they have, and—"

"Zombie-pet?"

Krael nodded. "While they were spying on me, I was able to see all of them. Usually, I can only see the boy-wizard, but this time, I could see the girl and the old woman, too; they must have been using some kind of magical amplifier. But the strange thing was that I could also see a zombie. The Crown of Skulls is linked to the magic plane, letting me sense other wizards, but I could see this one particular zombie, as well."

"They were probably in some special room built by the ancient wizards during the Great War. It likely lets them spy on us from a different world in the Pyramid." Kora smiled. "If the zombie were in the room with them, then he'd be visible too, right?"

"Perhaps," Krael said. "But I don't like mysteries, and I don't like that boy-wizard spying on us."

"So how do we stop him, husband?"

Now it was Krael's turn to smile. "Hopefully, I destroyed the artifact he was using to spy on us: the Eye of Searching. I poured my magic into it, trying to shatter the thing, so I bet the Eye shattered on the fool's face. Maybe if I'm lucky, the glass blinded him as well."

The wither king laughed cruelly. "Now let's continue toward Wizard City."

Krael and Kora continued floating toward their objective, the army and air force now catching up with them.

"Husband, with the Eye of Searching destroyed, is the link between you and the boy-wizard completely severed?"

Krael shrugged, then veered around a tall oak tree. "Watcher's link through the Eye of Searching should now be broken; he'll no longer be able to spy on us, I think." Krael smiled an evil smile. "But I can still sense him."

"You can?" Kora sounded surprised.

"The Crowns of Skulls lets me feel his presence. From this world, it is just a faint sensation in the backs of my skulls, but when we get to the Far Lands, I'll likely be able to sense exactly where he's hiding."

"That's fantastic!"

Krael nodded, grinning evilly, then slowed to a stop. They were at the edge of the Valley of Arrows. Many of the monsters on the ground seemed afraid, the arrows streaking back and forth across the valley looked deadly; they didn't know it was just an illusion.

Turning, Krael faced his army. "The arrows are a lie and do not exist. You need not fear, and I'll prove it. Where's the tiny wither named—"

"Kobael," Kora said.

"Right. Kobael, where are you?"

"Here," a high-pitched voice squeaked.

"Kobael, come forward, and go into the Valley of Arrows," Krael commanded. "Show the others the arrows are harmless."

A small wither floated out of the collection of monsters and headed hesitantly for the Valley of Arrows. Kobael moved into the magical image, letting the deceptive arrows pass through him, leaving him unharmed.

"You see, it's just a bit of trickery made by our enemies." Krael glared at the Valley of Arrows as if it were itself a mortal enemy. "Now, withers, get ready to fire your flaming skulls at the shield protecting Wizard City." Krael floated higher into the air, his eyes glowing with evil intent. "Once the shield opens, we'll go in and attack any golems or wolves left behind to protect the city. When they are all destroyed, the City will be ours."

The monsters growled and snarled, excited for the imminent battle.

"Now . . . FIRE!"

The withers concentrated their flaming skulls on the illusion, targeting a spot near the ground. The fiery projectiles smashed into an invisible shield, making it give off a soft orange radiance. The glowing spot grew larger as their projectiles continued to crash into the protective shell, straining its magical power. The illusion for which the Valley of Arrows was named slowly faded as the withers' attack drained the enchantments of their energy. Now, the withers could see through the illusion into Wizard City, where a series of sparkling buildings, all made of iron blocks, shimmered behind the protective shield. A group of iron and obsidian golems gathered near the glowing spot, ready to do battle.

Krael gathered all the magical power in the Crowns of Skulls and channeled it into his next attack. When he fired, the three flaming skulls shined with such intensity, all the other monsters had to look away. They slammed into the enchanted shield with a bang, causing it to finally rip apart.

A clap of thunder filled the cloudless sky as a huge gash tore across the barrier. The monstrous horde below Krael screamed with delight, then charged into the city, their battle cries echoing off the metallic buildings. Instantly, the legs on the iron golems extended, allowing the metal giants to reach up and grab the low-flying withers, pulling them to the ground, where, as they held the dark monsters, the obsidian golems stepped up and hammered on the captives with clenched stone fists.

The warped monsters on the ground attacked the golems with sharp teeth, pointed claws, and stone swords. Releasing the withers, the golems fought back, kicking and hitting their attackers, but there were just too many of them. Falling back, the golems tried to move into the streets, fleeing from the attackers, but a group of withers moved behind them, blasting them with their flaming skulls. The golems turned and reached up, grabbing an unwary wither or two to defend themselves.

"Monster on the ground . . . charge!" Krael shouted.

The warped creatures ran forward again; spidery monsters climbed up the golems as zombies and skeletons slashed at their metal legs, enveloping the golems in a storm of claws and fangs.

A golem staggered and fell to the ground. Before it could stand, thirty monsters swarmed atop it, devouring its HP in seconds; it disappeared with a pop, leaving behind a handful of iron blocks and three glowing balls of XP (experience points).

"Withers, ATTACK!" Krael roared.

A deluge of flaming skulls fell upon the remaining metal and stone defenders. Even the monsters held within their massive hands took damage as the deadly rain enveloped them all. One after another, the golems fell to the ground, their strength finally waning.

Finally, the last golem fell, adding to the litter of iron and obsidian blocks strewn across the streets, balls of XP glowing amongst the defenders' remains. With so many monsters and so few defenders, the battle had been decisive and brief. The last protectors of Wizard City were destroyed.

"Wizard City is ours!" Krael's voice boomed across the city, magically amplified by the magical power of his Crowns.

The monsters below him cheered, holding weapons and clawed hands in the air.

"Now, we must find the wizard's portal." Krael glared down at the monsters. When his eyes fell upon the tiny wither Kobael, he realized he couldn't remember if he'd seen the tiny monster actually fight during the battle. With a shrug, he continued.

"Tharus had his own portal linked to the Far Lands. It's hidden somewhere within Wizard City. Monsters on the ground, you are to go into every building and search for this portal. Rip every door off its hinges and break down every wall; this gateway to the Far Lands must be found."

Krael turned his attention to the withers. "My brothers and sisters, use your flaming skulls to tear the roof off every one of these iron buildings. Destroy everything in sight until you can peer into every room. With the golem protectors turned to rubble, there is nothing here to stop us." The monsters shouted and growled with savage glee.

"It is time to erase Wizard City from the surface of Minecraft. Go forth, my friends, and destroy everything!"

Hundreds of monsters instantly spread out, each finding their own doors to pound on with clawed fists until they buckled inward and shattered. Meanwhile, the withers floated across the city, sending down a hail of flaming skulls upon the iron roofs. Krael drifted up into the air with Kora at his side, watching the destruction.

"Back during the Great War, I would have never dreamed we'd be here, destroying the great Wizard City." Kora laughed with vengeful glee.

"Yes, I know, wife. And when we find Tharus's portal, we'll become an unstoppable flood, covering not just the Wizard City, but all the Far Lands with destruction."

An intense iridescent glow built up around the Crowns of Skulls on his three heads, the magic getting stronger and stronger as he channeled it into amplifying his voice. "I'M COMING FOR YOU, WATCHER, AND THERE'S NO PLACE FOR YOU TO HIDE!"

Both Krael and Kora laughed as they thought of all the violent, destructive things they would do to the Far Lands and their enemy, Watcher.

CHAPTER 7

They moved in silence through the wide, ancient corridor, the sounds of their footsteps and Er-Lan's claws clicking on the hard stone floor the only things they could hear. The purple glow coming from Planter, Mirthrandos, and Watcher cast a circle of shimmering light around the party; Mira's glow was much brighter, since she was the most powerful of the three.

They entered a wide corridor, maybe twenty blocks across, the ceiling twice that distance in height. Pieces of stone walls dotted the edges of the passage, most of them having crumbled over the years.

Watcher slowed and ran his hand over the remains of a mossy cobblestone wall. "What was this place?"

"This section used to be called the Market Place." Mira's scratchy voice filled the passage. "Wizards would trade spells or enchanted artifacts. Sometimes villagers would come down here, terrified of us, but hoping to get a cure for an ailing sibling or child."

"Did you help them?" Planter asked.

The old woman shrugged. "Sometimes, I suppose, if the problem seemed challenging enough."

"Challenging enough?!" Planter scowled. "You should have helped them regardless of the problem."

"You don't know what you're talking about." Mirthrandos glared at her, frowning. "If we helped every NPC whenever they had a problem, they would have been here in the thousands. Sometimes, people need to take care of themselves."

Planter shook her head in disgust. "You don't get it. When someone asks for help, they're baring their soul to you, letting you know they can't take care of their families, but they're willing to swallow their pride and ask for help. You wizards should have felt *honored* to help someone—they're putting their trust and hopes into your hands. But instead, your sense of superiority got in the way. You are totally—"

Suddenly, pain enveloped each of the wizards, and they fell to their knees as a spike of agony burrowed through each of their minds. Only Fixit stayed on his feet, rushing back and forth between Planter and Mira, trying to help. And then, as quickly as it came, the burning pain disappeared, leaving each dizzy and weak.

"What was . . . that?" Watcher gasped for breath.

Mirthrandos sighed, a look of sadness and fear on her wrinkled face. "He did it."

"Did what?" Planter asked.

"Krael broke through the shield surrounding Wizard City." She slowly rose on shaky legs. "We must have still been connected to him or the City somehow."

"Now we're certain, then: Krael knows about Tharus's portal." Watcher stood and helped Planter to her feet, then moved to Er-Lan and helped the zombie.

The ancient wizard nodded. "He's probably demolishing the city while we stand here talking. I'm not sure how much time we have."

"Do you think Krael knows where to look?" Planter reached down and patted Fixit gently on the head; the concerned mechite still had a worried expression on his tiny metallic face.

"I don't know," Mira said. "All of us scoured Wizard City after Tharus was killed, looking for his portal, but we never found it. Maybe he wrote some hints in a book or something; he was arrogant enough to do something like that."

"Figures . . . just like a wizard," Planter said, her voice filled with contempt.

Watcher shook his head. "Come on; we need to get back to the village. It's time to prepare for war. We need more weapons and more soldiers, and it's likely we don't have a lot of time."

He took off running, his companions following close behind. As he ran, Watcher could feel the faintest itch in the back of his mind, probably due to Krael—somehow, he could sense the monster with his magic. Glancing at Planter, he could tell she was feeling the wither king's presence as well, with the look of disgust on her face making it plainly evident.

"I hate feeling that monster in the back of my mind," Planter said as she ran. "It feels like—like a rusty nail tickling the back of my brain."

"You're right, that's exactly how it feels." Watcher glanced at her and nodded, expecting a smile in return, but all he received was a grimace.

I'm glad *I can feel Krael's presence in the back of my mind,* Watcher thought. *It reminds me of what we need to do, and maybe it'll be useful somehow.*

He smiled, but instantly turned his grin to a frown when Planter glanced at him. He didn't want to give her the wrong idea.

"It is getting brighter ahead," Er-Lan said from where he ran just behind Watcher.

Watcher nodded. "Yeah, we're getting back to the populated section of the Wizard's Tower."

Fixit streaked ahead of the others, his tiny legs a blur of motion. The mechite squeaked and whistled as he approached the homes the villagers had built against the walls of the ancient structure, the wolves in the village barking their replies.

"What's he doing?" Watcher asked.

"He's gathering the wolves and mechites." Mira glanced at him. "Fixit is likely telling the other creatures from Wizard City about the Great War that's about to start. Make no mistake about it, Krael wants to destroy every NPC and burn every village to the ground. This is exactly what happened before. The wither king back during the Great War was Kaza, not Krael. You likely don't know anything about that wither king."

Watcher shook his head. "No, we know a lot about Kaza. He imprisoned hundreds of NPCs, making them slaves."

"We destroyed that monster and saved all our friends," Planter said, a proud smile spreading across her face. But when Watcher glanced at her, she scowled and looked away.

The old woman nodded. "Kaza was the original king of the withers when they betrayed the wizards and joined forces with the monster warlocks. Krael's goal now is the same as Kaza's hundreds of years ago: the extermination of all villagers."

"That's just great." Planter's voice dripped with sarcasm. "More violence is just what we need."

"Well, we aren't gonna let Krael do this . . . not without a fight." A look of stern determination appeared on Watcher's face. "It's time we told the others what's going on; we have preparations to make."

Then, before any of them could respond, he sprinted toward the main gathering area in the base of the Wizard's Tower, thoughts of battle and death filling him with a terrible sense of dread.

CHAPTER 8

Watcher stepped into the base of the Wizard's Tower and was instantly enveloped in a cacophony of nervous chatter; the villagers had sensed something was happening, and they were scared. Afternoon rays of sunlight shone through the stained-glass windows at the top of the structure, painting the upper reaches of the interior with a palette of oranges, yellows, reds, and blues, but because it was late afternoon, none of the colors reached the Tower floor, leaving the NPCs in shadows, magnifying their fear.

Blaster pulled out a torch and placed it on a wall, Cutter and Mapper doing the same nearby. The flickering light calmed the NPCs a bit, but by the looks on their faces, Watcher could tell they were still uncertain and afraid.

Pulling a block of dirt from his inventory, Watcher placed it on the ground, then stepped on top and raised his hands. "Quiet everyone, quiet, please." He turned in a circle, catching the eye of everyone in the village, his calm expression silencing the crowd.

"What's going on, son?" Cleric asked. "The wolves and mechites got all excited, and a bunch of them went up to the forest; it seems like they're on guard, watching for something. What happened?"

"Well . . . Krael and his army of monsters are coming to the Far Lands soon, and we need to—"

The crowds exploded with questions and comments before he could continue. Some pulled swords from their inventory, while others fitted arrows to bowstrings and glanced at the entrance, ready to defend their families.

Suddenly, a voice boomed through the tower, accompanied by a loud clanking sound—Cutter had moved next to Watcher and banged his diamond sword against his iron chest plate, yelling at the top of his lungs, "BE QUIET! BE QUIET!"

The villagers, always afraid of Cutter's temper, slowly stilled their voices and looked up expectantly at Watcher, scared expressions on their square faces.

"I know you're frightened, but you need to listen to what I have to say so we can prepare."

The NPCs grew calmer as they stared up at Watcher.

"That's better." He gazed down at Planter and smiled. "Mira took us to a secret room called the Viewing Chamber, where we saw Krael and his army of monsters heading for Wizard City. We think the wither king is looking for a hidden portal within the city that'll let him and his army leave that world and come to the Far Lands." The NPCs glanced at each other and began to murmur, but with a stern look from Cutter, they went quiet. "A few minutes ago, we felt the withers break through the shield protecting Wizard City. Eventually, he'll find the portal and will bring his army here."

Mapper pushed through the villagers and moved closer to Watcher, his bald head reflecting the flickering light from the torches, which gave the ring of gray hair around the edge of his head a warm glow. "How many monsters are in his army?"

"Well, you remember he had maybe two hundred withers, right?"

Mapper nodded.

"Now, he has at least that many warped and distorted monsters on the ground as well." He turned and glanced down at the NPCs around him. "With Mira's wolves, mechites, and golems helping us, we might have a chance to stand up against either the withers or the ground forces, but not both. We need more soldiers."

"You gonna use your magic wand and clone a bunch of people?" Blaster smiled at Watcher as he thought about the Wand of Cloning, which had helped them on numerous adventures.

"It takes a lot of magical power to clone people." Mira's scratchy voice chiming in from the back of the crowd startled many of the NPCs. "I doubt we'd have enough strength to clone more than a dozen, and then all of us wizards would be too tired to fight." She glanced up at Watcher. "That's not a solution."

"So the first thing we need to do is recruit more NPCs." Watcher turned to his father. "Dad, I need you to form squads of NPCs and send them to every nearby village. Convince them to join our cause, and bring everyone here. If any NPCs stay in their homes, they won't stand a chance against Krael and his mob."

"I can do that, but how will I convince the other communities that this is truly serious?"

"We'll send an obsidian golem with each group." Watcher glanced at Mira, and she nodded. "That'll give the groups some protection, as well as something for the villagers to see; none of them have ever seen an obsidian golem, since they don't exist in the Far Lands. Maybe that'll convince everyone this is truly serious."

Cleric nodded. "I can do that."

"We also need people to start making potions and crafting weapons and armor." He glanced at the crowd, looking for someone to lead that effort.

"Leave that to me." Mapper raised a hand in the air.

"No, I have something else for you to do," Watcher said. "We need someone else."

"I'll take care of the potions and crafting," a voice said near the back of the crowd. It was Brewer.

The tall NPC moved through the crowds, pushing

others gently aside as he approached Watcher. He was easily a head taller than any of the other villagers; his dark green smock with its black stripe running down the center stood out against the brighter clothing around him. "No one brews potions better than I do. Most of the ingredients for potions of healing, rejuvenation, and swiftness are already in my chests. I'll get those made while I oversee the crafting of weapons and armor."

"Good." Watcher smiled.

"But, son, what will you be doing?" Cleric asked.

"I'll be leading a large squad of warriors out into the Far Lands." Watcher glanced down at Blaster, and the boy smiled excitedly.

"Why? What do you hope to find?" Cleric had a concerned expression on his wrinkled face.

"We're gonna try and find Tharus's portal in the Far Lands." Watcher stared down at his father. "If we can destroy it before they come through, then we'll stop the war before it even starts."

Cleric smiled and placed a hand on his son's shoulder, pride showing on his wrinkled face.

"If we can't find the portal in time, then we're gonna harass Krael's forces and slow him down while we try to evacuate the villages in his path. Hopefully, it'll give everyone here time to prepare for war."

"That sounds dangerous." The worried tone in Cleric's voice was obvious.

"Yeah, dangerous for Krael," Blaster said with an enthusiastic smile.

The other NPCs laughed, some cheering.

"Leaders, gather your volunteers and let's get to work." Watcher stepped off the block of dirt, then dug it back up with a shovel. "Mapper, where are you?"

"Here." The old man stepped forward.

"I need you to gather every map you have." Watcher put a hand on the old man's shoulder. "We need to figure out where Tharus's portal is located."

"On it." Mapper turned and ran toward his house.

"Watcher, I need you over here," Blaster said nearby.

Watcher turned and found his friend standing next to Fencer, who was staring at Blaster with adoring eyes. Watcher smiled; he always found Blaster's discomfort over Fencer's adoring attention hilarious.

"What's up?" Watcher asked.

"I told Fencer you had a special job for her." Blaster gave him a wink.

"Ahh . . . oh, yeah, that special project." He had no idea what Blaster was talking about, but went along with it.

"Come on, Fencer, it's down here." Blaster led Fencer and Watcher down a long passage, the torches on the walls throwing small clouds of ash into the air.

Watcher glanced at Blaster, hoping he'd tell him what was going on, but the dark-haired boy just shook his head and kept walking as two burly NPCs suddenly fell in behind the trio; obviously, they were part of the plan. Fencer seemed oblivious to what was happening; her loving gaze was completely focused on Blaster, unaware of the two new additions to their company.

Finally, Blaster reached a doorway and stopped.

"It's in here." Blaster pointed to the dark room. "Right, Watcher?"

"Ahh, yeah, this is the place." He glanced at Fencer. "Thanks for helping us with this. It's really important."

Blaster smiled and nodded. "This is imperative. I'm glad you can help, Fencer."

She beamed with happiness as Blaster gazed at her. Moving into the room, Fencer pulled out a torch and looked around. Before she could turn around, the two huge NPCs stepped into the doorway and stood with their hands on their hips, barring her from leaving.

"Sorry, Fencer, but I can't have you following us this time; it's too dangerous." Blaster shrugged, then turned to leave.

"Oh, no, you don't!" she shouted. "I'm going with you."

Blaster shook his head. "These are the two strongest NPCs in the village. They're twins, one named Chopper, the other Breaker; I'm never quite sure which is which. They're gonna keep you here until we're long gone. You can't go with us." He smiled as he backed away, Watcher at his side.

"I don't *think* so." Fencer glared at the two giants, then reached into her inventory and pulled out a wooden stick.

"What are you gonna do with that, little girl?" one of them asked.

"Watch and learn." She gave them both a smile, then went to work.

Using the stick like a sword, she struck Chopper in the stomach, but it just bounced off as if it had hit a block of stone. The NPC laughed, then reached out to grab her, but Fencer just attacked Chopper's arm, cracking the stick across his elbow. He shouted out in pain, but she wasn't done yet. Crouching, she spun across the ground with her leg extended. It caught Chopper at the ankles, sweeping his legs out from underneath him. The big villager fell backward, landing hard on the brick floor as Breaker now moved toward her, an angry frown on his square face. Fencer rolled across the ground away from him, then stood and rapped him across the top of his head; Breaker put his hands up to his stinging head, leaving his stomach exposed, so she drove her blunt weapon in his stomach, using the stick like a spear. The giant villager doubled over, groaning in pain and holding his belly. With a quick double strike, Fencer hit his knees, causing them to buckle. Breaker fell to the ground, landing right on top of Chopper with a thud.

With a satisfied grin, Fencer casually walked over the two incapacitated villagers and stood directly in front of Blaster.

"I think I'm gonna go with you." She stared at Blaster, then glared at Watcher. "Any objections?"

Both boys shook their heads, stunned by what they'd just witnessed.

"How did you learn to do that?" Blaster asked in disbelief.

"Cutter's been teaching me a few tricks so I can fight better."

"I'd say he's a pretty good teacher." Watcher was amazed.

"No . . . I'm a good learner." She smiled at him, then turned and headed back to the others, Watcher following behind.

After a few steps, Watcher glanced over his shoulder at Blaster. The boy was staring down at the big NPCs as they struggled to stand. Surprisingly, Watcher spotted a smile on Blaster's face, as if he were impressed.

"Come on, Blaster, it looks as if everyone's ready to leave." Watcher pulled Needle from his inventory and tapped it on the ground to get his attention. "Are you coming?"

Blaster nodded, then helped Breaker and Chopper up. "We're coming." He glanced at the two big villagers. "I guess you'll be coming with us now, but if a little girl can beat you up, I don't know what's gonna happen when real monsters actually show up."

"Monsters will take it easier on them than I did," Fencer shouted from up ahead, then laughed aloud, a satisfied sound echoing off the cold stone walls.

Watcher chuckled as well as a look of resignation came across Blaster's face. The young boy had just realized he couldn't stop Fencer from following him wherever he went.

"Come on, Blaster, speed it up. We have a monster army to find and destroy," Watcher said.

"Maybe you should just send Fencer after them." Blaster glanced at Fencer, the faintest smile still on his face. "She could probably take care of them all before we even get a chance to take out our swords."

"I hope so," Watcher said. "I really hope so."

Images of battle and death filled his mind as he thought about the impending war. *How many of my friends must die to stop Krael and his army?* he thought.

As many as is necessary, a scratchy voice replied in the back of his mind.

Watcher held his hands up and glanced at the Gauntlets of Life on his wrists; he knew that voice came from Taerian, the wizard trapped in the magical weapons. The Gauntlets gave off a bright pulse of light, then faded back to their normal, glowing state. The disregard for life that came from Taerian made him shudder, but maybe that was how he would have to think if they were going to win the Second Great War.

"Come on, Watcher, hurry up," Blaster shouted from up ahead.

Watcher realized he'd slowed to a stop while he was talking to the Gauntlets. With a nod, he sprinted through the cold passage, weaving around NPCs as he neared the main tower, then skidded to a stop next to Blaster.

"The few horses we still have in the village are all up in the forest waiting for us." Blaster removed his gray-colored leather armor and replaced it with his favorite: midnight black. "The other warriors are up there already."

Watcher nodded and headed for the steps, but Blaster grabbed his arm and stopped him.

"How about you do that cloning thing with some TNT?" Blaster pulled out one of the red-and-white striped cubes and placed it on the ground. "I have a feeling we're gonna need it."

Watcher nodded, then reached into his inventory and pulled out the Wand of Cloning. It was a bent and crooked stick with one end split into two, making the shape of a 'Y.' Tiny bands of metal wrapped around the ends, each glowing softly, giving off an iridescent glow. "Do you have a potion of healing?"

Blaster nodded and pulled out a splash potion, the red liquid sloshing black and forth.

"Stand back; I don't want to clone your foot accidentally." Watcher waved the wand over his head, allowing the magical power to build. Other NPCs gathered
around to watch, but kept a safe distance from the
young wizard.

The Wand grew brighter, making it hard for villagers to see, and many moved back a little farther, afraid
of magic. Watcher could feel the power building in the
Wand, but also feel it growing within himself. Suddenly,
pain blasted through his body as the Wand of Cloning
looked for energy to feed into its enchantments and
used Watcher's HP. A glass bottle crashed against his
diamond armor, cooling the flames of agony, but not
completely.

When he felt the time was right, Watcher pointed the
wand at the TNT and flicked his wrist once, then again
and again and again as a bright purple glow enveloped
the explosive block, making it impossible to see. He
continued the process as pain surged through his body,
his HP diminishing. Another healing potion shattered
against his back, the enchanted liquid doing what it
could to rejuvenate him, but it never seemed to elimi-
nate the pain completely.

Finally, as fatigue caused his legs to weaken, Watcher
stopped flicking his wrist and put the Wand back into
his inventory. The iridescent glow on the ground slowly
faded, revealing not just one block of TNT, but dozens.
The crowd moved closer and gasped in surprise as they
saw all the blocks, leaving the villagers uncertain what
to say. Chopper moved to Watcher's side and patted the
boy on the back, then cheered. The other NPCs added
their voices to the jubilation as more villagers patted the
young wizard on the back.

Blaster stepped forward and picked up the explosives, a huge smile on his face. "Good job, Watcher. I
hope we don't need all this."

Watcher just nodded, exhausted, then headed up
the stairs leading out of the ancient structure and up to

the forest overhead, with Blaster, Fencer, Chopper and Breaker following behind.

When they finally made it out the giant hole in which the Wizard's Tower sat, they found about three dozen villagers, all on horseback. Watcher found his horse, a dusty-gray mare with white markings around her hooves; it was the horse he'd gotten during the battle with the spider warlord at the Citadel of the Horse Lords. This horse had saved his life that day, as well as the lives of many others; Watcher was glad she was still here.

Pulling an apple from his inventory, he offered it to the horse; the animal gobbled it up instantly. Grabbing the reins, he swung up into the saddle and glanced at Mirthrandos. "Any idea where we go to find Tharus's portal?"

The ancient wizard shrugged. "I know the Overworld is about a million blocks to the east, so I'd guess it's to the west."

"Deeper into the Far Lands." Watcher nodded. "That makes sense. Blaster, why don't you take the lead? Let's head west."

The boy nodded and turned his mount, then gave it a gentle kick with his heels. Instantly, the animal took off at a gallop, the rest of the company following.

Watcher glanced at Planter; she looked scared.

"It'll be okay." Watcher tried to sound confident but did a poor job. He could still feel that jagged tickle in the back of his mind, reminding him Krael was still out there and wanted to kill them all.

CHAPTER 9

The party rode with light hearts, the sounds of animals in the forest making it feel as if life surrounded them, but as usual, they couldn't see any of them; the cows, chickens, and pigs were invisible amongst the oak and birch trees. Watcher knew many of those sounds came from the metallic wolves loping along with villagers; the animal sounds were how they communicated with each other. He always found it peculiar when he heard the sounds of animals but couldn't find them, but now he understood: it had been the iron wolves patrolling Minecraft for years, if not centuries. They were too stealthy to be seen as they protected all the worlds in the Pyramid of Servers, watching for another Great War.

Well, now they'd found one.

Every few moments, the ground shook, as if a giant's fist had slammed into the forest floor, but it was the heavy footsteps of the golems. The massive creatures tried to step lightly, but it was difficult when their bodies were composed of either iron or obsidian.

The forest thinned out, revealing a wide trail, a tall spruce tree standing out of place amongst the oaks and birches. At the fork in the path, small groups of warriors peeled off and headed in different directions, obsidian golems traveling with each. Watcher's group of NPCs, three dozen strong, followed the path to the west, a ring of mechites riding iron wolves around the villagers, the towering golems staying on the road to avoid the low-hanging branches.

His sister, Winger, rode at the front of the formation with Blaster and Mapper on either side, Fencer trying to push her way between the villagers to ride at Blaster's side. Mapper, always the courteous one, moved aside, making room for the young girl. Blaster scowled at the old man . . . it made Watcher laugh. Glancing over his shoulder at the sound, Blaster gave Watcher an angry glare, then shrugged and turned forward.

They followed the sun as it slowly settled toward the distant horizon, their shadows growing longer and longer. Watcher swallowed nervously. He knew where this trail led: toward a place he dreaded and would have been glad never to visit again.

"I hope the others can convince more NPCs to come to the Wizard's Tower and help us." Planter glanced at Watcher, her face creased with discomfort. "We need more troops for the war that's heading for us. But I feel bad about bringing others into the violence."

"Why?" Watcher asked.

"We may be bringing them to their deaths."

"If they stay in their homes, they'll be destroyed eventually, after Krael finishes us off." Watcher sighed. "They have no choice . . . like us. It's war or destruction for every villager; there's no other option."

"Come on, let's speed it up," Cutter shouted from up ahead. "The golems and wolves can easily keep up."

The big NPC kicked his horse into a gallop, the rest of the party following.

Er-Lan guided his mount next to Watcher's. "It seems like a long time ago when Er-Lan met Planter and Watcher on this very road."

"That was farther to the east, as I recall," Planter

said. "I think it was on the other side of the village in that direction."

The zombie nodded.

"I think it was when the zombies were trying to kill all of us." Cutter's voice had an angry edge to it.

"Bad times, indeed." Er-Lan nodded sadly.

"I wonder, now and then, why you let us capture you?" Cutter turned in the saddle and glared at Er-Lan. "I know zombies can be sneaky and quiet if they want, yet you just bumbled around in the forest that night, making lots of noise." He glanced at Watcher. "I bet he wanted to get captured." Cutter glanced at Er-Lan again. "Maybe you did it so that idiotic zombie warlord, Tu-Kar, wouldn't discover anything."

"Discover? What could be discovered?" the zombie replied, confused.

"Ahh . . . I don't know, that maybe you're a *warlock*, and you're really working for the wither king?" Cutter pointed at Er-Lan with a thick, meaty finger.

"Cutter, that's ridiculous. Er-Lan is our friend, and we've taken him into our family." Watcher glanced at the zombie and smiled reassuringly, then ducked as he rode under a low-hanging branch. "And the magic thing is absurd. Do you see him glowing like me, or Planter, or Mirthrandos? If Er-Lan were a warlock, I'd be able to sense it, and I don't detect any magic in him."

Cutter still glared at the zombie. "He's done some things that make me suspicious, like the last time we were in the Hall of Planes."

"You mean the time he saved all our lives by pushing Krael out of the portal?" Watcher replied. "That's your evidence? How could Er-Lan be working with Krael if he stopped him?"

"Well . . . he was glowing purple, like you and Planter." Cutter's voice was growing quieter.

"That was because my magic leaked into him," Watcher replied. "That wasn't because of Er-Lan, it was because of me, of course."

"Well . . ." Cutter shook his head but remained silent.

Blaster shouted something difficult to hear as he galloped back to the main party. Fencer rode right behind him, a huge, satisfied smile on her face.

"What did he say?" Watcher asked.

"Blaster said there is no one in the old village." Er-Lan glanced at the young wizard, a concerned expression spreading across his scarred green face. "Is something wrong?"

"I haven't been here since . . . you know, the attack." Watcher turned to Planter. "This might bring back some uncomfortable memories. Are you okay?"

She nodded but remained silent.

Everyone in the company could feel the tension from Planter and Watcher; both of them were clearly afraid of confronting the memories from that terrible day.

"You and me, together," Watcher said to Planter.

She nodded, her long blond hair shining like fine gold in the ruddy light of the setting sun.

They rode side by side into their village, the rest of the warriors staying back to give them some privacy. They headed first for Watcher's former family home. Winger kicked her horse forward and moved to her brother's side.

"You okay?" Winger reached out and put a hand on Watcher's shoulder.

He nodded but kept his eyes straight ahead.

When they reached the home, all three of them dismounted as the wolves and golems formed a perimeter around the charred remains of the broken structure. Watcher stared at the charred walls and shattered windows and wanted to weep, but he knew it wouldn't help, not now. So many painful memories started from this point on that terrible day. Using every bit of self-control, he choked back the emotions as much as he could and tried to look brave; by the looks on his friends' faces, he knew it wasn't working.

"This is it." Winger kicked a piece of the door. It

snapped off the hinge and fell to the ground. "These ruins are all that's left of our home."

"I thought destroying the zombie warlord, Tu-Kar, would have brought me some peace." Watcher scowled and shook his head. "But the empty place deep within my soul always reminds me of that terrible day when the zombie warlord attacked and shattered our lives. A feeling of despair still sits within me, festering, like a disease."

"It's okay, brother," Winger said. "We all did what we could that day, but we were outnumbered. It's not any-one's fault that the zombies took over our village and captured everyone."

"You don't get it," Watcher snapped. "You put up a fight; many people did. But all I did was lay here on the ground and pretend to be dead because I was afraid. I didn't do anything to help our friends and neighbors."

"You did rescue everyone." Mapper moved next to him and put an arm around his shoulder. "I'd say that's something. That's a big something."

"He's right." Planter stood directly in front of him, her emerald eyes filled with sadness, but also a bright spark of strength and courage. "You said you were gonna save everyone, and you did. If you hadn't convinced all of us to fight back, Winger and all of the villagers from here would still be in the mines, digging up gold for Kaza. You defeated that wither and probably saved all of the Far Lands. I'd say that's something to be proud of."

"Maybe, but how many acts of bravery will it take to erase the one moment of cowardice that I still regret?" Watcher lowered his gaze to the ground.

"Never regret your failures," Mira advised, her scratchy voice filled with wisdom.

"Why? Don't you think Watcher would want to forget that terrible day?" Planter glared at the ancient wizard. "We all want to forget it."

"I'm sure it was terrible, but our failures make us who we are." Mira turned toward Watcher. "If you don't learn from your failures, then you've failed twice. The defeats we experience mold and shape us just as much as our victories. For good or ill, we *are* the decisions we make. All we can do is learn from them and try to do better next time." She turned and smiled at Watcher, then grew very serious. "I should know. I have enough failures for all of us."

"What was learned from the failure that cursed Mira with eternal life?" Er-Lan asked.

"That wasn't a failure. I helped a little wither named Kobael to stay alive. Every day I think about that tiny wither. I hope he had a good life and escaped the violence of the Great War. But there's no doubt the punishment of eternal life molded me into who I am."

"How did it do that?" Blaster asked.

Everyone turned and found the boy behind them, his black leather armor allowing him to merge with the darkening background.

"With each loved one I watched grow old and die, I became more bitter, until I finally withdrew from the world and hid down in my underwater palace."

"So how is that a good lesson?" Blaster asked. "It sounds pretty miserable."

"For a couple of centuries, it was. But then I met you." Mira pointed her crooked, metal-banded staff at Watcher. "You awakened something in me that I'd completely forgotten."

"What was it?"

"Hope: hope that life can be worth living; hope that maybe I can help make the world a better place; hope that maybe . . . just maybe, my presence in this world will make a difference in someone's life. That's the gift you gave me, Watcher . . . hope."

"Wow, that's a lot," Blaster said. "All Watcher ever gave me was a headache from all his crazy plans."

Fencer punched Blaster in the shoulder. He flashed her a smile, then quickly looked away, abashed.

"Come on, we need to keep moving west," Watcher said.

"Ok, but first I wanna go to my house quickly."
Planter grabbed the reins of her horse and headed
deeper into the village.

She led them past the charred remains of house after
house, some of them just an outline on the ground, their
walls and floors burned to ash. Finally, they reached
her ruined home.

She moved to the entrance and gazed at the remains.
The bottom half of a wooden door lay on the ground,
the top half smashed into splinters. Stepping inside,
Planter glanced around at the destruction, Watcher
and Mira a step behind. Inside, furniture lay toppled
on the ground, much of it broken, as if a great battle had been fought here, which it had. A tear trickled
down Planter's cheek as she stared at the ruins, then
moved farther into the house, Watcher now at her side.
Kicking aside broken chairs and overturned tables, she
moved to a chest, its lid torn off. Tiny wooden carvings
lay inside; toys made by her father's caring hands, each
now broken apart, their shattered pieces scratched by
zombie claws.

"I wonder if they found it?" Planter said softly.

"Found what?" Watcher asked, but she ignored him.

She moved to the back room, her former bedroom,
then shoved aside the bed. The magical glow coming
from her arms bathed the dark room in a soft purple
glow. The tiny red embers dancing around the edge of
her dark-blue armor added a warm crimson hue to the
darkening room. Dropping to her hands and knees,
Planter moved across the floor, staring intently at each
wooden plank.

"Here it is."

She wiped away a layer of dust and stared down at
a square of wood, just a shade darker than the rest. It
was a dark oak plank, its color almost indistinguishable
from the surrounding spruce planks.

Rising to her feet, Planter held her hand out to
Watcher. "Give me an axe."

He reached into his inventory and pulled out an iron axe, then handed it to her. Raising the tool up high, she brought it down upon the dark plank, the razor-sharp blade digging into the wood, cracks forming across its wooden face. Her arms pulsed with lavender light as she swung with all her strength, hitting it again and again, causing slivers of wood to fly into the air, spraying her with their pointed ends until, finally, the dark oak plank shattered. Watcher peered over her shoulder. In the hole was a small chest. Planter dropped the axe and knelt, slowly opening its lid. The hinges creaked and groaned, complaining about the many decades they had been ignored.

"My mom told me to come back for this after I escaped our house during the zombie attack. This box contains a family heirloom passed down from mother to daughter for generations." She paused for a moment, overcome by emotions. "My parents bought me the time I needed to survive—bought it with their lives."

A tear trickled down her cheek. Watcher moved to her side, but she held up a hand, stopping him. He stood back, resisting the urge to wrap his arms around her and hold her tight, but that relationship was gone, and now they were just friends, and barely that. "I don't know what's in here, but my parents were willing to protect it with their lives."

Planter reached into the chest and pulled out what looked like a golden key. When she held it up in the air for the others to see, the iridescent glow around her body suddenly stopped pulsing and shot into the key. The gold artifact grew bright as the magical energy flowed into it, then flashed, giving off such a brilliant lavender burst that everyone had to shield their eyes. When the light faded, the key glowed just like Planter, the pulsing light in the artifact synchronized with her body, as if it were a part of her now.

Mira moved closer and stared down at the key. "You know what that is, child?"

Planter shook her head.

"That's Sotaria's Key." The ancient wizard nodded, her long gray hair swaying back and forth.

"You mean the wizard that made my magical shield?" Planter asked.

"She didn't just make them." Mira glanced at Watcher, then back to Planter, making sure both were listening. "Sotaria put a small sliver of her consciousness into each of the shields, spreading her power across many of the artifacts." She moved closer to Planter and lowered her voice. "Sotaria told us she made the key before she sent her mind and powers into her shields. I never knew its purpose, but she said it was critical this key never become lost, for it would one day be needed in the final battle. I thought when the Great War ended we'd seen the final battle, and the key had been used somewhere . . . but here it is. Maybe she knew the final battle—the *real* final battle—would happen now, in this time, instead of centuries ago." Mira glanced at Planter and extended a hand. "I think it best I hold on to that."

Planter glared at the magical artifact, a look of hatred in her emerald-green eyes, then brought her angry gaze to the ancient wizard. "My parents gave their lives to protect me and this key. I'm not giving it to anyone." She stuffed it into her inventory, eyes blazing. "I don't know what this key unlocks, but my parents were willing to defend it with their lives, and I'll do the same, even though I hate its magic as much as I hate my own."

Mira turned to Watcher, the side of her unibrow raised, as if asking a silent question.

"Don't look at me," he said. "Planter makes her own decisions, and I agree with her. That key has been in her family's care for, I don't know, generations? Her parents paid the price for that key; it stays with her." He glanced at Planter, hoping for a smile or some recognition, but she just stared at the now-empty box.

With one foot, Planter kicked the chest closed, then turned and headed for the broken door. "I've seen enough. This life is gone. Let's go; there's an army of villagers out there somewhere, and we just need to convince them to go to war with us."

They followed her out of the shattered home and into the now-darkened village; the sun had finished setting, allowing a tapestry of sparkling stars to spread across the heavens. The rest of their company was already mounted and waiting, some of the NPCs glancing about at the destruction; for many of them, this had been their village too. Painful emotions were etched on many of their faces as the villagers thought about loved ones they'd lost. The effects of the destructive act brought upon them by the zombie warlord would forever leave a scar on their souls; only time would heal their wounds. But how much time did they really have if Krael was coming?

"There's another village to the west." Blaster pointed with one of the enchanted curved swords he'd taken from Wizard City weeks ago. The weapon gave off a soft iridescent glow, bathing him in a lavender hue until, putting the weapon back into his inventory, he nearly disappeared, his black leather armor merging with the darkness.

"Let's move," Cutter boomed. "I want to be at that village before sunrise."

Without waiting for a response, Cutter kicked his horse forward, casting a suspicious glance at Er-Lan, then urged his horse to a gallop and headed out of the village, the rest of the company following close behind.

Fixit, on the back of an iron wolf, glanced up at Watcher and smiled, then let out a loud whistle. The wolves in the forest howled in response, then followed the villagers to the west, the protective ring of wiry metal fur and fangs guarding against threats.

Watcher nudged his mount forward, moving up to Er-Lan's side. The two companions rode in silence as the ground rumbled under the footsteps of the iron golems around them, the metal giants pushing through low-hanging branches with steel fists. Out of the corner of his eye, Watcher glanced at his zombie friend and wondered. With his magic, he could feel Planter and Mira up ahead; somehow, he could feel their energy through the fabric of Minecraft. But with Er-Lan, he could feel nothing.

Cutter's wrong. There's no way Er-Lan's a warlock, Watcher thought, shaking his head. *If he were, I would detect something, and I don't feel anything coming from him.*

Sometimes, emotions cloud what we see, a high-pitched voice whispered in the back of Watcher's mind.

Reaching into his inventory, Watcher pulled Needle from his inventory and stared down at it. "Dalgaroth, you have something to say?"

The enchanted sword remained silent, the soft purple glow from the weapon adding to the light coming from his body.

"What did Watcher say?" Er-Lan glanced at his friend.

Watcher shook his head. "Nothing, never mind." He returned the blade to his inventory and rode in silence, but the tiniest seed of doubt now lay planted deep in his soul; was Er-Lan really his friend, his family . . . or was he here for another reason?

I couldn't bear it if Cutter's suspicions were true, Watcher thought. *I refuse to accept it.*

Ignoring something doesn't make it go away, Dalgaroth thought to him. *Truth is still truth, even if it is unwanted.*

The wizard's thoughts made Watcher sad as he thought about that possibility. A tear trickled down his cheek as he rode through the forest, a dark sadness enveloping him in an icy embrace.

CHAPTER 10

The king of the withers floated across Wizard City
like a predatory beast stalking its prey and waiting
to strike. His three Crowns of Skulls grew brighter
and brighter as he drew magical power from the artifacts
and funneled it into his impending attack. He gathered
more energy, making the crowns shine brighter than
the sun . . . and then he fired.

With a malicious grin on each of Krael's faces, three
flaming skulls shot through the air. The terrible projectiles struck the roof of a towering structure and
exploded. The iron covering buckled under the blast,
then shattered, raining glowing metal cubes on the
street below.

Krael smiled at his wife, Kora, then moved over the
building and peered inside.

"What do you see?" Kora asked.

He scowled. "Nothing . . . again!" Frustration filled
the monster's booming voice.

Gathering more power, he fired upon the exposed
floor, tearing it to bits, revealing the room below; it was
also empty, with just the remains of broken furniture
now littering the interior. With his frustration rising,
Krael continued to drill furiously through the building's

innards, removing floor after floor until he reached the ground level.

"It's not here!" The wither king's angry voice crashed across the ancient city, his rage amplified by the power of the three crowns upon his heads.

"Don't worry, husband, you'll find the portal. I have confidence in you." Kora moved to her husband's side, her presence calming him.

Krael looked up from the broken remains of the building and gazed out across the city below. Flaming skulls rained down upon structure after structure, the thunderous explosions echoing off the ironclad buildings. His army of withers was spread out all across Wizard City, the dark monsters searching the tallest buildings for the all-important portal.

On the ground, distorted monsters with seemingly random combinations of body parts from different creatures flowed down the streets and alleyways, flushing out the few remaining protectors still in the City. Occasionally, an iron wolf or one of the tiny metal children would emerge from the shadows and charge at the invaders. They didn't last very long.

Glaring down at the shattered remains of the iron building below him, Krael's anger built. "This was the seventh building I've destroyed, the largest one still standing. I thought for sure Tharus's portal would be here. I don't understand it. If I were Tharus, I would have put the portal in the largest and tallest building, so all would know of my power." His anger and frustration grew stronger and more dangerous as his power began to grow.

"Husband." Kora's voice instantly had a calming effect on him. "Perhaps this wizard did not want the other NPCs to know of its existence. Maybe it was only meant for him and was not shared."

"Perhaps. Tharus was always arrogant, but selfish as well. When he cast the spells to create you and me, and all the other withers, I recall his companions telling

Tharus it was too dangerous." Krael turned toward his wife. "One of the other wizards said, 'What if they turn on us?' and Tharus said something about how weapons could sometimes cut the hand that holds them . . . or something like that. But the part I remember clearly was what he said next. He said, 'Then you better be prepared, as I am.' That struck me as strange at the time, but now I think I understand. Tharus had his portal back then, and he wasn't planning on sharing it with anyone else."

Kora nodded. "If that's the case, then he'd hide it not just from us, but from his fellow wizards as well."

"Wife, you're brilliant, as usual." Krael floated higher into the air until his crowns brushed against the magical shield encompassing Wizard City, which had already repaired itself, then stared down at the iron buildings.

"Brothers and sisters, listen to me." Krael's voice boomed across the city, amplified by his crowns. "Stop searching the largest or most elaborate buildings. Instead, your king commands you to search the smallest and most insignificant structures. It will be in these tiny and uninteresting buildings that we'll find what we seek." He drew on the energy in the Crowns of Skulls, then fired three flaming projectiles, one from each skull. They smashed into the ground, causing the ground to shake as if struck by a gigantic meteor. The blast shocked his army, putting a bit of fear in every eye. "Find the portal, or I will be displeased, and may decide to use my flaming skulls for something other than smashing buildings."

The monsters and withers all moved quickly, entering smaller structures and smashing down walls, looking for the portal that would allow all of them to move to the Far Lands and get the revenge they all sought.

"Where is that small wither?" Krael asked. "Wife, what was his name?"

"Kobael."

"Right." Krael's crowns grew bright with power.

"Kobael, come to me, NOW!" His voice exploded across the city, shattering the few panes of glass not yet broken.

A small wither floated up from the buildings, a timid look on his three faces. Krael could tell the tiny monster was terrified. . . . *Good*, Krael thought, *a little fear is a good thing, a lot of fear is even better.* He glared at the creature until it was nearby him.

"Yes, my king," Kobael said. The wither was perhaps half the size of Krael, and looked more like a child than a soldier in the wither king's war.

"I want you to find the smallest buildings and go inside to search them," the king said.

"Go . . . inside?" Kobael's voice cracked with fear. "But that means I'll be close to the ground."

All withers hated being near the ground; they were vulnerable to weapons or claws. Altitude meant safety to a wither.

"Are you refusing an order from your king?!" the wither king glared at Kobael, his eyes growing brighter, preparing an attack.

"No, sire." The tiny wither lowered his heads to stare at the ground. "I will do as you command."

"Good. Then get to work."

Kobael bowed his head, then descended to a small structure sandwiched between a pair of towering buildings. He glanced up at his king as he neared the ground, likely hoping for a reprieve. Krael laughed, then nodded at the minute wither. With a sigh, Kobael entered the structure, searching for the hidden portal.

"You should be nicer to that tiny wither, husband." Kora floated to his side. "He's cute and harmless."

"Cute and harmless are not what I need in this army," Krael said. "He will do his share, no matter how dangerous, or face the consequences. And, as you know, there is only one consequence for a wither who will not fight."

"Death." Kora's voice was barely a whisper.

"That's right. Death." The wither king smiled at his wife. "Kobael will do his duty, and of that I have no doubt."

Krael and his wife floated across the city, firing their flaming skulls at smaller structures. With each collapsed roof and empty interior, Krael's frustration grew.

"Do you remember the day when we stopped doing our duty to the wizards?" Kora asked after a while.

"Of course. It was our proudest moment." Krael laughed. "The looks on their faces when we abandoned them and moved to the monsters' side were priceless."

"I can still remember the terrible things the wizards were doing to the landscape." Kora's voice had a sad, distant quality as the memory played through her three heads. "They made those massive stone columns to come shooting up out of the ground. Remember how it sent all those monsters flying up into the air, only to fall back to the ground, to their deaths?"

Krael nodded, his eyes narrowing with anger. "They used that other weapon to warp the monsters together, making the distorted creatures we have on the ground with us now."

"It was terrible," Kora hissed. "It not only mashed the monsters together into horrific and painful ways, but it also distorted the landscape, bending trees and distorting houses and their occupants, remember?" Her eyes narrowed like Krael's. "The wizards didn't care how much harm they caused, as long as they made sure monsters suffered. If we hadn't abandoned them and joined the warlocks, they may have won."

"All that fool Tharus cared about was the destruction of every monster in Minecraft," Krael said. "I bet after he destroyed the monsters, he would have turned on us, but we didn't give him that opportunity."

"No, we didn't, husband."

"I heard Tharus talk about his 'Answer' many times when he still thought we were his friends." Krael laughed. "He had some master plan to destroy all monsters on every world in Minecraft. It would have been great to know how he was going to do it; we could use it against the villagers instead."

"But we don't need to worry about that anymore," Kora said. "Tharus has been dead for centuries."

"Perhaps, but there are still three wizards out there." An angry glare spread across Krael's three faces; it happened whenever he thought about Watcher and his wizard friends. "Monsters will never be safe while those three wizards live. When we find this portal, we'll flood into the Far Lands and hunt them down like the animals they are."

The two withers stared down at the street below as Kobael exited the building. The puny monster glanced up at his king and shook his heads.

"Go find another building and search, you fool!" the wither king shouted, hurrying him along.

Krael growled with annoyance, then floated to the next small structure and hovered over it as Kobael hesitantly entered.

"Husband, won't the NPCs be preparing for our arrival?"

"Perhaps, wife, but they might be a little busy with some friends I'm sending them."

"Friends?" Kora asked.

Krael laughed. "Like I mentioned before, with the Crowns of Skulls I'm able to whisper in the ears of monsters across all the planes of existence. Soon, the monsters in the Far Lands will be enraged enough to attack every NPC they see. Watcher and his friends won't have time to recruit while they're being attacked."

"That sounds brilliant."

"And when we get there and face that idiot, Watcher, I'll have a special surprise ready just for him."

"What is it, husband? Tell me."

"It's something the wizards started to make, but after our betrayal, they chose to keep it hidden." Krael smiled. "That arrogant fool Tharus couldn't help himself; he had to write it down in his books. His thirst for fame will be the source of Watcher's destruction."

Kora giggled as huge smiles spread across her faces.

"When we unleash these new creatures, the NPCs will likely just drop their weapons and flee, but that still won't stop us from destroying every villager in Minecraft." Krael smiled at his wife. "Soon, we'll be exacting revenge on the last three wizards, and then Minecraft will be ours."

Kora laughed. "Then come, husband, let's motivate our troops to work harder. I'm getting impatient and want to be in the Far Lands now."

Krael nodded, then fired a string of flaming projectiles near a group of spiders, leaving the skeleton heads on their fuzzy black bodies staring up at him in fright. "Search the buildings, you fools! Find me the portal before I get even more impatient and vent my anger upon the slowest monsters I see!"

Instantly, the creatures on the ground scurried about as fast as their distorted legs would carry them, darting into the many abandoned buildings lining the streets.

"Search the small ones first; leave no door unopened," Krael boomed, his amplified voice crashing like thunder. "Soon, we'll be in the Far Lands; that's when the real fun begins."

His three skulls laughed as he fired indiscriminately at the ground, encouraging his army to work harder or die.

CHAPTER 11

Watcher's nerves were stretched thin as he rode through the dark forest, the silvery light from the moon overhead giving the surroundings a magical appearance; but it did little to quench the young wizard's fears. Being out at night was always dangerous, even when surrounded by huge golems and a pack of metallic wolves, because nighttime was monster time in Minecraft. The villagers' nervous eyes searched the darkness, hoping to find nothing, but many had swords and bows drawn, just in case.

Guiding his horse around a large bush, Watcher avoided some fallen branches on the ground, hoping his horse would not step on them and make any unnecessary sound.

Crunch.

He glanced over his shoulder, only to find Er-Lan riding behind him, his horse trampling the branches into dust.

"Er-Lan is sorry," he whispered, the chain mail helmet on his head jingling ever so slightly.

Cutter moved his horse up to the zombie's side softly. "Be quiet. We don't want to attract any attention to us, especially at night."

"Er-Lan said sorry." The zombie lowered his gaze to the ground.

The big warrior just glared at the monster, then yanked on the reins and pulled his mount off to the right flank.

"Don't worry about Cutter, Er-Lan." Watcher leaned over and put a hand under his friend's chin, then slowly raised it up. "He can be a little scary, but you have nothing to fear. You're part of this community and a member of my family. Don't forget that."

The zombie nodded and gave his friend a toothy grin.

"Something's approaching," Winger warned in a low voice. She pulled out an enchanted bow and notched an arrow, then stopped her horse and pulled back on the string.

Watcher drew Needle from his inventory, ready to charge at whatever was nearing their company.

Something pushed through some bushes, the tiny branches cracking under the heavy footsteps. A strained silence spread across the forest, as if the entire biome were waiting for something to happen.

Watcher glanced at Mirthrandos, whose long gray hair was like a river of silver under the light of the moon. "Why didn't the wolves give us a warning?"

The ancient wizard just glanced at Watcher and smiled. "You need to trust them more. If there were something out there, the wolves would let you know."

Another branch snapped under a heavy footfall; it was closer than the last.

"Does anybody see anything?" Cutter's voice was barely a whisper.

No one answered. The NPCs glanced at each other nervously and moved closer together, all of them ready to fight.

Watcher urged his mount to the front of the formation, the purple light from his enchanted sword adding to the iridescent glow of his body and casting a shimmering glow around him, but the forest outside the circle of illumination remained bathed in darkness.

Just then, something emerged from the shadows: a broad white smile, seemingly floating in midair.

"Everyone seems so nervous . . . what's going on?" the smile said, then a hand reached up and removed a dark helmet, revealing Blaster's face.

"Stand down, everyone, it's only Blaster." Watcher lowered his bow and wiped his brow.

"*Only* Blaster?" the young boy said as he moved to Watcher's side. "That seems a bit insulting."

"We thought some monster was approaching," Watcher explained, shaking his head.

"Great . . . now I'm a monster?" Blaster laughed, but suddenly grew very serious as he stared at someone approaching from behind Watcher.

"Blaster, you're back and safe, I was so worried."

Watcher instantly recognized Fencer's voice. He glanced at Blaster and smiled. His friend returned the smile with a scowl.

Fencer urged her horse forward, pushing past Watcher until she was at Blaster's side. "I was so scared while you were scouting ahead." She lowered her voice. "I tried to follow you, but with your black leather armor and that black horse you're on, you disappeared into the darkness, and I had to stay with everyone else instead."

"Ahh . . . too bad." Blaster grinned.

"But now you're back. I can keep an eye on you and make sure you're safe." Fencer gave the young boy a huge, adoring smile.

Blaster cringed while Watcher smiled.

"What's up ahead?" Cutter's sudden booming voice startled them all.

Blaster glanced at the big NPC. "There's a village up ahead. We'll be there before sunrise."

"Excellent, let's get moving." Cutter glanced down at Fixit riding atop the iron wolfpack leader and nodded.

The little mechite squeaked and whistled a complicated pattern of notes and sounds, then nodded back at Cutter.

"OK, the wolves and golems are ready," Cutter said. "Everyone, forward."

The party moved as quietly as possible through the oak forest, trying to avoid trampling bushes or fallen branches. Watcher glanced over his shoulder and spotted Planter. Slowing his horse, he let her catch up to him, then rode at her side.

"I didn't see you when Blaster was sneaking up on us," Watcher said. "I could have used your shield up at the front of the formation."

"You know I hate using this thing." She reached into her inventory and pulled out the shield. The three black skulls across the front seemed more threatening than usual somehow, the red background across the shield the color of blood. "Whenever I connect to it with my magic, I feel like it's trying to draw my mind out of my body."

"That sounds terrible." Watcher had learned it was better to be understanding with Planter rather than bossy or judgmental. "And you can't block out the feeling so that you can use the shield? It's a really important part of our defenses."

"So it's more important that I am?" Planter's eyes flared with anger.

"You know that's not what I mean." Watcher steered his horse around a tall birch tree, Planter going around the other side. "But you must admit, that shield has saved our lives more than once."

"Of course I know that," she snapped. "But each time, it pulled my mind deeper into its dark recesses. I'm afraid I'll get lost in there and be trapped within the shield, like those wizards in all your weapons."

"I'd never let that happen."

"And how are you gonna stop it?" She glared at him, then ducked under a low-hanging branch. "I know this shield is important. I know its magic is powerful. But I also know that every time I use this thing's magic, it pulls me in a little deeper."

"I know." He reached out and gently put a hand on her arm, but she pulled it away with a scowl, then shoved the shield back into her inventory. Watcher sighed. "We'll figure this out together. You need to trust me and—"

"Here's the village," Blaster shouted from up ahead.

The forest thinned out, revealing a cluster of wooden homes, each with light spilling from the windows. A light brown path wove through the community, leading them past large animal pens and broad fields of wheat and carrots. Tall posts held torches, the burning sticks casting a flickering glow on the community.

Watcher glanced down, searching for Fixit. He found the mechite riding with Er-Lan; the mechanical child had somehow jumped up into the saddle with the zombie and was sitting in front of him.

"Fixit?" Watcher said softly.

The mechite glanced at him.

Watcher lifted a finger in the air, then moved it in a circle, as if encompassing the village. The little creature nodded, then gave off a long whistle, followed by three short ones and a squeak. A wolf somewhere in the darkness barked, causing Fixit to smile and nod his shiny head.

"What was that?" Winger asked, and Watcher jumped. Somehow, she'd snuck up next to her brother without him noticing.

"I asked Fixit to have the wolves and golems surround the village. They'll keep an eye out for monsters or any unwanted guests."

She nodded, then turned away and headed for the village well at the center of the community. Watcher followed her, then dismounted and had someone lead his horse away.

"I see a lot of lights, but is anyone home?" Blaster asked him. "I'm sure they know we're here. Maybe we should—"

"Here comes somebody." Watcher glanced around,

making sure his soldiers were watching the treeline and not him.

"Hello, strangers." An old NPC with short gray hair stepped out of the shadows. He wore a black smock, a wide gray stripe running down the center. "You are certainly welcome, but this is a strange hour for visitors.

"Yes, I know." Watcher stepped forward. "I would rather have come at a more convenient hour, but time is short, and we have little to waste."

"What's going on?" the village's crafter asked, beginning to sound alarmed.

More NPCs emerged from their homes, some with weapons and armor ready. *They're cautious,* Watcher thought. *Good.*

Ease them gently into the truth. Baltheron's deep voice resonated in his head.

Watcher had the urge to pull the Flail from his inventory to look at it, but he knew that it wasn't necessary to communicate with the ancient wizard trapped in the weapon.

What do you mean? Watcher replied.

Ease them gently into the truth, or you'll scare them. A scared villager will not believe the truth of your words. And hide your magic—that'll be sure to cause some panic.

Watcher nodded and pushed his magical power deep within his soul, causing his arms to dim. *That's good advice, Baltheron, thank—*

Before Watcher could finish the thought, Cutter stepped forward and spoke in a loud voice.

"There's an army of withers coming to the Far Lands." Cutter's steel-gray eyes stared down at the old crafter. "The Great War is underway again, and it will be here soon. You and all your villagers must come with us and—"

"Withers? The Great War? That's ridiculous," the crafter said. "The Great War is ancient history, and withers aren't even real anymore. No one has seen one of those monsters in the Far Lands for centuries."

"Well, I have some bad news for you: Krael, the wither king is—"

Watcher interrupted. "What my impatient friend is trying to tell you is that a wither king has been in the Far Lands. And now it'll be here soon, with a huge army of withers and other monsters. I know this sounds unbelievable, but we're telling you the truth; the Great War is on its way to the Far Lands, and it will crush this village, without remorse. Your only hope is to join us and fight."

"We aren't joining some army to fight an unseen enemy." Another NPC emerged from the shadows. This one wore a full set of iron armor and held a gleaming iron sword in his hand. He stared at Cutter as if sizing him up. More villagers emerged from their homes, some with children in tow. "We're a peaceful village, and we will only fight to protect our families."

A group of villagers emerged from behind Watcher and his companions, each of them heavily armed.

"The question is," the NPC crafter continued, narrowing his eyes, "are you friend or foe?"

"This is ridiculous!" Mira shouted suddenly. The ancient wizard stepped forward, her crooked staff clicking on the hard ground with every step. She moved in front of the angry NPC, then let her magic flow into her body, casting a wide circle of lavender light. At the same time, she brought the end of the staff down onto the ground. Everything shook as the magical weapon fired a cluster of tiny rockets into the air, where they exploded high overhead, filling the sky with a thunderous blast.

The NPCs glanced up into the air in shock, then brought their terrified gazes back to Mirthrandos. At the same time, the metallic wolves and iron golems pushed through the foliage and lumbered into the village.

"Those—those are . . . ." Crafter was completely shocked.

"Golems . . . yes, I know." Mira glanced at Watcher and smiled.

"And the wolves, they're metal," another villager said in wonder.

"Very true," Mira replied. "They fought in the Great War beside me and the other wizards. Now, is this enough proof, or do I need to have the golems smash some of your houses to convince you we're serious?"

Crafter shook his head, still stunned. "What is it you need?"

Watcher released his grip on his own magic, allowing his body to glow again. Crafter stared at him now, eyes wide with surprise.

"You too?"

Watcher nodded, then glanced at Planter. She stepped out from behind a group of warriors, her arms and body giving off an intense lavender glow.

"There's three of you?" The crafter looked confused.

"We're gathering an army to find the wither king and his forces," Watcher said. "Our plan is to slow him down a bit while others make preparations for battle. Anyone who stays here in the village will likely be destroyed when Krael and his horde of monsters pass through. So, I have to ask you, do you choose to come with us and live, or do you want to stay here and choose death?"

He stepped closer to the crafter and extended a hand to him. The gray-haired NPC glanced over his shoulder at his friends and neighbors, many of them nodding. He brought his gaze back to Watcher and the soldiers in his company, then finally sighed and nodded. Glancing down at the glowing hand, the crafter extended his own and shook it.

Watcher smiled and was about to say something when Crafter's face took on a look of surprise and shock as a squeaking sound filled the air, followed by a loud howl. Turning, Watcher found Fixit yelling at the top of his lungs, hanging on to the silver fur of the wolf as it sprinted straight for him.

"Fixit, what's the problem?" Watcher glanced at Er-Lan. "What's Fixit saying?"

The zombie stepped out from behind Blaster and approached his friend.

"Look out, there's a zombie," Crafter yelled when he saw Er-Lan. "We need to—"

"Relax, Er-Lan is a friend and part of our community. You have nothing to fear." Watcher turned toward the zombie. "What did Fixit say?"

"Fixit says monsters are approaching from the south. There is little time; they will be here in a few minutes." Er-Lan glanced at Crafter nervously, then stepped back behind Blaster.

Watcher turned to Cutter. "We need to get ready. Get people building some defenses. We need archer towers." He glanced at Blaster. "You have time to build a few surprises."

Blaster just smiled and took off running toward the south side of the village with Fencer on his heels.

Watcher took a step toward Crafter. "We need your people. Keep those that cannot fight in hiding. We may not know what we're facing, but we'll stand against it together."

Crafter glanced at his iron-clad villager companion and nodded. The NPC banged his sword against his iron chest plate, causing a dozen more soldiers to come charging out of a nearby house and gather around him. Then Crafter pointed to the south and took off running toward the edge of the village, the rest of the warriors following.

Watcher streaked through the village. Ahead of him, Planter ran with Er-Lan and Fixit at her side. When they reached the edge of the forest, they found a wall already under construction between two large homes. Steps went up the walls, allowing archers to mount the sloped roofs, while warriors stood atop the fortifications with arrows already notched to bowstrings.

A villager moved to Watcher's side. "Why would the monsters attack now?"

The young wizard shrugged. "I suspect the wither king is somehow responsible, though I don't know how that's possible, since he's still in another plane of existence."

"Well, whatever he did, that wither obviously knows what he's doing." The villager pulled out an iron sword, then put on chain mail armor. "We haven't had an attack by monsters for maybe twenty years, and now, all of a sudden, this happens? I don't believe in coincidence."

"Me neither." Watcher nodded in agreement. "We'll deal with this attack, then figure out what to do next."

Suddenly, a silver wolf emerged from the tree line, a mechite hanging on to its thick, wiry fur. The metal animal easily leaped over the cobblestone wall, then skidded to a stop next to Fixit. The tiny creature on its back gave off a series of squeaks and whistles, Fixit nodding as he listened, then glanced up at Er-Lan. An expression of fear covered the zombie's face.

"What is it?" Watcher asked.

"The mechite says there are many monsters coming, more than the NPCs in this village." Er-Lan reached down and patted the mechite on its head. "The wolves can slow them now."

"No. We won't risk anyone unnecessarily." Watcher glanced down at Fixit. "Have all the wolves and golems come into the village, send half there and the other half there." He pointed to a pair of large buildings.

Fixit nodded, then gave off a shrill whistle. Wolves and golems emerged from the forest and moved into the village, the NPCs from the community looking shocked at what they were seeing. Watcher nodded in satisfaction, then turned and searched their troops. He spotted Planter near the back, shaking, as if she were terrified. Waving his hand, Watcher motioned for her to come next to him. She sighed, then pushed through the crowd of warriors, her eyes cast to the ground.

"Planter, we're gonna need your help." Watcher pulled out his enchanted bow, then gestured with it for her to do the same. With a reluctant smile, she drew her bow, standing up tall.

"Here they come," an archer shouted from the rooftop nearby.

The smell reached them first: the odor of rotten meat left out in the sun. Watcher held a hand over his nose, trying to block out the stench, but it did little good. Soon, the clattering of bones began to echo through the forest, with the clicking of spiders audible in the treetops. A wave of panic spread through Watcher as he imagined this battle going very wrong.

I'm responsible for these people. I can't let them down, he thought. He stood up straight, trying to look brave, but inside he was terrified. *If I can't stop this mob of monsters from the Far Lands, what hope do I have at stopping Krael?*

The sounds of monsters crashing through the undergrowth filled the air, amplifying everyone's fear, but the NPCs remained silent. They all knew they had to stand and fight to protect those behind them hiding in the homes.

The cold fingers of doubt wrapped themselves around his soul, his fear feeding its icy grip, until Watcher didn't know what to do. Then, paralyzed with uncertainty, the young wizard did the only thing he could do: wait for the battle to crash down upon them.

He wouldn't have to wait long.

CHAPTER 12

"**H**ere they come—I can see them through the trees," one of the archers said from the rooftop.

Blaster jumped up on top of the fortified wall, his enchanted curved swords absent.

"Get down from there, Blaster." Fencer moved to the wall and pulled on the hem of his pant leg. "The monsters will be here any minute."

Turning, Blaster just glanced down at her and smiled, then leaped off the wall and stood in front of it, waiting for the wave of fangs and claws to smash upon their fortifications. Fencer screamed, then scrambled onto the wall and stared down at the boy.

"What are you doing?!"

Blaster gazed up at her and smiled, then held a redstone torch high in the air. "My dad had a saying: 'Surprises are so much more fun when there's a big bang.'"

"You're insane." Fencer glared at him, then jumped down and stood at his side. "If you're gonna be stupid and just stand here, then at least I can try to protect you." Fencer drew an enchanted curved sword; it was one of the weapons she'd taken from Wizard City. She pulled out a wooden shield and held it in her left hand, then stared at the forest, the crashing footsteps of the approaching monster horde filling the air.

"I think now's a good time," Blaster said with a mischievous grin.

"A good time . . . a good time for what?" Fencer asked, confused.

Blaster smiled, then placed the crimson torch on the ground. Instantly, a line of redstone powder turned bright red, the glowing dust stretching off into the forest. A group of zombies showed their faces through a copse of trees and snarled . . . that was the last thing they did.

Blocks of TNT, hidden behind bushes or buried under sheets of grass, came to life, surrounding the monsters with their fiery embrace. The zombies went from angry to terrified as the blast threw them through the air, burning away their HP until they disappeared, leaving only glowing balls of XP falling to the ground.

"Is that all you were planning on doing?" Fencer asked.

Blaster raised a hand, signaling her to wait; the growing smile on his square face suggested the show wasn't over.

More explosions rocked the forest, tossing more monsters and debris into the air. With each detonation, Blaster laughed like a child opening a present, at times jumping up and down with excitement.

"I love TNT!" he exclaimed to Fencer, the young girl smiling at him. "It's almost over. We need to get back behind the wall."

Blaster placed a block of dirt on the ground as the last of the TNT detonated in the forest, then climbed up onto the wall, turned, and extended a hand to help Fencer. Her smile grew even wider at the offer, causing the boy to pull it back quickly, letting her climb atop the wall without any aid. Once she was behind the wall, Blaster dug up the dirt block with a shovel, making the wall unscalable again.

"Here they come," someone shouted from a rooftop. "They look a little beat up now, but really angry."

Just then, a horde of spiders, zombies, skeletons, and endermen charged out of the forest and crashed against their barricade. Immediately, pointed shafts rained down upon the monsters, the archers firing as fast as possible. Skeletons replied with their bows, forcing the NPCs on rooftops to move back and seek shelter.

"Planter, help the archers." Watcher pointed to the roof.

Relief covered Planter's face as she put away her magical shield and pulled an enchanted bow from her inventory. Nodding, she climbed the steps to the top of the house, then fired down at the monsters, her arrows wreathed in flame.

"Archers, aim for the skeletons," she ordered.

They launched their projectiles as quickly as possible, targeting the bony creatures. With the monsters bunched together against the wall, if they missed a skeleton, their arrows almost always found another monster. Screams of pain filled the air, but the monsters refused to yield; they just kept trying to destroy or climb the stone wall.

"What's driving them?" Winger asked next to Watcher. "It's as if they're insane."

Watcher was about to answer when a pair of black, fuzzy legs appeared atop the wall, each tipped with a wicked curved claw. The legs dragged a massive spider to the top, its eight eyes flaring red with crazed hatred.

Before he could even think, Watcher drew the Flail of Regrets and charged, his body blazing with magical power. He swung the weapon over his head, allowing his magic to flow through the wooden handle and metal chain until it settled into the spiked cube, which was glowing bright.

The spider before him paused for a moment, shocked at what it was seeing; that was its first mistake. Using every bit of his strength, Watcher brought the weapon down upon the creature. He missed; the fuzzy black monster leaped out of the way at the last instant. It then turned and charged at his sister, Winger; that was its second mistake. As the spider's claws sliced through the air, heading for his sister's head, Watcher dashed forward and held the Flail's handle in the air, blocking the attack before anyone was hurt. Then, spinning, he brought the weapon down onto the monster, the glowing ball smashing the monster and its HP. Struggling, the spider tried to regain its feet, but Blaster was there with his two curved swords, taking the last of the monster's health. It disappeared, leaving behind three glowing balls of XP.

"More are coming over the walls," Winger shouted in warning.

"Good." Watcher smiled. "Everyone, back up!"

The warriors gave ground to the approaching spiders. At the same time, the cobblestone blocks in the wall finally shattered under the claws of the zombies. The green monsters along with the few remaining skeletons moved through the debris and followed their spidery companions. Endermen teleported back and forth, trying to get into the fight, but they couldn't attack unless they were attacked first, or were stared at by an NPC.

"Keep moving back!" Watcher shouted.

"No, don't retreat!" Cutter stepped forward, his diamond sword slashing at the spiders with lethal precision.

"Cutter, retreat!" Watcher tried to get to his friend's side, but a spider was in the way. "Stay with everyone else."

But the big warrior refused to retreat; it wasn't something he did very well, and Watcher knew it. Suddenly, a green body streaked past, then stopped right behind Cutter; it was Er-Lan. The zombie grabbed the back of Cutter's armor and pulled him backward, toward the rest of the villagers.

"Hey . . . what's happening?" Cutter tried to look over his shoulder, but a spider stepped near, distracting him. He slashed at the monster as he moved backward, allowing more monsters to flow into the village after him.

"Keep going back . . . keep retreating." Watcher glanced at the large buildings to the left and right; they were almost there.

Another spider charged toward Cutter, but Blaster appeared at his friend's side, the boy's enchanted blades carving paths of destruction through the monster's bodies. The two continued to retreat as the horde flooded into the village.

Fencer ran across the spiders' bodies, stepping lightly on their fuzzy backs, as if they were part of some parkour course. She landed next to Blaster, her curved sword, like Blaster's, glowing bright with magical enchantments. Slashing at the monsters like a skilled warrior, she kept the creatures from attacking Blaster's flanks, helping them retreat faster.

Watcher glanced at the buildings again, then raised a fist into the air. "NOW!"

Suddenly, wolves and golems from the left and right charged into the fray, catching the monsters by surprise. Before the shocked attackers could respond, Watcher shouted again, "CHARGE!"

The NPCs closed in from the front, while the wolves and golems attacked from the sides, nearly surrounding the monsters. Watcher hoped they would just retreat, but he saw the same look in all of their terrible eyes: pure, uncontrolled rage.

As he reached the monsters, Watcher swung the Flail with all his strength, smashing zombies and spiders. Winger stepped up to his side, her enchanted bow humming a song of death. The *Flame* enchantment on the weapon set each of her shots ablaze, making the pointed shafts do extra damage. Because of Blaster's TNT, only a single hit was required to destroy most of the monsters.

"Run away," Watcher shouted at the monsters. "Don't just fight and die."

A zombie stared at him, then snarled viciously. "The voices say NPCs want to destroy our children. We'll never let you do that."

"We don't want to—"

The zombie didn't listen. Instead, it dove at Watcher with its sharp claws extended, reaching for his throat and catching him by surprise.

Suddenly, a wall of purple flames enveloped Watcher. Glancing to the left, he found Planter at his side, her magical shield in her grip. She grimaced, then sent more power into the shield. Monsters threw themselves at the enchanted barrier, but the iridescent purple flames projected by the magical artifact just burned away the monsters' HP.

"Planter, move forward!" Watcher grabbed her arm and stepped closer to the monsters. "They'll see your shield and run away."

She sighed and stepped forward, staying at his side.

The monsters, seeing the magical duo, charged at the two wizards, but none of them stood a chance.

Suddenly, Mirthrandos appeared atop one of the houses, her crooked wooden staff held over her head. She pointed it at the monsters, then poured her magical power into it. Tiny, glowing projectiles shot from the end and bombarded the monsters. As they struck, black smoke rose from the creatures' seared skin, the monsters howling in pain until they disappeared as their HP burned away.

Finally, the last of the monsters perished, leaving the village and surrounding forest eerily quiet. Watcher glanced around, seeing countless glowing balls of XP on the ground; they all seemed to be from the monsters. But then he spotted a pile of discarded items on the ground, then another and another; it was the inventory of fallen villagers, the only things left marking their existence in Minecraft. Tears welled up in Watcher's eyes, but he knew he couldn't cry, not now; there would always be time for tears later. . . if there was a later.

Bending over, Watcher picked up an iron sword and held it in the air. "This is what Krael sends us; death and destruction."

"Why do you think this was Krael's doing?" Blaster asked.

"Did you see the crazed expressions on their faces?" Watcher bent down and picked up a bow that lay surrounded by the XP of countless monsters. "These weren't normal monsters; they were insane, thirsting for our destruction. One of them said something about voices whispering to them, telling them we were gonna destroy their children."

"Why would the monsters think we'd do something that terrible?" Planter stuffed her magical shield into her inventory, a look of relief washing across her square face, then looked down at the dark blue armor still wrapped around her body. She reached up and tried to pull the sparkling helmet off her head, magical red embers dancing around its edges, but it didn't move. With a scowl, she turned to Watcher.

"I'm telling you, it must be Krael," Watcher said. "Somehow, the wither king is whispering things in the monsters' minds, making them hungry for violence." He looked up toward Mira. "It's possible, right?"

The ancient wizard's long gray hair swayed as she nodded. "With all three Crowns of Skulls, that wither possesses a lot of magical power. Who knows what he can do with it?"

"This is a great talk and all, but I think we should be moving." Blaster put his enchanted swords into his inventory. He glanced at Fencer, then stared down at the ground, eyes wide; glowing balls of XP from the many monsters she'd destroyed littered the ground around her feet. "Which way do we go from here?"

Watcher glanced at Mirthrandos. "What do you think?"

The ancient wizard shrugged. "I guess we keep going deeper into the Far Lands."

"I think we need a better plan than just heading in some random direction." Blaster stepped away from Fencer and moved to Watcher's side. "Let's look at some maps."

With a nod, Watcher scanned the sea of faces around him. "Mapper, where are you?"

"Here." The old man pushed through the crowd until he reached Watcher. Then, reaching into his inventory, he pulled out a map, its edges frayed and torn, as if it had been ripped from a larger sheet. "You remember this map?"

"Sure. It's the magical one we took from the forest mansion," Watcher said.

"Touch it, so we'll know where we're at." Mapper extended the frayed map.

With an extended finger, Watcher touched the ancient chart. A purple spark leaped from his finger and danced on the edge of the map, then disappeared. Instantly, the image on the map blurred and slowly resolved, showing the terrain around them, the villager at the center. Watcher placed two fingers on the paper and drew them together, causing the map to zoom out until the village was just a faint dot, the biomes of the Far Lands looking like swaths of cloth in a strange and colorful quilt. Sections of forest could be seen butting up against patches of desert and areas of frozen tundra. Every biome in Minecraft was represented on the map, but one of them seemed strange.

"What's that sickly green spot?" Watcher asked.

Mapper shook his head. "I don't know."

Mira jumped down from the house, surprisingly agile for an ancient wizard. She peered over Mapper's shoulder. "I think I know what that is. Zoom in on it."

Watcher placed two fingers on the strange section of the map, each next to the other, then separated them quickly; the map zoomed in until that bizarre section was visible. "It looks like a swamp, but the color is weird."

"That's because it's not just any swamp." Mira brought her gaze to Watcher, her bright green eyes boring into his blues. "It's called the Poison Swamp."

"Poison Swamp?" Watcher was confused. "Why would a swamp be poisonous?"

"Many thought it was Tharus's doing." She glanced at Er-Lan. "Some claim it was the monster warlocks . . . no one is sure. The paths leading through that swamp curve in all directions like a maze. Those who have entered were never heard from again."

"That sounds like a wonderful place." Blaster grinned sarcastically.

"I may not know much about wizards and magic," Mapper said. "But if I wanted to hide a portal somewhere in the Far Lands, in the middle of a mazelike poisonous swamp would seem like a good place."

Watcher nodded. "Mapper, you're probably right. If we could get there before Krael and his army of monsters comes through, we could destroy the portal and stop this war before it even starts." He glanced at his companions, all of them nodding in agreement. "I say we head for the Poisonous Swamp; it's in the right direction."

"You mean deeper into the Far Lands?" Winger asked.

"Yep, and on the way, we stop at every village we can find and bring those NPCs to our cause."

"Agreed," Mira said.

Watcher waited for objections, but he heard none. "Alright, then. Gather everything you'll need; we leave in five minutes."

The villagers murmured to each other as they headed to their homes to gather what they needed for war.

Glancing down at the map again, Watcher got an uneasy feeling. That tingling sensation was still there in the back of his mind; he could feel Krael, and he felt certain the wither could sense him as well. Were they doing the right thing? Or were they running directly into the jaws of the beast? Uncertainty and fear spread through Watcher's body, igniting every nerve with anxiety, but he knew there was no other choice; they had to go to the Poisonous Swamp and find Krael, even though it would likely cost many lives.

CHAPTER 13

Krael snarled as he fired his flaming skulls into another small building, peeling off the roof as if it were paper. Floating over the half-destroyed structure, he peered into its interior . . . nothing, again. Krael glared down at the empty room, his anger causing the Crown of Skulls on each of his three heads to glow bright.

"I grow frustrated, wife." The wither king glanced at Kora. "It must be here, but there are thousands of buildings in Wizard City; this is taking too long."

"I'm sure we'll find it soon. The arrogant wizards cannot hide anything from the great king of the withers." Kora's soothing voice always seemed to calm Krael's rage.

"You have such patience, Kora. I admire that," Krael said, and his wife beamed with pride at the compliment. We must find that portal. I can feel that idiotic wizard across the Pyramid of Servers. He's likely getting ready for our invasion, and the longer this takes, the more prepared he will be."

"Is there something we can do to hinder him?" Kora asked.

Krael gave her a knowing smile. "I'm already doing it. The monsters in the Far Lands grow restless because of the messages of hatred I've been whispering in their ears. The dim-witted monsters think these thoughts are true." Krael's smile grew even bigger. "I've been saying the NPCs want to destroy all their children. You can't imagine the anger that's blossoming within these monsters as a result. I can sense their rage . . . almost taste it." The wither king smiled. "It's delicious."

"That's brilliant." Kora's voice made Krael beam with pride.

"The monsters will attack Watcher and his foolish companions at every opportunity. By the time we get to the Far Lands, the NPCs there will already be too scared to help that pathetic wizard and his puny band of followers. We just need to find that por—"

Suddenly, a distorted enderman with the arms of a spider and the head of a blaze appeared on the roof nearby, the monster wrapped in a mist of purple teleportation particles.

"My king, I think the portal has been found," the enderman said. "Follow me."

The dark monster teleported down to the street, Krael floating through the air as he followed. The shadowy monster then teleported to the end of the street and waited for his king. As Krael approached, the monster disappeared, then materialized at the door of a small structure, far from the center of Wizard City. The building had the same iron walls all of the structures did, though this one was only six blocks high and as many wide. An iron door set in the middle of one wall was the only feature on the cube-shaped structure. No lever, button or pressure plate was visible to allow them to enter. As Krael moved near, he spotted a strange green light seeping around the edges of the door, a faint humming from inside.

"Everyone, get back." Krael's voice boomed off the buildings lining the street, echoing back and forth, making it seem as if there were many Kraels speaking at once. The Crowns of Skulls gave off a bright lavender glow as his power built, filling the wither's body with energy.

And then he fired.

A flaming skull smashed into the door, causing it to bend inward and glow a soft orange. The wither fired again, sending two more skulls at the metal barrier. The iron door glowed brighter and brighter, denting under the assault, then shattered into a million shards, a cloud of dust and smoke billowing into the air. Instantly, green light from within the tiny building flooded into the street, painting the stone-covered ground and iron walls with an emerald hue.

The wither king glanced at the nearby withers. "Where's Kobael?" He floated higher into the air·and shouted. "KOBAEL, COME HERE NOW!"

The tiny wither emerged from behind a tall structure, an expression of perpetual fear on the small monster's faces, as always.

Krael scowled at the small creature. "Go into that building and tell me what you see."

Swallowing nervously, Kobael bowed. "Yes, my king."

The wither shook nervously. To refuse an order from Krael was to invite death. With a sigh, Kobael descended to the door and floated into the tiny building. Almost instantly, the creature emerged again.

"I told you to go in and check it out, you fool." Krael scowled at the wither.

"The portal . . . it's there." The fear painted across Kobael's dark skulls was replaced with expressions of relief. "It's sitting right in the center of an empty room. There are no traps anywhere in sight."

"Excellent." Krael smiled at his wife who floated nearby. "All monsters, come to my voice. Our portal has been found."

The wither king's voice boomed across Wizard City. A cheer rose into the air as the monsters ran toward his voice, his withers flying across the rooftops like an unstoppable flood.

Krael floated high into the air, making himself easily visible to the approaching mob. The withers headed directly for their leader, while the warped and distorted monsters on the ground ran through the streets, coming from all directions. Their pounding footsteps echoed off the tall buildings, making it sound as if they were in the middle of a thunderstorm.

"Go through the portal, my brothers and sisters. The Far Lands yearn to be conquered."

The monsters snarled and growled as they charged into the squat building. Krael descended and watched the monsters file into the glittering portal, his angry glare making them move faster. When the ground forces had all passed through the magical doorway, the withers descended and moved into the building, their skulls glancing about nervously in all directions, looking for threats. They didn't like the confines of the iron-clad structure, but knew if the King's command were refused, it would likely mean their deaths.

When the last of the floating creatures passed through the portal, Krael and Kora approached the doorway.

Krael glanced at his wife. "This will mark the end and the beginning."

"The end and the beginning of what?" she asked.

He gave her a vicious grin. "The end of the Great War started by the ancient wizards hundreds of years ago, and the beginning of the new Great War started by me." He laughed.

"And also, the beginning of another historic event."

"What?"

This time Kora gave the evil grin. "The extermination of the last wizards in Minecraft."

"Wife, you are perceptive, as usual." Krael beamed with pride in his mate. "Come, it's time for us to go to the Far Lands again. I have a little gift for that fool Watcher."

Both withers chuckled with evil glee as they passed through the portal and began the destruction of the Far Lands.

CHAPTER 14

As the group rode, a chill suddenly spread across Watcher's skin like the slow creep of the arctic tide as it moves inland, freezing everything with its icy touch. The sensation made his flesh feel cold and lifeless, as if his body were dying, but the feeling also spread inward, to his very soul. They were in a cold taiga biome, the ground and soaring spruce trees all covered with snow, but it wasn't the chill in the air giving him this terrible feeling; it was something else, something . . . evil.

Pulling on his reins, Watcher brought his mount to a halt, then drew his weapons, Needle in his left hand and the Flail of Regrets in his right. Scowling, he turned in the saddle and stared at Planter; she had the same expression of horror on her face. She pulled out her bright red shield, the three wither skulls across the center staring out at the environment as if they were alive. A look of pained resignation spread across Planter's face as her magical power built, making her body give off a bright iridescent glow. She sent the magic into her shield, igniting a wreath of purple flames dancing along the edges of the wooden rectangle.

"Did you feel it too?" Watcher asked.

She nodded, but remained silent.

"Mira . . . I think—"

"I know . . . he's here." The ancient wizard's scratchy voice was edged with fear. "Krael must have found Tharus's portal." She gave off a low growl. The wolves heard it and did the same, the metallic animals feeling her frustration. "I told that arrogant wizard having his own, unprotected portal was dangerous, but he just denied its existence." She turned to Watcher. "Now he's let untold numbers of monsters into the Far Lands. I knew Tharus's overconfidence would be his undoing, but I didn't think it would be ours as well."

"Maybe we should find out how many monsters the wither king has," Blaster suggested.

"You're so smart." Fencer urged her horse closer to the boy's side and smiled, their legs brushing against each other.

Blaster grimaced and moved away from her; some of the NPCs giggled.

"I think you're right, Blaster." Watcher reached into his inventory and pulled out the Eye of Searching, then glanced at Planter. "Last time I used this, Krael made it burn my skin, so we need to be fast. You have healing potions?"

She nodded, her blond hair spilling down her shoulders, the morning sun making her locks appear like a golden waterfall.

Watcher jumped off his mount and sat on the ground, leaning against the trunk of a tall spruce. His breathing grew rapid as he thought about the imminent pain to come, each exhalation forming billowing clouds of fog in the icy air.

Planter dismounted and moved next to him, a splash potion of healing held at the ready. Her arms and chest gave off a bright radiance as magic flooded her body. She glanced down at the iridescent glow, a look of disgust spreading across her square face.

Watcher glanced up at her; she nodded. With a sigh,

he wrapped the leather straps around his head and tied them at the back, then positioned the glass lens over his eye. Instantly, the artifact gave off a flash of purple light, then reached into Watcher's HP and took what it needed. He groaned as pain seeped through his body, his skin feeling as if it were aflame. Planter held the splash potion of healing over Watcher, but he shook his head.

"Not yet," the young wizard groaned; he could still withstand a little more.

Closing his eyes, he concentrated on Krael. Instantly, an image of the wither king appeared in his mind. The monster was floating across what looked like a poisonous bog. Stagnant pools covered the ground with a sickly shade of green, a putrid mist clinging to the poisonous surface. Behind him, his army of withers floated, likely two hundred strong. They smiled down at the foul landscape as if they enjoyed the terrible biome.

"I can see the withers, they're—" Watcher groaned, gritting his teeth to hold back a scream. He glanced up at Planter and nodded. A liquid splashed across his shoulders, easing some of the pain. "They're floating across some kind of foul, stagnant pools—the water's colored a terrible green."

"It's poisonous swamp far to the west," Mira hissed. "I knew it."

"Are there any of the other monsters with him?" Blaster asked.

Watcher closed his eyes again. The image of Krael appeared, the monster's skulls each showing vicious grins. Imagining himself moving away from the wither king, Watcher made the image zoom out, allowing more of the swamp to come into view. He gasped in shock. "Yes, he brought those distorted monsters with him. I can't see them all because of a pale mist covering the ground, but some of them are visible. I bet Krael probably has a hundred of them with him . . . maybe more."

"You mean those things that were part skeleton, part zombie, part . . . whatever?" Cutter asked.

Watcher nodded.

"This just gets better and better." Blaster laughed.

"What do you mean part skeleton, part zombie, part . . . whatever?" Winger asked.

"They're a mishmash of body parts, something the wizards created during the Great War." Planter glared angrily at Mira. "The wizards discarded them in that world when they thought the War was over, letting them suffer through their lives. Now, they're with Krael, which means apparently we must fight a ground force as well as an air force."

"There's time for recrimination later." Mira glanced at Watcher. "Find the portal. We need to know if any more monsters are coming through."

Watcher nodded, then closed his eyes again and concentrated. Needles of pain jabbed at his skin as the Eye of Searching took more HP. Agony swept over his body, but Watcher pushed the pain aside and focused on Krael. The image appeared again. Drifting to the back of the army, Watcher moved higher into the air. Finally, a rectangle of iron blocks came into view, a sparkling sheet of green energy filling the ring; it was empty.

"No more monsters are coming through." Watcher gave a sigh of relief. "Krael just has the monsters I've seen on the ground and in the air."

He reached up and was about to remove the Eye of Searching when something dark flashed past his view. A cold, prickly sensation spread across his body, like a thousand frozen spiders crawling across his skin.

"Krael," he whispered.

Watcher turned his view and moved backward, bringing the king of the withers into sight, his three Crowns of Skulls glowing bright with magical energy.

"I see you, boy. You *still* think you can spy on me with that pathetic Eye without me knowing . . . ha!" Krael laughed, his eyes filled with vicious hatred. "I'm coming for you and your friends, and if you think this is my entire army, then you're a bigger fool than I thought. Soon, I'll crush you and that pathetic girl with the shield and the old woman, but not until I destroy every other NPC in the Far Lands. You'll be forced to watch their suffering while I punish them for their crimes."

"What did they do?!" Watcher demanded. "What did the NPCs of the Far Lands ever do to you?"

"They exist, and for that, they will be punished. And after I've forced you to watch all their suffering, then it will be your turn. Prepare to meet your doom."

The wither king's three crowns grew bright with power, then he shot a ball of magical energy straight at Watcher. Instantly, searing heat enveloped the Eye of Searching again. Watcher pulled the enchanted artifact off his face just before it shattered, throwing tiny shards of glass across his face; the Eye of Searching was gone.

"That discussion didn't seem like it ended well." Blaster didn't give Watcher a sarcastic smile this time.

"No, it didn't." Watcher stood and tossed the now-useless leather straps on the ground. "We need to find more troops. There's a large village to the northwest, in the Extreme Hills biome; my dad told me about it once."

"That'll put us closer to Krael and his army." Planter sounded scared.

Watcher nodded. "I know, but if we don't get to that village before Krael, they'll never know what hit them. Those monsters will wipe out every man, woman, and child. We have to get there first and evacuate that village, then try to slow that monster horde and give the villagers back at the Wizard's Tower time to prepare."

"We're with you, Watcher." Blaster nodded.

"Yeah," Fencer added, throwing a grin towards Blaster.

The young boy cringed; Watcher smiled.

Planter just shook her head, the glow from her body getting dim.

"Planter, are you alright?" Watcher asked.

She shook her head. "I don't have a good feeling about this. Something, deep inside, is telling me to run."

"I know, I'm scared too," Watcher said.

Fixit moved next to her and purred, driving the worried scowl from Planter's square face. The tiny mechite attached a sharp knife to his right wrist and held his hand up high, flashing a confident smile to the young wizard.

Reaching down, Planter ran her fingers through Fixit's soft metallic hair. "I feel better knowing you're there to protect me, Fixit."

The mechanical child smiled, then turned to the wolves and whistled. Three of the majestic animals moved next to Planter and stared up at her, their eyes filled with strength.

"Fixit told them to protect Planter," Er-Lan said. "Now, Planter has four protectors."

"Four?" Winger asked.

Sharp claws slowly extended from the zombie's fingers. Cutter reached for his sword, but Er-Lan ignored him. "Er-Lan is the fourth. Nothing will be allowed to harm Planter."

Planter nodded. She reached down and patted each of the metal animals on the head, then hugged Er-Lan. "I feel better knowing you're all there for me." She glanced up at the rest of the villagers and smiled. "All of you, too."

The NPCs smiled. Planter stared down at her glowing arms again and the smile instantly faded.

"If we're gonna do this, then let's get it done." Blaster nodded to himself, then drew his two enchanted curved swords and jumped back into the saddle. "I think it's time we rode hard. I don't like the idea of trying to fight those monsters at night."

"Agreed." Cutter's voice boomed across the frozen landscape. He glanced down at Fixit. "We'll need perimeter guards and forward scouts."

Fixit whistled the commands to the other mechites, wolves, and golems, then jumped up onto the back of one of Planter's wolves and glanced at Cutter impatiently.

"Fixit is ready, so let's get going." Planter smiled down at her protectors, then mounted her horse and urged it forward.

The rest of the NPCs drew their weapons and nudged their mounts in the ribs with their heels, moving them to a gallop.

Watcher climbed into the saddle as the company rode past. He looked at every face, some appearing strong and brave, while others looked terrified. They all knew Krael was out there with his monster horde, and when their forces clashed, a terrible battle would ensue.

How many of them will die because of my decisions? Watcher thought. There was a time when he'd been just an insignificant, almost-invisible villager who no one noticed or cared about, other than Planter. But now, he was the one to decide if they fought or ran, if they charged into battle or used some kind of trick that would turn the tide; he was the one to decide who lived or died. The weight of this responsibility was almost unbearable . . . it made his soul ache.

But Watcher knew they had to fight now. Those back at the Wizard's Tower needed time to prepare, or all was lost.

That scratchy, jagged itch in the back of his mind told him something terrible would happen soon, but what, he didn't know. Which of the villagers would never see home again? Watcher would find out soon enough, and then he'd have to add those lost lives to the growing list of dead heroes etched forever into his memories.

CHAPTER 15

Krael floated through the sweltering air as tiny cubes of sweat ran down his dark forehead, most of the moisture evaporating before it reached his eyes. He wanted to wipe his brow somehow, but with his lack of arms, it was impossible.

"I hate desert biomes," he growled.

"I like them." Kora looked at her husband and smiled. "The lack of life makes them seem clean and fresh."

"But what about the cacti? They're alive."

"Well, sure, the cacti are indeed alive," Kora said. "But with all those razor-sharp spines, what's not to like about them?"

"Yeah, I guess." Krael glared up at the oppressive sun overhead, then surveyed their surroundings. "I can hear the echo of magic in this desert. Likely, Tharus created this desert as an additional obstacle."

"An obstacle for what?" Kora asked.

"If anyone were to go looking for Tharus's portal, they'd have to cross this sweltering desert. It would probably dissuade the curious from venturing too close to the poison swamp and his little secret."

Kora nodded.

"That's what I would have done, but I would have

added more monsters and—" Krael suddenly stopped speaking and glanced around, as if looking for something, then stared straight down at the sandy ground. "This is a good spot."

"A good spot for what?" Kora moved to his side, floating back-to-back with him, watching for threats.

"Withers, gather around me." Krael's voice boomed across the lonely desert. "Keep the ground forces away." The wither army formed a wide circle around their king, then fired flaming skulls at the ground, encouraging the monsters to keep back.

"What are you doing, husband?"

"Something important." Krael slowly moved toward the ground, Kora descending with him. "Below the sand, there are layers upon layers of stone, stretching all the way down to the limit of Minecraft. I can sense those layers through the Crowns of Skulls."

He moved closer and closer to the ground until his stubby spine rested on the hot sand. Kora stayed a few blocks off the ground, afraid to be too low.

The wither king closed his eyes and concentrated, the three Crowns on his heads glowing brighter and brighter until the lavender glow even pushed back on the yellow rays of the sun, painting an iridescent circle on the sand. Some of the blocks within the sparkling circle started to smoke, their tops turning black as the powerful magic charred their speckled faces.

Krael's breathing grew strained as he inhaled and exhaled faster and faster to take in enough air to support the terrible strain on his body. Sweat poured down his dark heads, flowing across his closed eyes and leaking into his mouths; the tiny cubes tasted salty and warm.

Krael's magic allowed him to sense the rock beneath the sand. It stretched down many blocks until it merged with the bedrock layer at the bottom of Minecraft, where, just below the bedrock, Krael felt something dark and terrifying . . . the Void. Fear nibbled at the edges of his senses as his magic probed the deadly Void; no creature could survive the Void, not even Krael.

I wonder if the Crowns of Skulls would keep me alive in that terrifying darkness? he thought, but knew he'd never attempt that test, it would be foolish and possibly fatal.

With a deep breath, Krael poured his magic into the bottom of the bedrock, sending a message across the thin layer between life and death, between Minecraft and the Void, letting it expand in all directions. Concentrating his power, he pushed the magic as far as possible, letting it infect as much of the bedrock layer as his power would allow. When the magic had spread as far as it could, Krael took another deep breath, then gave the sheet of magic a push upward, back toward the surface. His enchanted message slowly seeped through the blocks of sand, rock, dirt, and gravel, percolating up through the dark layers of the Far Lands until it reached the air and bubbled into awaiting ears.

At that moment, Krael's army of mismatched creatures suddenly froze and listened to the whispering voice in their malformed ears. They growled and snarled as the words formed in their minds, making them angrier and angrier.

"What's happening?" Kora asked.

Krael floated back up into the air. "I whispered my message of hatred to all the monsters in the Far Lands." He glanced at Kora, a satisfied grin on each of his ashen skulls. "I was already bending the minds of a small number of monsters in this world, but now, my message is reaching many thousands of monsters. Soon, they'll start attacking every NPC village. As long as my magical spell resides down there in the bedrock, it will continue to play, driving the monsters of the Far Land into a violent rage."

"That's fantastic," Kora said, her six eyes beaming with pride.

"In addition to distracting and weakening the NPCs,

my whispers of rage will drive many monsters to us, swelling our ranks until this army is bigger than anything seen during the Great War."

The other withers around Krael smiled, then bowed their heads to their king in recognition of his greatness.

"Where do we go now, husband?" Kora asked, looking around.

"First, there is another task I must perform." The wither king glanced at the monsters surrounding him. "All of you should back away from me."

The withers floated back, pushing the monsters on the ground away as well.

Krael closed his six eyes and focused on his magic. As before, the Crowns gave off a purple glow, its radiance growing brighter and brighter until the nearby monsters had to turn away, the intensity too great. Some moaned in fear, afraid the King's magic might cause them harm.

Ignoring the sounds of terror from his horde, Krael pulled as much magic as he could from the three Crowns. He felt as if he were burning from the inside, the magic searing his nerves, but he kept drawing on the incredible power held within the three enchanted artifacts.

Nearby, a monster screamed in terror and fell to the ground, fainting from fear. It made Krael growl with annoyance.

When he thought he'd drawn as much power as he could possibly contain, Krael focused his mind on the Far Lands, then released his hold on the magic. An iridescent blast of energy flowed out from the wither king, washing over the monsters around him and then traveling outward into the landscape.

Opening his eyes, Krael watched the wave of magic speed away, the unstoppable storm of shimmering power growing dimmer as it spread outward. It grew fainter and fainter until it was no longer visible, but Krael knew the energy had not diminished; there was enough power in that spell to flow in an ever-widening circle, spreading through the Far Lands until, eventually, it would spread into the Overworld.

"What was that, husband?" Kora slowly moved to his side.

"I've sent out a spell to modify the monsters of this world." Krael smiled, pleased with himself. "The monsters on this plane of existence will no longer be burned during the day; they'll now be impervious to the harsh rays of the sun. Let that throw a little fear into the hearts of the villagers."

Krael floated higher into the air, his wife at his side. "There is an extreme hills biome to the east of here. There we will gather more monsters . . . and meet an old friend." Krael laughed as if he knew a secret.

"An old friend . . . what are you talking about?" Kora glanced at the other withers, looking to see if any understood.

"I can clearly sense that fool, Watcher." Krael smiled. "When we were on a different plane of existence, he was but a tickle in the back of my mind, but now, I can sense his presence. I don't understand how it's possible, because I didn't know the Crowns of Skulls could do it. When Tharus created these Crowns, their original purpose was to find magical weapons made by the monsters, but when I wear them, they give me the ability to sense my enemies." He turned and scanned his army, a satisfied expression on his three skulls. "We'll have a little reunion with that boy-wizard and his other magical friends soon enough. In a single attack, the last wizards of Minecraft will be destroyed, leaving us free to take the Far Lands for ourselves!"

"Fantastic, we'll end this war sooner than I thought." Kora smiled at her husband.

"End it sooner, ha . . . it has only just begun." Krael laughed. "After we destroy the wizards and exterminate all villagers in the Far Lands, then we'll cleanse the Overworld of their NPC infection, too. And after this world is sterilized, we'll move to the other Planes of Existence until every NPC is gone." He glared at the landscape around him. "I'll make them regret ever trying to imprison my wife in that Cave of Slumber."

Kora nodded, but a concerned expression had settled on her three faces. "Husband, don't you think too much killing might be—"

"Soon, we will rule everything!" Krael called out, interrupting her.

The monsters on the ground and those floating in the air all cheered for their king.

"Follow me, my friends," Krael said, his voice amplified by his Crowns. "There's a desert village nearby that I can feel with my magic. We'll crush the NPCs there, then look for more villages as we close in on the boy-wizard and his friends. You'll be feasting on a wizard's XP soon."

The creatures cheered again, then headed to the east, every one of them moving as fast as they could, with delicious thoughts of violence running through their twisted minds.

CHAPTER 16

Watcher shivered. They were in a frozen river biome, the ground rock hard and nearly flat with occasional mounds of snow here and there. The horses' hooves made crunching sounds with every step as they broke the thin layer of ice on the ground. The air was icy cold. The constant east-to-west breeze flowing through Minecraft felt as if it were filled with razor-sharp needles—tiny shards of ice, almost too small to see, floated on the wind, each frozen sliver managing to find exposed skin.

Watcher stood up in his stirrups and scanned the surroundings, looking for threats. Ahead and behind the company, iron and obsidian golems lumbered along, their huge metal heads scanning the area for monsters. All around them, the silvery fur of the iron wolves reflected the afternoon sun, making the animals appear to glow.

To his right, a river sliced through the landscape like a slithering blue snake, turning one way, then another as the waterway carved a circuitous path around hills of snow. The river's frozen surface was like cerulean glass, the transparent blue ice showing the chilly water underneath.

A sudden howl cut through the silence. Watcher glanced down at Fixit, and the tiny metal child smiled, then whistled and chirped a string of notes. He glanced at Er-Lan.

"Fixit says the wolves like it out here," the zombie said. "With a clear field of view, monsters cannot sneak up on the villagers."

"What else does that little metal child say?" Cutter's sudden voice was loud, as usual; it startled both Watcher and Er-Lan. "How do we know that zombie is telling us everything it says?"

"Why would Er-Lan lie? He's one of us." Watcher looked over his shoulder at the big NPC in frustration. "You need to stop accusing him of being some kind of traitor. He's part of our village, and he's part of *my* family."

The warrior kicked his horse forward and moved up next to Watcher.

"Even if he's lying about what he is?" Cutter's steel-gray eyes bored into the young wizard's blues.

"What . . . you mean he's not a zombie?" Watcher smiled.

"You know what I mean!" Cutter leaned forward and glared at Er-Lan, then brought his gaze back to his friend. "He did that thing in the Hall of Planes, and—"

"Are you still worried about that? The time when Er-Lan pushed Krael back through the portal and saved all our lives?"

The hulking NPC just nodded.

"I told you before—my magic leaked into him. That's the only explanation, and I wish you'd just believe me and leave this alone." Watcher scowled.

"Well, it's funny."

"What's funny?"

"Your magic has never leaked into anyone else, has it?" Cutter paused for a second, then continued, not letting the young wizard respond. "Oh, wait, I think you *thought* your magic had leaked into Planter when she used that magic bow from the skeleton warlord."

"You mean this?" Watcher reached into his inventory and pulled out the Fossil Bow of Destruction. It had been constructed by the monster warlocks before the Great War and had served Watcher well many times since he'd taken it from the skeleton warlord. He handled it carefully, knowing if he grabbed it too firmly, the magical weapon would reach into his HP for power, just like the Eye of Searching. That was something he'd like to avoid.

"Yeah, I considered that as a possibility at first, because something had to make it so Planter could use this bow without dying." Watcher stuffed the enchanted weapon back into his inventory. "So what?"

"But that wasn't the case, was it?" Cutter veered around a large mound of snow, then guided his horse across a frozen river, its hooves clattering on the icy surface. "Your magic leaking into Planter wasn't actually the answer, was it?"

Watcher shook his head. "You know as well as I do that it wasn't my magic that allowed Planter to use the Bow. It was the fact that she's a wizard, like me."

"Ah, I see, so you thought your magic had leaked into Planter, but it didn't; actually, she was a wizard." Cutter's voice was growing louder, his anger rising. "So why don't you think it's the same with that zombie?"

Watcher glanced at Er-Lan and gave him a reassuring smile; the zombie looked scared. "I just know. Why isn't that good enough for you?"

"Because when that zombie shows his true colors, villagers are gonna suffer." Cutter glared at Er-Lan. "I'm not gonna let that happen, no matter what you believe."

Watcher sighed. "Cutter, I wish you'd just trust me and—"

Suddenly, the sounds of screams echoed in the young wizard's head. It made his head spin as a sickening dizziness spread through his body.

"Help . . ." Watcher's pleading voice was weak as he fell off his horse.

"Watcher, what's wrong?" Cutter leapt off his horse and knelt at the boy's side.

The other NPCs gathered near, staring down at the boy.

More shouts of agony and terror echoed through his mind. Watcher could almost feel the pain these ethereal voices were feeling as their cries for help went unanswered. Sweat poured down his face, his body feeling burning hot as if he were trapped inside a raging inferno, yet at the same time, a merciless cold dug its claws into his skin. A potion of healing splashed across his armor, the liquid seeping quickly between the diamond plates and soaking into his skin, but it had no effect.

"I can hear them dying," Watcher whispered. "Krael . . . he's killing villagers somewhere, and no one is there to help."

Distantly, Watcher felt as something was clasped around his neck. It was a thin chain of some kind with a cold stone dangling on the end.

"This is a blocking stone . . . I made it myself." Mira stared down at Watcher, slowly lifting his head and cradling it in her lap. "In a moment or two, it'll help with the sounds."

Watcher looked up at the ancient wizard, her warm eyes trying to hide the fear she felt for him.

Another group of screams slashed through his mind, but this time, they were softer. Maybe it was because of the blocking stone, or maybe there just weren't as many NPCs still left alive in the besieged village.

The dizziness faded, leaving Watcher feeling empty and ragged—like a wet cloth wrung out too many times. Slowly, he sat up.

"What happened?" Planter stood over him, her emerald-green eyes filled with concern and fear.

"Krael . . . he's started his destruction." With help from Mira and Planter, the young wizard climbed to his feet. "That horrible wither is destroying a village some-where. I could hear the screams of his victims . . . it was terrible." He lowered his gaze to the ground. "And I couldn't do anything to help those poor souls."

"What could you have done?" Mira put a hand under Watcher's chin and raised his head until his eyes met hers. "You're here and Krael is . . . who knows where?"

"It doesn't matter." He glared at the ancient wizard. "I did nothing when the zombie warlord attacked my vil-lage, and many people were hurt. I can't just let others suffer because I wasn't there . . . Something must be done. I can't bear hearing them suffer."

Watcher lifted the chain around his head. A fac-eted gemstone as black as night hung on the end of the chain, shimmering with magical power. He raised the stone and slid it under his chest plate, then turned to Mira. "Thank you. That amulet helped a lot."

The old woman nodded. "Somehow, you're linked to Krael; it's likely your magic mixed with his somehow during a battle. The blocking stone will muffle the suf-fering of his victims in your ears. Just keep wearing it and it'll give you some protection from those sounds."

"Okay." He turned to Blaster. He was about to speak when one of the forward scouts shouted, "I see the extreme hills up ahead!"

A villager wearing white leather armor and riding a white horse came galloping up to the company. Blaster rode out to meet him, also wearing white to blend in with the environment. The two NPCs spoke briefly, then the scout turned and headed back into the frozen land-scape while Blaster returned. Fencer rode out to meet the young boy, but he ignored her and headed straight for Watcher.

"She said that—" Blaster started to say.

"She?" Cutter interrupted.

"Yeah, she." Fencer caught up to Blaster and moved to his side. "That's Farmer, and *she's* one of our best scouts. Isn't that right, Blaster?"

The boy just grunted and refused to look at her, though Fencer's smile was already beaming.

"Yeah, as I was saying, Farmer saw the village. It's right at the boundary between this biome and the extreme hills. We can just make it there by sunset if we hurry."

Watcher nodded, then glanced at the rest of their company. They were all cold and exhausted. Many of the NPCs slumped in the saddle, tired from the journey. Some rode double; the last village hadn't had enough horses to accommodate everyone.

"OK, let's get everyone moving faster," Watcher said, then glanced at Cutter.

The big NPC nodded, then moved to the left flank to talk to some of the warriors. After a short discussion, the soldiers charged ahead, probably to reach the village first and make sure it was safe.

Standing in his stirrups, Watcher looked around at the rest of the NPCs. "The extreme hills village is just up ahead. From here, we gallop as fast as possible. I want to get there before dark; I'm sure all of you can understand."

They nodded.

Watcher glanced down at Fixit. "Let's get the wolves and golems moving as fast as possible."

The little mechite smiled and let out a series of shrill whistles. The ground suddenly shook as the golems switched from walking to running.

"Come on, everyone," Watcher shouted. "We ride for the extreme hills village."

Kicking his horse into a gallop, Watcher sped across the frosty ground, his mount's breath billowing out in soft white clouds. He drew Needle as he rode, hoping he wouldn't need the weapon when they reached their destination, but he'd learned many times, Minecraft had a way of throwing obstacles at you whether you're ready or not.

CHAPTER 17

An eerie silence sat atop the village like a sheet
stretched too tight, about to rip. Many of its
inhabitants glared up at Watcher and his friends
as they rode into the extreme hills community; it was
clear they weren't welcome here.

Planter moved her horse up next to Watcher. "This
isn't the warmest reception we've ever received." She
turned in the saddle and glanced around at the others'
faces. "What did we do?"

Watcher shrugged. "I'm not sure."

Ahead, a group of NPCs gathered near the community's well. One of them wore a black smock with a wide
gray stripe running down the center; he was the village's crafter. The NPC's dark eyes glared suspiciously
at Watcher and Planter and Mira, their glowing, magical
bodies making them stand out.

Watcher guided his horse toward the well, then dismounted and handed his reins to a young boy, who led
his horse away.

"Hello." Watcher held out a hand to the village's
crafter. The crafter looked the young wizard over with a
skeptical eye, but then the old NPC's eyes grew wide with
shock as Fixit approached on the back of an iron wolf.

Watcher glanced down at the mechite. "Set up a perimeter around the village. We don't want any surprises."

Fixit nodded, then whistled and tweeted, his commands piercing the cold air. The wolves with their shiny metal riders shot out into the darkening landscape, some of them climbing the steep hills bordering the community. The ground rumbled as golems marched out and took up positions at the mouths of the numerous valleys leading into the village. The passes were lined with steep hills of stone and gravel, each now sparkled with the silver bodies of wolves and mechites.

"You giving the orders in our village?" The crafter glared at Watcher as if offended.

"Well, it's just that . . . you see, we're here because—"

"And how dare you bring all these warriors and weapons into our village?" The old NPC took a step toward Watcher. "Soldiers and swords always attract violence. Whatever you're involved with, it isn't welcome here."

Cutter pushed through the villagers and stared at the old crafter. "There's an army of withers and monsters coming this way. If you don't want to be squashed flat, then you're gonna leave this village and come with us."

"What?" one of the NPCs exclaimed. "We aren't leaving our homes." He was a large villager, like Cutter, with bulging muscles straining the sleeves of his smock. "Withers are just a myth these days; they haven't been around since the Great War. And I don't see any monsters attacking us." He turned and glanced at his neighbors. "Do any of you see an attacking mob?"

The other villagers all shook their heads, then brought their accusing stares back to Watcher.

"We don't see any monsters or withers here." The crafter shook his head. "I don't know what kind of game you're playing, but we don't like it." He pointed at Watcher's arms. "And what's up with the purple glow? Are you sick?"

Watcher was about to reply, but Fencer stepped forward, her enchanted curved sword in her hand. "He's a wizard, just like Planter, and—" Fencer glanced around until she spotted Mirthrandos and pointed, saying, "—she's one too."

"Wizards . . . here, in our village?" The crafter laughed. "There haven't been any wizards since the Great War, and now you're telling me they're standing right here, before us. . . . Ha!"

"Where do you think all these iron wolves and the mechites and the golems came from?" Fencer pointed at Mira. "Mirthrandos is the strongest wizard in all of Minecraft, and if she says monsters are coming, then you better believe it."

"Be quiet. You're a foolish child who doesn't know anything," the big villager said.

Blaster instantly stepped in front of Fencer and glared at the big NPC, his two swords drawn.

Planter moved in front of the young boy. "Listen, we aren't trying to trick you. It's true, we're wizards, though I wish it weren't . . . but it is. And soon, Krael, the king of the withers, is gonna descend down upon this village and destroy everything and everyone. He's decided to exterminate all NPCs, and your village is likely in his path."

Watcher moved to Planter's side. "Soon, he'll be here, and—"

The young wizard suddenly grunted and grabbed the back of his head.

"What's wrong?" Winger rushed forward and caught her brother as he fell to one knee.

Just then, Planter and Mira cried out in pain as well and fell to their knees, expressions of agony on their faces. Watcher forced his way to his feet and moved to Planter's side. With his arms under her shoulders, he slowly lifted her to her feet.

"What's happening?" Mapper asked. "What's going on?"

Glancing at the old man, Watcher shivered as a feeling of icy dread slithered across his soul. "He's here."

The young wizard's voice sounded thin. He spoke louder. "Krael's here. That means his army is here too."

Instantly, Cutter drew his huge diamond sword and held it over his head. The other members of their company drew their weapons as well, many putting on armor and pulling out shields as the NPCs took up defensive positions along the sides of buildings, each scanning the area, looking for their attackers.

"I don't see any monsters." The village's crafter pushed through the crowd and stood directly in front of Watcher. "Is this some game? I don't know what you're trying to do, but we—"

The majestic howl of a wolf cut through the air.

"The monsters are coming," Er-Lan said as he moved up next to Watcher.

"A zombie!" one of the villagers shouted.

"This is Er-Lan." Watcher put a hand on the zombie's shoulder. "He's our friend and is no threat."

"For now, maybe," Cutter muttered under his breath nearby.

Another courageous howl echoed off the steep, rocky hills surrounding the village.

Watcher cast Cutter a warning glance, then turned to Er-Lan. "What are they saying?"

"The wolf says the monster army is—"

A group of howls filled the air, their metallic voices filled with strength, but now edged with the sound of fear.

"Ha ha ha . . . look what we have here!" a scratchy voice suddenly shouted from high overhead.

"Krael!" Watcher glanced into the air, searching for his enemy. The blue sky blushing a deep red as the sun nestled itself behind the western horizon.

"I see my old friend, Watcher." The wither king's scratchy voice reflected off the steep mountains, making the monster's location difficult to find. "You seem to be glowing more, wizard. Perhaps your powers increased . . . Good! Now you might finally be a worthy opponent."

Watcher pulled out the Fossil Bow of Destruction, holding it lightly; he wasn't ready for the enchanted weapon taken from the skeleton warlord to dig its magical claws into his HP . . . not yet.

"We're ready for you, Krael," Watcher shouted. "Why don't you come out and show yourself?" He glanced at Crafter and whispered, "Get your people ready to run. Maybe we can lose the monsters in all those narrow canyons." He pointed to the extreme hills surrounding the village, their steep, rocky faces already bathed in darkness.

"Run . . . from what?" The old villager shook his head. "We aren't going anywhere."

Suddenly, an explosion rocked the village as a wooden structure at the south end of the community erupted in flames. A black skull streaked through the air and hit the building again, its detonation shattering the roof.

"Monsters," Krael screamed from somewhere overhead, "ATTACK!"

Wolves growled and snarled as the monster horde charged into the village from the south. The iron and obsidian golems thundered through the streets, heading for the attacking mob as wolves from other parts of the village converged on their foe.

"Quickly, get all your people to the north side of the village." Watcher didn't wait for the crafter to reply. Instead, he gripped the Fossil Bow of Destruction in his left hand and pulled back the string; a magical arrow instantly appeared and, just as quickly, pain erupted throughout his body, the enchantments in the weapon demanding their price.

A wither floated into view, its body difficult to see as the sun finished sinking behind the horizon. Watcher aimed, then released. The sparkling shaft sliced through the air and hit the monster, taking all of the creature's HP. The wither disappeared, expressions of surprise on its three shadowy faces.

Cutter and Blaster streaked by with Fencer just a step behind, the enchantments on their weapons covering the ground with a shimmering purple hue. Watcher sprinted after them, his arms glowing brighter as his magic built. Pounding footsteps filled the air behind him as the rest of his warriors followed, their armor clanking as loud as the lumbering golems three huge steps behind.

Nearby, wolves snarled and howled, their iron teeth making crunching sounds as they came down upon monster limbs. Whistles and screeches from countless mechites added to the cacophony; the tiny metallic creatures were already fighting somewhere up ahead.

Watcher darted around the corner of a wooden building and skidded to a stop, stunned at what he saw. Planter rounded the corner just behind him and nearly collided with the young wizard, and she, too, was terrified at what she beheld: a massive horde of monsters was charging out of one of the narrow valleys, only the sheer walls keeping the creatures from overwhelming the defenders immediately. A powerful stench floated across the defenders, preceding the sharp claws and pointed teeth; the putrid odor of decaying flesh and unwashed bodies was almost too much to bear.

The mob was composed of every mismatched possibility of monster parts: spiders with zombie heads and skeleton arms, endermen with baby-slime heads, skeletons with blaze heads . . . they were all horrific. But even more terrifying than their appearance was how many there were; easily a hundred monsters were descending upon the community, each intent upon destruction.

A group of warriors flowed past Watcher and Planter. They formed a line and moved into the valley, pushing back on the monsters' advance, their blades and bows helping to defend the wolves and mechites already joined in battle. Blaster and Fencer fought side-by-side, their enchanted curved blades streaking through the air, almost too fast to see.

"How do we stop this many monsters?" Planter turned to Watcher, her green eyes filled with fear and desperation.

Watcher groaned in pain as he fired the Bow of Destruction again, the magical arrow streaking into the fray, piercing multiple bodies. His HP was getting dangerously low. Firing one more shot, he put away the Bow and pulled out the Flail of Regrets, the glow from the enchanted weapon turning the night around them into an iridescent day. "We have to use our magic to keep our friends safe."

Tiny whispers of pain and fear flittered through Watcher's mind. The blocking stone was limiting the volume of the NPCs' shouts in the back of his head, but their real voices were near and loud enough for the young wizard to hear every one. NPCs were dying, right here, and Watcher wasn't sure if he could protect them.

He pulled out a healing potion and drank it quickly, then glanced at his friend.

Planter groaned as she reached into her inventory, grabbing the magical shield with her left hand. "I hate this thing. Every time I use it, I feel like I almost lose a little piece of myself."

"I know, but we have no choice." Watcher put a reassuring hand on her shoulder, but she pushed it aside with a scowl. "We have to slow Krael's army to give those back at the Wizard's Tower time to prepare for battle; that's where we're making our final stand."

"It seems like we might be making our final stand right here." Planter's voice cracked with fear.

"I know." Watcher nodded, a determined expression covering his square face. "Come on; it's time to fight!"

Without waiting for a response, Watcher charged toward the angry mob, every nerve electrified with fear. He could hear Planter's footsteps behind him; it was reassuring, but did little to help his terror.

How are we going to stop this many monsters? Watcher thought as he ran. *I'm sure the withers are out there somewhere too, just waiting to rain death and destruction upon us.*

The shouts of pain from both villagers and monsters filled the air, adding to the overwhelming weight of responsibility on Watcher, but he knew there was no other choice. Screaming at the top of his lungs, the young wizard dove into the fighting, the magical glow from his body making the terrifying scene seem like a dream.

No—more like a nightmare.

CHAPTER 18

The sounds of battle filled the air: steel clashing against claws, fanged mouths snapping shut upon flesh, shouts of pain and fear . . . they all added to the terrible cacophony of destruction.

Watcher crashed into the horde of monstrous bodies, his enchanted flail streaking through the air like a blazing purple meteor. The intense glow coming from the spiked cube forced many of the monsters to look away, which was a huge mistake. Without mercy, the young wizard smashed the blinded and vulnerable distorted creatures with his enchanted weapon, causing multiple monsters to flash red as they took damage.

"Get the wizard!" A skeleton with an enderman head snarled. "Krael promised a reward to the monster who—"

Watcher didn't give the monster a chance to complete the sentence. Swinging the flail in a wide circle, he pushed the monsters back, giving some of the NPCs on the battle lines a chance to take a breath, then turned and moved to Cutter's side. As he did, the big warrior destroyed a zombie just as it reached for Watcher's back, its razor-sharp claws scraping the back of his armor before it disappeared.

"Pay attention!" Cutter reprimanded him.

Watcher nodded, then smashed a group of slimes, the huge gelatinous cubes splitting into smaller ones; they didn't last long.

Then, a terrible odor wafted across the NPCs as a new contingent of zombies and skeletons charged at the villagers' battle lines. Watcher braced himself for the attack, but before he could act, a pair of flaming arrows streaked past his head and hit the lead monster in the horde. The burning shafts ate away at the creature's HP, causing the beast to scream in pain. Picking up its bow, the skeleton aimed at Watcher, but was silenced by another pair of flaming arrows. Watcher knew they came from Planter and his sister, Winger. He glanced over his shoulder and smiled back at the two of them, then faced the monster horde and swung his weapon again.

A group of monsters tried to close in on Blaster and Fencer, but none dared to get very close; the duo fought like a lethal, well-oiled machine, each protecting the other's back while they wreaked havoc on the wall of claws and fangs surrounding them. Watcher tried to reach them and help at first, but there were too many monsters in the way. He glanced at Blaster and saw a huge smile on the boy's face as he destroyed monster after monster, Fencer starting the damage with her curved sword, leaving the killing stroke to her companion. It seemed as if both Blaster and Fencer were enjoying it.

"More monsters coming through the valley!" Winger shouted from a nearby rooftop.

Watcher backed up, allowing other NPCs to take his place. Then, jumping into the air, he placed blocks of dirt under his feet until he could see far into the extreme hills biome.

What he saw shocked him. Monsters, shoulder to shoulder, choked the narrow pass as far as he could see. There were at least a hundred of them, and likely more coming; they'd never be able to hold this ground for long. Besides, defeating this mob wasn't their plan, anyway; they just needed to slow them down long enough to give those at the Wizard's Tower time to prepare their last stand.

Turning around, Watcher surveyed the opposite end of the village. Some of the inhabitants, mostly women and children, were heading in that direction, terrified expressions on their square faces.

"Watcher, they need your help down there."

The young wizard turned toward the voice. He found Winger pointing at a huge cluster of spiders scaling the steep walls of the stone valley, hoping to get around the NPCs' formation and attack them from behind.

Shoving the Flail into his inventory, Watcher pulled out the Fossil Bow of Destruction again. Instantly, the warlock-made weapon stabbed at his HP as he drew back the string. Concentrating his mind on the lead spider, he fired, then drew and chose another target. Pain exploded throughout his body again, but he didn't care. He had to stop the spiders from getting behind his friends.

Running to the left flank, Watcher kept firing, his health dropping dangerously low. Suddenly, a bottle shattered against his back, a soothing liquid soaking through his armor. He drew back the string and fired again, aiming at a distant spider. The glittering shaft went through four spiders before it hit its mark, destroying them all. Watcher smiled, then glanced over his shoulder.

"You okay?" Mapper held another healing potion ready in his hand.

Watcher nodded, then glanced around, looking for Blaster. He spotted the boy and motioned for him to come near. "There are too many monsters approaching from the valley. I'm sure Krael and his withers will open fire soon, too. We have to retreat while we have only one army to fight."

"Got it, what do you—" Blaster stopped to slash at a large spider-zombie, blocking its curved claws with one blade while he attacked with the other. After three swings of his sword, the monster disappeared. "Sorry . . . what do you need me to do?"

Glancing at the villagers around him, Watcher smiled. "You think you could plant some surprises to cover our retreat?"

Now it was Blaster's turn to smile. Before Watcher could say a word, the young boy took off running. "Fencer, Builder, Mapper, come with me, NOW!"

Watcher pulled a healing potion out of his inventory and drank, then ran toward Cutter. He pushed his way through NPC defenders until he reached the big warrior's side. Then, shoving the Bow into his inventory, he pulled out Needle and slashed at a huge zombie. The magical blade bounced off the monster's long claws, the zombie snarling with hatred in its eyes. Before it could attack, Cutter brought his diamond sword down upon the creature, erasing it from Minecraft.

"Cutter, we need to hold out a little longer. Blaster needs—" Watcher ducked under a zombie's attack, then struck it with Needle. The glittering blade tore through the monster's leather armor and sank into its rotten flesh. Before it could back away, Watcher hit the terrible creature again, taking the last of its HP.

"What were you saying?" Cutter kicked at a skeleton, breaking its ribs, then destroyed it with a quick jab of his diamond blade.

"I was saying, we need to hold out a little longer. Blaster is preparing something to cover our retreat."

"Retreat?! We just got here, and it's just getting fun!" Cutter gave Watcher a vicious grin, his eyes filled with a lust for battle.

"There are lots more monsters coming through that valley up ahead. We'll never be able to hold this position. We must—" Watcher stopped and pulled a shield out with his left hand just in time to block the iron axe swung by some kind of gigantic misshapen skeleton thing.

An NPC to Watcher's left stuck the dark skeleton with an iron sword. The creature made a sickening crunch as the blade's keen edge snapped its ashen bones. Before Watcher could finish off the monster, it turned toward the villager and attacked, enraged. The monster's axe shattered the NPC's armor, then tore into his HP. Shouting, the villager tried to protect himself, but it was too late. The dark skeleton attacked a second time, too fast for Watcher to help, taking the last of the doomed NPC's HP. Screaming in terror and agony, the villager disappeared, his armor and weapons clattering to the hard stone ground.

"NO!" Watcher charged at the monster, smashing into it with his shield.

The huge skeleton attacked again, striking the shield, but this time, Watcher anticipated the attack and shoved the shield into its weapon. The head of the axe cut through the shield and protruded through the back, getting stuck. The shadowy monster tried to yank the axe free, but it wouldn't budge, just as Watcher hoped. Pulling back on the shield, the young wizard yanked the weapon from the creature's bony grasp. The skeleton glared at Watcher with rage burning in its lifeless eyes and extended a gnarled, bony hand toward Watcher's throat. But it never reached its goal. Needle moved through the air like a bolt of enchanted steel lightning, carving through the monster's bones and destroying its HP. The monster disappeared from sight.

Growls from more monsters filled the air as reinforcements charged through the valley, adding to the horde's numbers. Some of the creatures pushed toward the edges of the NPC battle line, trying to break through. Watcher spotted Mirthrandos at one end of the battle lines. She swung her crooked wooden staff like an experienced warrior. A pair of iron golems stood at her side, their shining metal fists sending attackers high into the air.

If they get behind us, we're goners, Watcher thought.

Push hard, a high-pitched voice said.

"Needle, is that you?" Watcher asked in a low voice.

A vindicator suddenly charged straight at Watcher, its dark brown vest and silver buttons covered with dirt and grime. Swinging its enchanted axe, it aimed straight for the young wizard's head. Raising Needle, Watcher blocked the attack as he allowed his magic to build, causing his body to glow brighter and brighter. He then drove the magic into Needle and brought it down upon the monster. Raising its enchanted axe, the vindicator tried to block, but the magic pulsing through Needle was too powerful. The enchanted blade shattered the axe, then destroyed the monster as well.

Push hard, the enchanted weapon said again.

"What are you saying?" Watcher was confused. "Dalgaroth, what do you mean?"

Push hard against the monsters. The ancient wizard's throughts sounded nervous, as usual, his high pitched voice screechy in the back of Watcher's mind. *After the push, pull back. It will confuse the monsters for a moment, giving you a chance to disengage.*

Got it, Watcher thought.

Drawing on his magic, Watcher took a huge breath and shouted as loud as he could, his magic amplifying his voice. "EVERYONE, PUSH FORWARD AND ATTACK!"

With the Flail of Regrets in his left hand, and Needle still in his right, he charged toward the monsters. The NPCs, seeing his advance, cheered and charged as well. They pushed hard against the wall of claws and fangs, fighting with renewed ferocity. Unsure of what was happening, the monsters backed up, expressions of fear on their scarred and terrible faces.

"BLASTER, I HOPE YOU'RE READY!" Watcher shouted, then gathered his magic again. "EVERYONE RETREAT, NOW!"

As one, the NPCs turned and ran from the attacking mob, none of them waiting to see how the monsters would respond.

"HEAD FOR THE NORTH SIDE OF THE VILLAGE!" Watcher's voice filled the air like thunder.

The NPCs sprinted between the buildings, heading for the opposite side of the community. As they ran, Watcher spotted blocks of TNT in the ground, with thin lines of redstone dust extending from each. He smiled.

"Hurry . . . run!" Planter shouted.

Watcher spotted her up ahead with Blaster and Fencer. The women and children were already fleeing into the next steep valley, each terrified of the destructive wave of monsters about to crash down upon them. Behind them, Watcher and the soldiers made it to the valley and stopped, setting up defenses. They placed blocks of stone across the valley opening, creating a hastily built wall that would slow the monsters and allow their archers to whittle down their numbers. Watcher moved into the valley, leaving the builders to finish the fortified wall while he scanned the steep hills, looking for any spidery sneak attack.

Suddenly, the TNT behind them exploded, enveloping the charging monsters in their fiery grasp. The world shook as more blocks detonated, tearing a huge crater in the ground. Monsters shouted in surprise and pain as their HP was blasted away, slowing their pursuit.

Then, another explosion rocked the landscape, but this one sounded different, and instead of an aroma of gunpowder, this blast was accompanied by the smell of death. The ground heaved up as another explosion crashed down, knocking most of the NPCs off their feet. A nearby building burst into flames, the walls and roof completely engulfed.

"That wasn't TNT," Watcher said to Planter as he stood.

She shook her head and was about to speak when a malicious laugh filled the air.

"You think you can escape my forces, fool?" a voice screeched from somewhere overhead.

Watcher glanced up at the night sky. Sparkling

stars decorated the heavens as if it were a king's cloak. Watcher stared at them as he stood, stunned for a moment by their glittering beauty, but as he gazed upward, the stars disappeared, blotted out, as if a dark tide of some sort were spreading across the sky.

"Withers," the young wizard gasped.

A purple glow enveloped one of the shadowy creatures. Watcher knew that was his enemy, Krael. With lightning speed, he pulled out the Fossil Bow of Destruction.

This is your chance to destroy Krael. Dalgaroth's voice filled his head, the wizard's perpetual nervousness driven away by the opportunity.

Taking a deep breath, Watcher pulled back on the string, holding the image of Krael within his mind and allowing the Bow to use it to aim. Pain blasted through his body, making his arm shake. Watcher gritted his teeth, trying to ignore the agony. Closing his eyes, he slowly released his breath and let go of the string. The glittering arrow leapt off the bow and streaked straight toward the purple glow.

"It's gonna hit him." Watcher's voice was barely a whisper. "This could be the end of the war. It could mean—"

Suddenly, a flaming skull shot out of the shadows and struck the magical arrow, causing both to explode in the sky, turning night to day. Watcher gasped when the light illuminated the hundreds of withers floating around their king, all of their eyes fixed on the villagers.

Watcher stuffed the Bow back into his inventory, then turned and glanced at the NPCs. "Everyone, RUN!"

The NPCs saw the terrible sight overhead, too, and needed little encouragement; they ran into the valley, ignoring the snarls and growls coming from the approaching horde of monsters on the ground.

"Leave the barricade and run," Watcher shouted. "We can't fight the monsters on the ground *and* in the air. Run for your lives, everyone!"

An explosion shook the ground as a flaming skull detonated behind him, tearing their fortified wall apart as if it were paper.

The NPCs sprinted through the canyon, their eyes peeking skyward, looking out for the next attack. Ahead, Watcher spotted Planter and bolted to her side.

"What are we gonna do?" she asked. "As soon as the withers fly over these hills and get overhead . . . we're dead."

"Watcher, you gotta think of something." Winger had her enchanted bow in her hand, firing random shots up into the air, hoping to hit something. "What do we do?"

Watcher stared into her bright blue eyes; they were filled with panic, just like his own.

Baltheron, Dalgaroth, Taerian, help me. Watcher pleaded to the wizards trapped within his weapons, but they said nothing . . . it was hopeless. He knew a few arrows would never bring down the withers or stop them from attacking.

They had lost. A tear tried to free itself from his eye, but the young wizard choked back his emotions, refusing to let the tiny cube of moisture free.

With a sigh, Watcher glanced up at the sky as he ran, waiting for death to envelop them all.

It was over.

CHAPTER 19

Watcher sprinted through the valley with Planter at his side, their magical glow painting the ground and rocky walls with an iridescent hue. A flaming skull shot over one of the peaks lining the trail, slamming into the rocky wall on the other side. Blocks of gravel fell down the steep sides of the valley, filling the path with debris, a cloud of dust choking the air.

"Keep running!" Watcher shouted.

"No." Planter's voice was soft . . . and sad. She stopped running and turned to face the approaching monsters.

Watcher skidded to a stop. "Planter, what are you doing?!"

"What I must." She glanced at her friend, an expression of fear and grief covering her beautiful square face. "If the shield takes my mind, just remember me as I was when we were kids, not what I've become."

"What are you talking about? We need to run!"

He grabbed the back of her glittering deep-blue armor, the red sparks drifting up from the chest plate and helmet looking like tiny embers floating up from a magical fire. He pulled her backward, expecting her to resist, but she just walked backward with him, calmly, as if the storm of death about to crash down upon them didn't actually exist.

As she shuffled backward, Planter pulled out her magical shield and held it over her head. Her body grew brighter and brighter until it was impossible to look at her. Watcher turned away as he kept pulling her through the narrow passage, the rest of the NPCs now far up the trail ahead of them.

"Look, my two favorite people waiting for me . . . how nice!" Krael floated over the hills lining the valley. "I just wish the old hag was here, too . . . oh, well. You better say goodbye to each other while you have the chance."

Watcher pulled out Needle and pointed at the wither, who glared down at them, the Crowns on his three skulls glowing bright. Krael was about to attack when Planter's shield exploded with magical power, a sheet of purple flames covering the duo.

"Help me keep going backward," Planter whispered. "We need to protect the others."

A trio of flaming skulls smashed against the enchanted shield, but the lavender flames over their heads kept burning bright.

"Can you run?" Watcher asked.

Planter nodded, then turned, keeping the bright shield over her head, its edges blazing with power.

They took off sprinting through the valley as Krael fired at them.

"Destroy the wizards!" Krael screamed.

More withers floated up over the steep hills and added their flaming skulls to the attack, but Planter's shield of flames kept them safe. They followed the trail, going around a bend and suddenly stopping—the NPCs stood waiting in formation, each with a bow in their hands, pointed skyward. As soon as the withers turned the corner, the air was filled with pointed shafts. The projectiles hit many of the withers, doing some damage, but not enough. All it did was distract and slow the flying mob.

Blaster ran to Watcher's side, his black leather armor making him hard to see in the darkness. "There's a cave up ahead—maybe it'll give us some protection."

"How far is it?" Watcher asked.

The boy sighed. "Far."

Nearby, Winger fired at a wither, the *Flame* enchantment on her bow igniting the shaft when it left the string. For a moment, Watcher thought it looked like a golden rocket.

"Rockets . . . of course." Watcher grabbed his sister. "Winger, do you have any fireworks?"

She reached into her inventory and pulled out one of the red-and-white striped tubes. "This is the only one."

"That'll be enough." Watcher set it on the ground and pulled out the Wand of Cloning.

A wave of flaming skulls crashed down upon them but stopped high in the air; Planter's shield was covering the entire group of villagers. Many of the NPCs ducked in fear as parents wrapped their arms around their children.

"Everyone, back up." Waving the Wand over his head, Watcher allowed his magic to build. Pain filled his body, but the young wizard didn't notice; his attention was completely focused on his task. He flicked the wand over and over again, duplicating the rockets. When the glow from the wand receded, he found stacks and stacks of rockets on the ground.

"Everyone, grab some rockets." Watcher grabbed a handful. "We'll shoot them at the withers to cover our retreat."

"Will it work?" Blaster asked.

"It better. We don't have any other options, and Planter is getting tired."

More flaming skulls smashed into the shield of purple flames; the magical barrier was starting to flicker.

"Hurry," Planter moaned. "The shield is searching for something, and all it can find is my mind. It's pulling me into its darkness."

"Everyone, follow Blaster and run for the cave."
Watcher's voice, amplified by his magic, boomed off the
steep walls of the valley. He turned to Planter. "It's okay,
you can lower your shield."

Planter's arm slumped to the side, the magical shield
clattering to the ground. Watcher bent over and picked
it up, then put an arm around her and ran, following
the rest of the NPCs.

"I see your pathetic shield failed," Krael hissed.
"Perfect. It's time for your destruction. Withers . . . ready
. . . aim . . ."

"Fireworks, everyone, NOW!" Watcher set a rocket on
the ground as he ran, then placed another and another.

Countless villagers did the same, launching their
rockets into the air. The tiny striped tubes flew up into
the air and exploded in the faces of the withers, showering them with burning embers and temporarily blinding
them with intense light. They screamed in pain and
shock. Then, just when they thought the blasts were
over, another wave of rockets streaked into the air,
exploding in their dark faces again, forcing many of the
creatures to move behind the peaks of the extreme hills
to avoid being hit.

Mixed in with the fireworks were Mirthrandos's
magic missiles. The old woman stood in the center of
the pass, her body ablaze with magical energy; it was an
awesome sight! She pointed her staff at the dark terrors,
then extended it. Blazing streaks of power streamed
from its end. They shot into the dark sky, guided by
her magic. When they struck the withers, the ribbons of
magical energy wrapped around the withers like shimmering snakes; the monsters flashed red, taking damage, which drove even more of them away.

"There's the cave!" Planter pointed up ahead.

Most of the villagers were already inside, moving
deeper into the dark passage to make room for the rest
of the ragtag army. Watcher ran as fast as he'd ever run,
Planter's feet pounding the hard ground next to him. He

placed down rockets on the ground as he sprinted, hoping the tiny missiles would keep the terrible monsters back.

A golem ahead of him suddenly stopped, then turned and walked toward the withers, its mighty iron arms held in the air, trying to grab one of the nearest creatures. The withers just laughed and bombarded the metal giant, allowing the rest of the army to bolt into the dark cave, Watcher and Planter arriving last.

Facing out of the tunnel, Watcher stared at the golem. Flaming skulls were hammering at the creature, causing its metal skin to dent and crack. It glanced back at him and smiled in acknowledgment just as a new attack took the last of its HP. The mighty creature fell to the ground and shattered, sacrificing its life so that Watcher and the rest of the NPCs could make it to the cave. Here, they were safe from the withers overhead, but they were also trapped.

"That poor golem." Planter stared at the three balls of XP floating off the ground. "It died for us."

She glanced at Watcher, as if expecting him to say something wise, but he remained silent. Staring at the XP, Watcher was stunned by the creature's selfless act; the golem had knowingly gone to its death to save a bunch of strangers.

How could he do that? Watcher wondered.

Sacrificing for others is the most noble of deeds. Baltheron's deep voice was like distant thunder in the back of Watcher's mind. *Sometimes, sacrificing yourself is the only way to help those you love. That was why myself and the other wizards sacrificed our bodies so that our minds and our magic could be stored in these weapons, and we could be here for you in this time, to see things finally finished.*

But you were never able to see your loved ones again.

True, but they survived the Great War, and that made the sacrifice worthwhile. Baltheron paused for a moment, as if recalling an old memory, then continued.

We believed in what we fought for, and our sacrifice, hopefully, will let us finally see things come to completion.

Watcher shook his head. *I don't understand.*

Baltheron laughed. *Hopefully, you'll never need to.*

A vile laugh filled the air. Krael slowly descended to the ground and allowed the golem's XP to float into his body.

"You're all trapped, like a bunch of silverfish in a hole." The wither king laughed again. "Thanks for making it easy for me." He glared straight at Watcher, his six eyes blazing with hatred. "Now . . . it is time for all of you . . . to die." Drawing magical energy from the three Crowns, the wither king fired the most powerful flaming skulls ever created in Minecraft straight for the cave opening.

Terror filled Watcher's mind as he stared at his death approaching, and all he could think to do was close his eyes, hoping the end would be swift.

CHAPTER 20

Planter took a step toward the cave opening and lifted her shield and screamed as loud as she could. Her magic flooded into the enchanted artifact, adding to the shield's power as it burst into a wall of purple fire. Krael's flaming skulls smashed into the fiery barrier, exploding on contact and filling the cave with thunder and heat, but no one was harmed.

"You did it!" Watcher exclaimed. "Planter, you saved us!"

He put a hand on her shoulder and she flinched, as if afraid to be touched. She glanced at him, tears streaming down her face.

"It's pulling me in. The shield is in my head." Another wave of flaming skulls smashed against her magical shield, but the wall of purple flames held firm. "It's searching my mind, and when it can't find what it's looking for, it goes deeper and deeper into my memories." Planter reached out a free hand to Watcher. "It . . . hurts."

Watcher took her hand. "I'm here, Planter. I won't leave you." He stood at his friend's side, but didn't know what else he could do to help. "Move farther back into the cave. Maybe that'll make it more difficult for Krael to attack."

They stepped farther back into the cave, the light from Planter's shield and body adding to the iridescent glow from Watcher's, pushing back on the darkness.

"Looks like we're trapped in here." Winger moved to Planter's side and put an arm around her waist. "Planter, you're keeping us—"

Another attack exploded against the glowing shield, sending a wave of heat washing over the villagers.

"You're keeping us alive, Planter. Keep it up." Winger kissed her on the cheek, then turned to look at Watcher, waiting for his orders.

"Better than . . . being out there with the withers." Mapper's voice cracked with fear.

Watcher nodded. "Is there any way out of this cave?"

Cutter stepped forward. "I searched it, the back of this thing is solid rock."

"No, there must be an exit." Er-Lan turned to Watcher. "Zombies have been here, Er-Lan can sense it."

"Oh, you can sense other monsters, yet you never told us that." Cutter glared at the zombie; the air was thick with tension. "I wonder what else you're keeping secret?" The big warrior sounded as if he were accusing Er-Lan of a crime.

"Er-Lan does not hide anything from—"

"Your squabbles aren't important right now." Mirthrandos banged the end of her staff on the ground. The tip instantly gave off a bright light, driving away all of the darkness. "If Er-Lan says this is a zombie place, then there must be tunnels leading deeper into the hills." She pointed at Cutter. "Take that pickaxe I know you carry and go find the tunnels. If necessary, make your own tunnel. Leaving from the front isn't—"

Another explosion rocked the cave, causing dust and debris to fall from the ceiling; it made Watcher cough.

"—leaving from the front isn't an option," Mira continued. She glanced at Watcher. "We need a plan."

Watcher moved to the middle of the cave and turned in a circle, looking at the scared faces staring back at him. Iron and obsidian golems stood near the back of the group, their tall bodies hunched over. The metal wolves with their mechite riders all gazed at Watcher, expressions of fear on their shiny faces. Everyone was scared, but they expected him to somehow save the day. An uncomfortable silence spread through the chamber, periodically interrupted by flaming skulls hammering against the side of the mountain and Planter's shield.

"How did Krael know we'd be in this village?" Winger asked. "That scems like an unusual coincidence."

"I think Krael can sense me somehow." Watcher hung his head low. "He's probably here because of me. All of the death and destruction happening here is because of me. If all of you follow me . . . you'll likely die. Maybe I should just go out there and let the wither king destroy me."

A hopelessness spread through Watcher's soul as he spoke, making the responsibility for keeping these people safe feel like a leaden cloak pushing him into the ground.

"I don't know what to do anymore." The young wizard's voice was weak, barely audible over the constant explosions outside. "I've destroyed everything I hold dear." He glanced at Planter, who looked away. "Maybe if I give up, Krael will leave all of you alone."

"Quit feeling sorry for yourself!" The angry voice belonged to Fencer. "I can't believe that at one time I idolized you. The person I cared about back then wouldn't just give up . . . he'd do something and fight. Giving up is just surrendering to your fear, and that's pathetic. I'm not willing to accept defeat." She stepped up to Watcher, put a hand under his chin and raised his head until he was looking straight into her eyes. "Quit fighting Krael's war and start fighting yours." She stepped back. "Figure out how Krael knew you were here and fix it!"

I know how Krael is tracking you. Dalgaroth's high-pitched voice spat out the words quickly.

"You do, and you're just now telling us?" Mira sounded furious.

"Who are you talking to?" Blaster asked, confused.

Watcher drew Needle from his inventory and held it in the air.

"Ahhh . . . talking to your toys again." Blaster smiled at him, but Watcher didn't smile back.

"Well?" The ancient wizard stepped closer to Watcher and banged her staff on the shining blade to hurry Dalgaroth along. "Spill it!"

I was there when Tharus created the three Crowns of Skulls, Dalgaroth said. *He made them to find the magical weapons created by the monster warlocks.*

"So?" Mira was getting angrier, the purple glow from her body getting brighter.

So, Krael is using the Crowns to sense something carried by our young wizard. Dalgaroth's voice was filled with anger.

"The Bow of Destruction." Planter glanced over her shoulder, her face covered with sweat, the magical wall of purple fire from her shield still repelling more flaming skulls.

"Of course!" Mira exclaimed loud enough to startle the other villagers. "He can sense the presence of that terrible weapon." She turned to Watcher. "You have to get rid of it, or Krael will keep following you to the ends of Minecraft."

Watcher pulled the Bow from his inventory and stared down at it. *This was all my fault. I kept this stupid bow to use its power, and now it's gonna get us all killed.*

"Can the Bow be destroyed?" Winger asked.

Mira shook her head. "The enchantments the warlocks wove into that weapon are likely too powerful."

Winger glanced at her brother. "Then what do we do?"

Sometimes, sacrificing yourself is the only way to help those you love. Baltheron's deep voice was filled with compassion, making Watcher feel as if the ancient wizard was giving him a warm, reassuring hug. *I sacrificed myself for my friends, and now you must do the same, or all will be lost.*

"I don't know if I'm strong enough to do that," the young wizard said, his voice barely a whisper.

"Strong enough to do what?" Planter gazed at Watcher, her emerald-green eyes filled with worry. Another explosion pounded her shield, making her take a step back. Someone threw a splash potion of healing on her back, but it did little to relieve the anguish on her face.

Watcher stared down at the bow, then turned toward the tunnel opening. *How will I get out the door? They'll see me right away.*

Use the cloak. The Gauntlets of Life flashed as Taerian's scratchy voice filled Watcher's mind.

"The cloak?" Watcher was confused.

"Of course—the cloak." Mirthrandos pushed through the crowd and stood next to Watcher. "We all suspected Tharus had somehow added a potion of invisibility to it, but we weren't sure. He probably used the cloak when he went to his portal to teleport to the Far Lands. No one ever saw him walk through the city . . . he'd just appear in different places."

Watcher reached into his inventory and pulled out the glittering purple cloak. The elaborate gold stitching sparkled in the bright light from Mira's staff. Watcher attached the cape to the shoulders of his diamond chest plate, then let it hang down his back.

As he put it on, a sadness spread through him like nothing he'd ever experienced before. He knew when he ran out of the cave, every wither and monster would hunt him down until he was cornered and destroyed. If he just ran out and dropped the bow, Krael would know Watcher was still alive, and he'd figure out another way to track him down and destroy him. There was only one solution, and it terrified him.

I'm gonna miss my friends, Watcher thought. *I don't want to die. Not yet.* He glanced at Planter, her eyes cast to the ground. Watcher knew she could hear these thoughts, but he didn't care. *There are so many mistakes I need to make right, and now I'll never get a chance. The sadness within me almost makes me welcome what's to come.*

I know how you feel. Baltheron's voice was soft and comforting in his mind. *We'll be with you until the end.*

A tear started to trickle out of Watcher's eye, but he wiped it away, refusing to cry. He stood up straight and turned to his sister. "You have to get back to the Wizard's Tower and make sure they're ready. Krael will head there after I'm gone."

"Gone . . . you aren't gonna be gone." Winger's blue eyes started to tear up. "You're just gonna sneak out and get rid of that bow, then follow us . . . right?"

Watcher gave her a small nod, but he knew she could see the lie in his eyes. The sadness within him had now become a dark cloud settling itself upon his soul.

"I'll fly back to the Wizard's Tower to make sure they're ready, then come back here and find you." Winger pulled out a firework rocket from her inventory and held it up. "With all these rockets, I can fly home to the Tower and get back here in no time. I will not abandon you."

"Fly all the way to the Tower?"

"Sure, it's no problem," Winger said. "The rockets give you a speed boost, so you never have to touch the ground."

"And you can still use your hands while you're flying?" *Was it possible?*

"Watcher, what are you talking about?" Blaster put a questioning hand on the young wizard's shoulder. "Don't you think there are more important things to worry about right now than flying?"

Watcher didn't reply. The black cloud of sorrow permeating his mind seemed to part just a bit, allowing some rays of hope to illuminate the dark recesses of his soul.

"Rockets . . . Elytra . . ." His thoughts became a hurricane of ideas, of possibilities, of ways out, but the solutions were just out of reach, hidden by his fears. "But how do we get high enough?"

"Watcher, what are you talking about?" Cutter moved closer and peered down at the boy in confusion.

The ideas were coming faster, each playing through his mind at high speed. The young wizard no longer stared at the ground with a slumped posture and a look of defeat on his face. Gradually, he stood taller, hope and determination giving him strength. He couldn't quite make out all the puzzle pieces in his mind, but he knew there was a solution there, and he just had to figure it out.

Suddenly, he realized they had a major weakness . . . slow ground troops. "Horses . . . where are the horses?" The young wizard glanced around the cave. The only horse was a pack mule with two wooden chests strapped to its hips.

"They all bolted when the fighting started," the village's crafter said. "This old mule is all we have left."

Watcher tried to focus on all the ideas in his head, but there was something still missing, and he knew the problem: he was afraid. If he came up with a plan, the wrong plan, then it might get everyone killed. How could he handle that responsibility?

But then a distant, maniacal laugh percolated through Planter's shield and trickled into Watcher's ear.

"Krael," the young wizard whispered, too softly for anyone else to hear, and the shadow of fear and uncertainty covering his inner self began to evaporate, replaced with anger.

I can figure this out . . . I must figure this out. He gritted his teeth, the rage within him barely kept in check.

"The destruction caused by Krael must be stopped." Watcher's voice sounded more like a hissing steam vent than a voice, his fury driving his words faster and faster. "Horses are the problem. Where do we get more—"

And then he went silent as the last part of the plan fell into place. He knew the answer, but it was risky. Extremely risky.

Watcher nodded to himself, then moved to the cave wall and stepped up onto a block of stone as a series of flaming skulls hammered the side of the mountain over their heads, causing more dust to fill the air.

"They're trying to burrow through the side of the mountain." Planter took another step away from the entrance, keeping the shield in place. A group of withers peered into the entrance, waiting for Planter's magical barrier to drop. "Once they drill deep enough, they'll be able to smash us from above, or just bring this mountain down on our heads." She glanced at Watcher. "I don't know what we're gonna do."

"I do." Now Watcher stood tall and strong, his chin held high. The magical power flowing across his arms and chest now covered his entire body. "I'm tired of playing Krael's game." He glanced at Fencer and smiled. "We run away from him, then attack, then run again and hope we get lucky and stop him; it isn't enough. We've watched our friends perish before our eyes, destroyed by Krael's withers or by his army of distorted monsters . . . well, I say no more." He scowled at the villagers, mechites, and golems. "I'm tired of reacting to whatever the wither king does. It's time he danced to our tune."

"But how do we fight his army in the air and that massive horde on the ground?" Cutter sounded scared for the first time. "I'm all for fighting them, but I'd hope there's some plan that doesn't end with all of us dying. What trick do you have up your sleeve that'll let us stand toe-to-toe with them?"

"Yeah, what's your plan?" another villager asked desperately.

"How do we do it?"

"What's your trick?"

"What do we do?"

The villagers fired question after question at him, their fear barely held in check.

"I'll tell you how we'll do it." Watcher's voice was clear and strong, like the wizards of old. "We'll use speed."

CHAPTER 21

Watcher jumped up onto the mule and pulled the wizard's cloak tight around his body, allowing it to drape across the animal's back.

"Are you sure this is a good idea?" Planter gave him a worried glance.

"Don't worry; I know what I'm doing."

"You really expect me to believe that?"

Watcher shrugged, then turned to Winger. "As soon as I draw the monsters away, fly to the Wizard's Tower and tell Mapper to head to the Citadel of the Horse Lords with as many NPCs as he can find. We need horses, lots of horses, and if he can't get there and get back in time, then we're—"

"Don't worry, little brother. I'll take care of it." Winger pulled out her Elytra wings and strapped them to her back, then pulled out a rocket and held it in her hand. "As soon as the withers fly away, I'll head out."

Watcher nodded. "Good . . . I'm counting on you."

"What about the rest of us?" Fencer asked.

"All of you need to get back to the Wizard's Tower and make sure the defenses are ready. If the monsters get inside, then we're done for." Watcher turned and peered down at Planter. "I'll try to get back as quickly as I can."

"You mean *if* you can." Planter's voice was filled with venom and worry.

With a nod, Watcher turned back to the rest of the NPCs. "I'm not gonna be afraid of Krael and his mob anymore. The Far Lands is a peaceful world, and the wither king and his army need to go. I think it's time they were evicted."

The NPCs cheered, some of them banging their weapons against their armor.

Suddenly, a group of metal wolves moved to surround the pack mule, each with a mechite rider on their backs, Fixit at the front.

"What do you think you're doing?" Watcher glanced at Mirthrandos.

"They're gonna cause a little commotion to help you get out of the cave." The ancient wizard nodded her head. "They know what's at stake, and they're gonna help. My wolves can be quiet when they want to, but they can also be pretty loud, too." She laughed. "Don't worry about them, you just worry about you." Mira moved closer and put a hand on the boy's back. "You make sure you get back to the Tower safely; there are a lot of people worried about you."

Watcher looked down at the wizard, an expression of determination on his face. "Don't worry, you haven't seen the last of me."

"Good," Blaster said, "because I'd miss being part of your crazy plans. They always seem to involve mass numbers of monsters trying to eat our faces, and I always love that."

He gave Watcher an infectious smile, which made Watcher giggle, the laughter quickly spread throughout the cave as the group's fear and dread morphed into determination.

Once the laughter stopped, Watcher stood up in his stirrups and stared down at the NPCs, mechites, wolves and golems. "This isn't over," he said. "The only thing Krael accomplished here was to make me mad, and it's a mistake to make a wizard mad." He turned to Planter and nodded. "Let's do it."

Gathering his magic, Watcher poured every bit of his power into Tharus's cape. A tingling sensation spread across his body, slowly leaking into the mount beneath him. Planter gave him one last glance over her shoulder, though she wasn't sure where to look; he and the mule were now invisible. She sighed, then lowered her shield.

As the magical barrier faded, Watcher dug his heels into the mule, forcing it to sprint toward the cave entrance, the wolves right behind. The metal creatures quickly sprinted through the valley away from the villages, with Watcher following as quickly as he could.

"The wizard is moving!" Krael shouted. "Everyone, look for that cowardly boy; he's trying to get away."

"But what about the other NPCs?" another wither asked.

"I don't care about them." The wither king's voice grew louder, magically enchanted by the Crowns of Skulls. "Destroy Watcher first, we'll deal with the puny villagers later."

Watcher smiled. The valley was dark, the magical cape hiding the iridescent glow coming from his body. Nearby, a howl cut through the air, followed by another one off to the right. Some of the monsters on the ground snarled at the sound, their clawed feet pounding the ground, anxious to find their prey.

A flaming skull smashed to the ground behind Watcher, tearing into the hard stone ground . . . but it missed. It made Watcher laugh.

"I hear you, boy-wizard." Krael's screechy voice filled the air.

Glancing over his shoulder, he spotted the monster in the dark sky; the glow from the Crowns made him easy to see. Flying next to him was another wither, who had a feminine look, her shoulders brushing against Krael's.

That's probably his wife, Watcher thought. He urged the mule to go faster; moving slow would mean death. He pushed the animal to its limit, the old mule's breathing strained. After ten minutes of dodging flaming skulls, the valley opened up to a forest . . . perfect. Wolves howled in the distance, baiting the monsters to pursue them; some of the distorted creatures did just that.

Watcher wove between gigantic spruce trees, trampling clusters of ferns under the mule's hooves. Glancing over his shoulder, he spotted Krael and his wife in the air behind him. Far to the left, another wither moved into the dimming moonlight, but this one was much smaller than any of the others in the air. *I remember someone saying something about a small wither . . . I just don't remember what.*

Focusing on the task at hand, Watcher guided the mule around a cluster of mossy cobblestones, the speckled podzol soil around it dotted with brown mushrooms.

Another barrage of flaming skulls smashed into the forest far to his left; the withers were now just firing randomly, hoping to hit him with a lucky shot.

"I think we've gone far enough, my friend." Watcher patted the animal on the neck. Then, releasing the reins, Watcher guided the animal with his knees as he reached into his inventory. Pulling out a long piece of rope and the Fossil Bow of Destruction, he tied the cord to the enchanted weapon. As he did, an explosion shattered a tree to his left, blocks of leaves falling in all directions.

"I know you're there, fool," Krael screeched. "I can sense your presence! When the sun finishes rising, I'll be able to see you, and then your cowardly retreat will be over."

Watcher glanced to the east. The horizon was glowing a warm orange, the glittering stars having been driven from the sky. Soon, the sun would be up.

Do you think the cape will protect me in the full sunlight? Watcher's thoughts shook with fear.

The ancient wizards trapped within his weapons remained silent, which meant they weren't sure . . . *Great.*

Holding one end of the rope in his hand, the young wizard tossed the Bow behind him, letting the enchanted weapon clatter onto the ground, the rope spooling out until it dragged behind them by a dozen blocks. Reaching up, he removed his enchanted diamond helmet and held it in his hand.

"Now we slow down and hope Krael's aim is good," he whispered to his mount. Relaxing his knees, Watcher let the animal slow from a gallop to a trot. He glanced at the eastern sky again; the sun was now peeking over the horizon, half of its yellow face shining down upon the land.

"Here we go, boy." The young wizard patted the mule on the neck reassuringly, then yelled as loud as he could, "Wither, your aim is as pathetic as your flying! I'm out here walking through the forest and you can't even hit me with your skulls. The other withers must be laughing at your incompetence."

A scream of rage pierced the brightening sky. Watcher glanced over his shoulder and saw Krael glowing brighter than he'd ever seen before, using every drop of magic from the Crowns of Skulls.

The young wizard swallowed nervously. Fear surged through Watcher's body, pulsing through his veins like liquid fire. His heart pounded heavily in his chest, getting faster and faster.

He glanced over his shoulder just as Krael fired, sending three skulls, each wreathed in bright blue flames, streaking down toward him. They looked as if they were heading straight for him.

"Go, mule . . . go!" Watcher urged the terrified animal to a gallop.

And then, close behind him, the explosion from the fireballs echoed through the land. The ground shook as if it had been hit by a giant meteor, sending a wave of heat washing over the mule and rider. Trees shattered, then instantly turned to ash. Blocks of podzol and stone and dirt flew into the air, then came hurtling down, pelting Watcher.

Quickly, Watcher let go of the rope and threw his helmet backward over his shoulder as hard as he could. It clattered to the ground far behind, tumbling into the deep crater now carved into the ground. Grabbing the reins, Watcher slowed the mule, then brought it to a stop behind a thick spruce. Patting the animal on the neck, he moved his mouth near its upright ears and whispered. "We need to be quiet now, my friend."

Watcher held the reins firmly in his hands, keeping the mule hidden behind the dark tree trunk. Leaning forward, he peered around the spruce. Krael cautiously descended down to the treetops, his three skulls looking in all directions. He peered at the crater, its depths clogged with smoke and ash.

"Someone go into this crater and see what's at the bottom." Krael glanced around, then gestured to another wither, the small one Watcher had seen earlier. "You, Kobael, go down there and tell me what you see."

The tiny wither moved down to ground level, a frightened expression on each of its skulls as it flew over the crater, then disappeared into the hazy smoke.

"Well . . . what do you see?" The wither king's voice sounded anxious. "Tell me, fool, what's down there?"

The little monster floated back up into the air and stared up at his king. "There's an enchanted diamond helmet, all covered with soot."

"Is that all? Speak! Your king commands it!"

"There's also something I've never seen before. It looks like a bow, but it's made of what looks like ancient bone."

"That's the Fossil Bow of Destruction." Krael smiled. "I gave it to the skeleton warlord a long time ago, but that pathetic boy-wizard took it from him."

"So, if it's here, in this crater," the tiny wither floated up into the air, moving away from his king, "then that wizard must be—"

"He's dead!" Krael's voice boomed across the land-scape. "I killed the wizard."

The other withers cheered, shouting out their king's name. Watcher watched, still hidden, as Krael glanced proudly at another monster, probably his wife. She smiled, then floated next to him, brushing her shoulder against his affectionately. On the ground, the distorted monsters arrived at the scene, their warped bodies easy to see in the morning light.

I hope they can't see us, Watcher thought.

Remain still, Baltheron said quietly in his mind. *They shouldn't be able to see you, but they might smell you, so don't move.*

The monsters gathered around the crater, many of them growling and snarling, their voices filled with a thirst for violence. Their numbers shocked Watcher—there were still far too many for Watcher's army to fight. Either Blaster's TNT hadn't done as much damage as he'd hoped, or Krael had far more warriors than anyone suspected.

One of the monsters, a giant spider with the head of a zombie and two skeleton arms, stepped away from the crater and took a step toward Watcher. The creature sniffed the air for a moment, then took a step closer.

Oh, no, I think it can smell us.

Don't move. Baltheron's thoughts were like thunder in Watcher's mind.

But it's coming closer. I think I'm gonna make a run for it.

NO!

The monster took another step closer.

It's moving right toward me. It knows I'm here. We should run. Watcher was terrified.

NO! If you run, they'll hear and catch you.

Watcher's fear morphed into panic. *I'm gonna do it. I'm gonna—*

Suddenly, from off to the north, a majestic howl pierced the forest, and the monsters grew silent, all of them turning toward the sound. The spider-zombie-skeleton-thing stopped and stood motionless. Another howl filled the air, but this time a second wolf added its voice to the song, then another and another and another, until there was a choir of wolves all howling as loud as possible.

"The villagers must have escaped the cave." Krael floated higher into the air, then turned toward the sound. "Don't just stand there, you idiots, go get them!"

The warped monster instantly moved to the north, chasing the sounds echoing through the forest. The terrible spider-thing glared in Watcher's direction once more, then slowly turned and scuttled off toward the wolves, the animals still howling with pride.

Watcher's heart finally slowed, the fear igniting every nerve fading away. He'd done it . . . Krael thought he was dead.

"Now we have an advantage," Watcher whispered to himself. "I'm looking forward to seeing the wither king again, but this time on my terms and in a place of my choosing."

A quiet squeak caused him to turn to the right. Moving out from behind a bushy fern, Fixit sat atop an iron wolf. The mechite smiled at Watcher, holding a fist high in the air, and soon another wolf emerged from behind a bush, the mechite on its back also holding his fist over his head. Six more of the animals darted quickly through the forest and stopped next to Watcher and his mule, all of the mechites sitting proud and strong on the back of their wolves. Watcher knew these wolves had saved his life, and he would be forever grateful.

Sitting up in his saddle, the young wizard held his fist over his head in response to the mechites.

"Friends, it's time we taught these monsters what happens when they mess with a wizard and his friends."

The mechites looked up at him and smiled, the wolves wagging their tails.

"Follow me to the Wizard's Tower, everyone. We have a battlefield to prepare." Watcher smiled. "And I have a little surprise in mind for my friend Krael."

Yanking on the reins, Watcher pulled the mule around and headed for home, a circle of metallic protectors at his side.

CHAPTER 22

The tiny wither floated within the branches of a tall spruce tree, out of sight from the other withers and the king. Kobael knew Krael was insane, the wither king's thirst to continue a war that ended many centuries ago had driven him mad. Yes, Kobael saw the insanity, yet he still followed Krael, for what else was a tiny wither to do? The only person who had ever cared about him had disappeared into the forest with the other villagers after being trapped in that cave; he'd never find Mira again.

Krael floated high over the forest as his monsters searched for the escaped NPCs.

"Why haven't any of those monsters returned?" Krael turned to his wife. "They should have found those NPCs by now. Their wolves foolishly give away their position by howling."

"Perhaps the wolves were a ruse, husband." Kora looked up at Krael with adoring eyes. "I think we may have been tricked."

"Are you telling me you think that foolish wizard rode out of that cave just to distract us, so the others could escape? I don't believe it." Krael's eyes grew brighter as his frustration built. "A wizard would never sacrifice himself for a bunch of ordinary villagers."

"How do you know, husband, that the wizard was actually killed?" Kora asked.

"We found his bow and his enchanted helmet."

"We? Who found them?"

Krael glanced around at the withers floating in the air, then screamed, "Kobael, come to me, NOW!" Kobael took a deep breath and moved out from between the branches. With his heads hung low, he flew toward his king, fear enveloping his ashen bones.

Why does he want me . . . does he think I know something about the wizards? Kobael's thoughts were a maelstrom in his mind, all the terrible possibilities slamming into his soul at once. *What if he thinks I was helping Mirthrandos, the ancient wizard who saved me so many centuries ago?* The wither shivered with fright, then floated below his king, looking up at his terrifying skulls.

"I am here, my king." Kobael bowed.

"My wife, Kora, is not convinced that pathetic wizard Watcher is dead." Krael moved closer to the little wither. "Tell her what you saw."

Kobael glanced at Kora, the peaceful expressions on her three skulls easing his fear a bit. "When I made it through the smoke, I reached the bottom of the crater. Floating off the ground was the skeleton warlord's bow, and—"

"You mean the wither king's bow." Krael scowled at the tiny monster.

"Yes, of course, I apologize, my king. I saw the wither king's enchanted bow, as well as an enchanted diamond helmet. I could tell the helmet had powerful spells woven into it."

"And because of those two items, you proclaimed that Watcher was dead?" Kora now moved closer, the peaceful looks on her faces getting angrier.

"All I did was report what I found." Kobael swallowed nervously. "We know that wizard carried the bow and had enchanted armor; we all saw it."

"But what about the rest of his armor, or that magical

sword he carried, or even his XP?" Kora now scowled at Kobael. "What about all that?"

The diminutive monster lowered his heads. "I assumed they were destroyed by Krael's overwhelming power. I only saw the helmet and bow." He slowly backed away from the king and his wife.

"I'm not certain the boy-wizard is gone, my husband," Kora said.

"Of course, he's gone . . . I destroyed him, my wife. I can sense it." Krael's bony chest puffed out with pride. "Withers, come closer. Your king has commands for you all."

The army of shadowy monsters moved closer, but Kobael drifted farther away, ducking amongst the tree branches and hiding in their shadows.

"Brothers and Sisters, that fool of a wizard, Watcher, is finally dead, and now it's time to punish the rest of the villagers."

The withers nodded, some smiling with evil glee.

"We will exterminate every NPC and all their villages. And while we're at it, we'll flatten their forests and farms and grassy hills until the land is barren. The NPCs of the Far Lands will learn the penalty for disobedience to their king . . . me."

The withers screeched with excitement, some firing flaming skulls into the air.

"And once we have destroyed the Far Lands, we'll move inward, toward the Overworld, annihilating everything, until this world is a barren, lifeless wasteland. Then, once everything is dead on this plane of existence, we'll go back to the Hall of Planes and move from world to world, destroying everything . . . everywhere. Soon, my friends, the Pyramid of Servers and all the worlds within it will belong to the withers, with each of you ruling your own world."

The flying monsters cheered louder.

"But we need not try to do this with just this army." Krael closed his eyes, and the Crowns of Skulls grew brighter and brighter until finally a blast of magical energy spread out in all directions. Like a glittering purple wave, the spell flew outward, washing over all the monsters, then continued to spread. Within the wave was a message from Krael: "Monsters, meet your king at the ancient church. That is where the last battle of the Great War will begin. Any monster who refuses this command will be destroyed."

Kobael was shocked by the message; the wither king was forming a massive army. It would be larger than any ever seen in Minecraft. The NPCs wouldn't stand a chance.

"He's insane," Kobael whispered. "If he destroys too much, he'll destabilize Minecraft. The Pyramid of Servers could collapse, destroying the entire Minecraft universe." The tiny wither moved into the foliage of a tree and peeked out between the branches. Many of the withers were beginning the destruction already, firing their flaming skulls at the forest beneath them. "He must be stopped, or it'll mean the death of everything."

I know what I must do, Kobael thought. *I must warn the remaining wizards and the other NPCs, even if it means my death. Hopefully, I can tell the villagers Krael's plan before they attack me.* And then an idea popped up within his mind. *Yes, maybe she can help . . . but will she?*

It was his only hope.

Slowly descending to the ground, Kobael flew under the leafy canopy, staying out of sight as he headed to the east, searching for the NPC wizards and their army, and likely his death.

CHAPTER 23

I t was dark. The moon was directly overhead, but clouds were masking the light from its lunar face, making the Far Lands darker than usual, which was perfect for monsters. Watcher moved slowly through the birch forest, his head turning to the left and right, searching for threats. He'd heard many creatures of the night lurking about, their muffled growls and moans easy to hear in the quietude of the forest. Without the iron wolves with him, Watcher would have had to battle groups of spiders, zombies, and skeletons. That wasn't much of a concern, for his weapons and armor were enough to protect him; his worry was that one of the monsters might spot him and report it to Krael. Watcher knew the wither king thought he was dead, and he didn't want to spoil the surprise he had in mind for that terrible monster.

Pain-filled whispers echoed through his head; Krael was likely destroying another village. Fortunately, the blocking stone from Mira was still doing its job; he could barely hear the shouts of agony.

Great . . . more villagers perishing, and I can't do anything to help them. Rage filled Watcher's soul, pushing the terrified whispers of despair into the dark recesses of his mind, making them almost inaudible.

Up ahead, the forest biome was ending, the dark green grass covering the rolling hills beyond it almost black in the darkness.

"Woof," a nearby wolf said. Watcher pulled on the reins of the mule and moved next to a tree, using it for cover. He glanced down at Fixit where the mechite sat firmly on the silver animal's back. Fixit raised his arm and removed his hand, then attached a sharp knife to the empty wrist socket. He pointed the blade to the right, then gave Watcher a series of squeaks and soft whistles.

"I wish I understood you, but I don't. I'm guessing the wolves smelled something that way?" Watcher pointed to the right.

Fixit nodded his tiny head, his fine, silvery locks of hair bouncing like strands of taut wire.

"Are they moving toward us?"

The mechite shook his head.

"Are they going away?"

He shook it again.

"So, they've stopped nearby?"

Fixit nodded vigorously.

"Well, we can't just sit here and wait for them to leave, and we certainly can't cross the open grasslands with an unknown force nearby." He glanced down at the mechite again. "We need to go see who they are. I think everyone should be armed and ready for battle, just in case we stumble into some hostile mobs."

Fixit nodded, then gave off a series of soft whistles. The other wolves moved silently through the forest and gathered at Watcher's side as each mechite fixed blades to their wrists.

Watcher jumped off the mule, holding the animal's lead in his hand. Pulling a wooden fence post from his inventory, he planted it into the ground, then attached the rope to it. The mule peered at Watcher with its deep brown eyes.

"Don't worry, I'll be back."

The animal nuzzled his soft, gray nose against Watcher's neck. Patting the animal gently on the neck, the young wizard turned and stalked through the forest. Dried leaves and sticks cracked under his feet, each sound causing the wolves to glance at him, annoyed expressions on their steely faces. He tried to be stealthy like the wolves, but it was difficult even to see the forest floor in the darkness.

Just then, the clouds overhead drifted apart from where they'd been clustered in front of the moon, allowing the lunar body to bathe the landscape in its silvery light. Faint shadows stretched out from the base of the trees, giving the forest floor a striped appearance. Watcher placed himself within one of these shadows, hoping to remain unseen by whatever was out there.

A stick cracked up ahead. Hushed voices whispered something, but the sounds were difficult to identify; were they monsters or villagers? Watcher pulled out the wizard's cloak and put it on. Gathering his magic, he sent his power into the glimmering cloth, letting it wrap around him. A tingling sensation, like a thousand microscopic spiders crawling across his skin, spread all over his body as he became invisible again. Fixit glanced up at Watcher, then nodded and smiled.

Quietly, Watcher drew Needle from his inventory.

I hope the glow from the magical blade is also hidden by the cloak. For a moment, Watcher considered putting the sword away, but in the end, he kept it out; he'd rather take the risk and be ready for an attack . . . just in case.

More voices came from off to the right; they were deep and rumbly. *Was that a zombie?*

He stared into the dim forest, hoping to see something. A moment later, a shape moved from tree to tree, as if trying to remain unseen. Watcher moved toward it, his nerves stretched to their limit. More sticks cracked, behind him this time . . . he was surrounded.

Watcher stopped in the shadow of a tree and turned, looking for enemies. A dark shape moved closer. *It's completely black; it must be an enderman.* The dark creature kept coming closer, skulking through the shadows and trying to remain hidden. Nearby, the wolves remained still and silent, waiting for Watcher to give the word to attack. Slowly, the young wizard raised his sword over his head, ready to strike as the shadowy creature came closer and closer until . . . a smile crept across the dark face.

"You know, that invisible cape doesn't stop you from casting shadows." The creature reached up and pulled off a dark helmet, revealing Watcher's friend, Blaster. "You should be more careful."

When he got over his shock, Watcher reached out and hugged his friend, a confused expression on the boy's face.

"Oh, sorry." The young wizard pulled his magic from the cloak; instantly, he rematerialized. "Where are the others?"

"This way." Blaster walked off, not waiting for a reply. "We've been searching the woods for you, so everyone'll be glad you've returned. We were all afraid you were . . . you know."

Watcher smiled and patted his friend on the back, nodding. "Wait, I need to get my trusty mount."

"You mean that crusty old mule? Set it free; that creature is of no use to us."

"Are you kidding?" Watcher laughed. "That 'crusty old mule' saved my life. He stays with me."

Watcher ran back to where the animal was tied up, then rode it to Blaster. By now, the wolves were clustered around the young boy, all the metallic animals wagging their tails. "Where to?"

"This way." Blaster turned and ran through the forest, weaving his way around the trees, moving as quietly as the wolves. Behind him, the mule's hooves pounded the ground as it galloped clumsily through the forest.

Watcher was certain everyone could hear him coming, which was good; he wouldn't want to startle an archer and get an arrow through his head.

He found the NPCs clustered together in a group at the edge of the forest. Obsidian golems patrolled the perimeter, their dark shapes difficult to see, even in full moonlight.

"Watcher's back!" someone shouted.

The young wizard dismounted and was enveloped by a cheering crowd.

"Hey, keep your voices down," Cutter growled as he pushed through the crowd and wrapped his huge arms around the young wizard in a gigantic hug; it was hard for Watcher to breathe. "We all heard the explosions and thought Krael got you."

Cutter released his grip, allowing Watcher to suck in a lungful of air.

"I never thought that." Planter pushed through the crowd of villagers and stood in front of Watcher. "You're much too stubborn to get killed before the last battle even begins." She smiled at him, for the first time in a long time, then lowered her voice angrily. "You had me terrified." She punched him in the chest, her fist making the young wizard's diamond armor ring like a bell; the NPCs laughed. "Don't ever do that again."

Before Watcher could reply, she turned and stormed off.

"I can see everything is back to normal with you two," Blaster said with a smile. "Did the wither king take the bait?"

Watcher nodded. "Yep. He thinks he killed me, so now we have a small advantage."

"I hope it evens the odds a bit." Mapper stood behind the young wizard, his voice shaking nervously. "He has a lot of monsters with him; we need every advantage we can get."

Watcher turned and nodded at the old man in agreement, then reached out and grasped his wrinkled hand. "We'll be alright."

"If you say so," Mapper replied doubtfully.

"Don't worry, Mapper." Blaster smiled. "With Watcher back, Krael will be no problem."

Fencer suddenly pushed through the crowd and stepped in front of the old man, facing Blaster. "Blaster, you're back. I was so worried you had run into some monsters and they'd taken you away from me."

"I could only hope." Blaster rolled his eyes.

"Oh, don't say that." She took him by the arm and led the boy away.

Blaster just glared helplessly at Watcher as the young wizard laughed again, enjoying his friend's misery.

"Cutter, why are you just waiting here on the edge of the forest?" Watcher moved to the edge of the grasslands and peered across the wide clearing. Nothing was moving out there.

"We were waiting for the moon to come out from behind the clouds." The big warrior moved to his side. "Being out in the open and not being able to see the withers seemed like a bad idea."

"I agree." The young wizard nodded. "But the moon's out . . . let's get moving."

"Right." Cutter drew his diamond sword and waved it over his head.

Instantly, a silvery wave of wolves charged forward across the rolling hills, spreading out into a giant V-shaped formation. Behind them, the villagers moved forward, followed by the golems at the rear. As soon as he crested the first large hill, Watcher spotted a village in the distance. Warm yellow light flickered between the buildings, the torches trying to keep monsters from spawning nearby.

The company crossed the grassy clearing and entered the village just as someone started banging on an iron chest plate with a sword, sounding the alarm.

The wolves and golems formed a ring of iron around the village, the obsidian giants following Mirthrandos as Watcher and his troop drew their weapons and headed to the center of the community. There they found an NPC standing next to the village's well, banging on his armor with a sword.

Watcher put away his weapons and held up his hands. "You don't need an alarm. We're here in peace."

As he spoke, villagers burst out of the wooden structures, each fully clad in armor with weapons in their hands. Archers appeared upon rooftops, their pointed shafts aimed at the grasslands surrounding the village. An NPC with a black leather tunic dangling across his brown smock approached Watcher; he was clearly the village blacksmith.

"What do you want here?" Blacksmith asked.

"We're here to warn you. There is a huge army of monsters and withers likely heading this way. You stand no chance of surviving any attack." Watcher waved his arms over his head, signaling for his people to put away their weapons. "They've already destroyed many villages, and yours will probably be next."

"We can defend our community." Blacksmith scowled at Watcher. "A bunch of strangers aren't going to make us leave our village. This has been our home for generations, and—"

A panicked and terrified voice suddenly filled the air. "Run! They're coming! Everyone, run!"

A young villager with a tattered and ripped red smock streaked into the village. He ran right up to Cutter and grabbed his arm. "They destroyed my village. Everyone is dead, and those monsters aren't stopping for anything."

Cutter grabbed him with his two meaty hands and shook the NPC, trying to get him to calm down. "Slow down and tell us what happened."

The NPC slowed his breathing and calmed himself, then said, "Monsters attacked our village. There were at least forty of them, if not more. I've never seen groups of different monsters work together before, but they acted as if they were all part of the same village or clan, or whatever monsters have."

Watcher turned to the terrified villager. "Were there any withers or distorted monsters that looked as if they came out of a nightmare?"

The villager noticed Watcher's glowing arms and a look of surprise spread across his dusty face.

"Don't worry about me," Watcher said in a calm voice. "It's safe. Tell us what you know."

"No, I didn't see any withers, just regular monsters . . . you know, spiders, zombies, skeletons . . ." The villager took a bottle of water that was offered and drank, then continued. "But the strange thing is, the monsters were all saying something about krill or kale or . . . I don't know, but they all were saying it, and—"

"It was Krael." Watcher's voice was soft, a touch of fear to it.

The villager nodded, eyes wide. "Yeah, that's it. How did you know?"

Watcher turned to the blacksmith. "Krael is the king of the withers, and he's the one leading all these monsters. They want to wipe all our villages off the map and take the world for themselves."

"That sounds like something out of the Great War," the muscular Blacksmith said.

Watcher just nodded. "That's exactly what it is. If you and your people stay here, you're doomed." He took a step toward Blacksmith and held his arms up for all to see. "I'm a wizard, and so are Planter and Mirthrandos." He pointed the other two out. "We're gathering every NPC we can find and heading for the Wizard's Tower. It is there where we'll make our stand. You need to evacuate your village, and everyone must come with us. There's no other option."

"The monsters completely overwhelmed our village." The young NPC wiped away tears with a torn red sleeve. "When I saw it was hopeless, I ran, but I can still hear the screams in my mind. The rest of the village stayed and fought, including my parents." He started to weep. "But they didn't stand a chance." The young boy looked up at Watcher. "I'm a coward."

"It is not cowardice to save one's life." Er-Lan stepped forward, scaring most of the villagers when they saw he was a zombie.

Watcher held up his hands to calm them, and put an arm around the zombie's shoulders, showing he was a friend.

Er-Lan moved closer to the young boy and put a clawed hand on his shoulder reassuringly. "Sometimes bravery and sacrifice can lead to a pointless death. Life is too precious to just let it go to waste. There are times when it is better to run, rather than throwing one's life away."

"And there's also times when you need to stand and fight, that is, if you trust the villagers you're fighting with." Cutter glared at the young zombie, his voice booming through the village. "Warriors must be able to trust those with them in battle. You can't just run away because *life is too precious.* Sometimes you need to hold the line. I'd expect every NPC to know that, but I'm not surprised a zombie doesn't."

"Obviously, both of you are right." Watcher moved between Cutter and Er-Lan, hoping his presence would lessen the tension. "It's clear Krael is recruiting more monsters to his banner, and it's likely they'll be here soon." He glanced around at the villagers, many of them children. "I think it would be bad if he caught us here. It's best if all of you come with us, really. We have safety in numbers, and when we get back to the Wizard's Tower, we'll be safe."

"Safe?" the refugee asked.

"Well . . . safer than here. I don't think any place is safe while Krael and his monster army are lurking around." Watcher glanced at the village leader. "We need to move, fast. Have your people gather all the food, potions, weapons, and armor you have; we're leaving."

"But this is our home," the blacksmith said, his voice now just a whisper.

"It'll be your grave if you stay," Blaster said.

Planter punched the boy in the shoulder. "Try to be just a little sensitive, if you can."

He shook his head, the black curls bouncing about like shadowy springs. "Nope . . . can't do it." He gave her a smile, which she didn't return.

"What do you say? If any of you want to come with us and live, then collect only what you need. You have two minutes."

With a sigh, the blacksmith nodded, then turned and headed for his home, the other NPCs doing the same. Blaster moved to Watcher's side, Fencer following along, of course. "You think we can get to the Wizard's Tower without getting caught by Krael and his monsters?"

Watcher nodded. "Yeah, if he were nearby, I'd feel his presence. I think he and his army are far from here."

"Then why did you tell these people they have to leave?" Fencer sounded confused and angry.

"Eventually he'll pass by here, and these NPCs are just about helpless without magic like Planter and I have. If we leave them here, they're doomed . . . eventually." Watcher glanced at his troops. "Warriors, form a perimeter with the wolves. We don't want any surprises."

The soldiers spread out, forming a wide circle around the village with the wolves and golems.

The villagers returned with their belongings in less than a minute; clearly, they were a disciplined group . . . *Good*, Watcher thought.

"OK." Cutter tried to keep his voice quiet, which was a challenge for him. "Let's go."

The party continued to the east, alternating between running and walking. Around him, Watcher saw far too many children.

How am I gonna keep all these kids safe? Krael doesn't care if it's a man, woman or child; he'll kill them all. Watcher shuddered as images of what might happen played through his head.

Worry not about all the possibilities. Baltheron's deep

voice boomed through his mind. *Instead, choose your goal, and figure out how to make it come true.*

But what if— Watcher thought but was cut off.

There is no if. Choose your goal and make a plan. A goal without a plan is just a wish, and wishes won't help you with the wither king, but plans will, so figure it out!

The voice went silent again, and Watcher knew the discussion was over, but it didn't help his uncertainty or fear. The number of lives he was responsible for was growing larger and larger, and the weight of that responsibility felt like it was about to crush him.

But, instead of falling into despair, Watcher did what Baltheron suggested: he planned. The horses were the key to fighting the creatures on the ground, but what would they do about the withers? Those dark monsters could just bombard them from overhead, annihilating everyone and everything.

As he thought, pieces of a plan started coming together, but timing would be everything. If his trick didn't work, none of them would survive.

CHAPTER 24

Krael stared down at the parched landscape, the undulating sand dunes like pale waves frozen in place by some magical spell. A hot, dry wind drifted across the land, carrying with it dust and biting sand, which stung as it struck his exposed, ashen bones; he loved the bleak emptiness of this biome, but could certainly do without the heat and grit.

They'd left the forest biome in frustration when the monsters had been unable to find the other wizards and NPCs. Their escape had infuriated Krael, causing the wither king to destroy a couple monsters as a lesson to the others for their incompetence. Now, they were searching the land, looking for more recruits as they headed for the ancient church, their meeting place.

"Look up ahead, husband," Kora said. "A desert village. I had hoped we'd get to destroy another one, but it seems a group of monsters already beat us to it."

Krael nodded. "These monsters likely obeyed my command and attacked the village. By the looks of the ruins, I suspect they destroyed this place several days ago."

Ahead, a desert village sat atop a large dune, a scant few sandstone walls marking where the structures had once stood. Piles of tools, weapons, and armor floated on the ground throughout the area, remnants of the deceased NPCs. Krael moved closer to the ground, then motioned his army of warped and distorted monsters to charge forward first. The creatures instantly obeyed, for to do anything else would invite a swift death.

When the wither king entered the village, his monsters surrounded the shattered community and took control. The current inhabitants—the zombies, skeletons and spiders who had destroyed the village—were now all clustered around the well, trying to find shade; they were still not accustomed to being unharmed in sunlight.

"Foolish creatures," Krael murmured, shaking his head.

"What did you say, husband?"

"It was not important, Kora."

Krael flew to the center of the shattered village, then floated above the tiny well. "Get away from the well; it's about to be destroyed."

The monsters glanced up at the wither king, then quickly bolted away just as he fired a trio of flaming skulls. The projectiles hit the structure's square sandstone roof and exploded, tearing a huge crater into the ground. When the smoke cleared, Krael descended closer to the ground and glared at the monsters.

"I have made you immune to the effects of the sun. As long as I wear these crowns, the daylight will not harm you. I will not allow you to cower in the shadows; it makes you look pathetic and weak, and my monster army IS NOT WEAK!" His voice echoed across the sweltering landscape. "Any monster hiding in the shadows for fear of getting burned will be destroyed."

The monsters nodded and moved away from the walls, stepping cautiously into the sunlight. When they realized they wouldn't catch fire, they relaxed and stared up at their leader in awe.

"Now, I commend you, my friends, on the destruction of this village." Krael found the largest zombie and stared at the monster, assuming this was the group's leader. "Did any escape?"

The monster shook his head. "After the battle, many of our brothers and sisters went in search of other villages. Hopefully they found more prey." The zombie gave the wither a toothy, evil grin.

Krael moved closer to the ground, knowing the withers in the air were ready to attack if any monsters threatened their king. "Using the Crowns of Skulls, I have sent out another message to the monsters of the Far Lands, commanding all to join our army and destroy the NPCs. Those nearby will feel my pull and come here. Monsters farther away will meet us at the old church built by the idiotic wizards hundreds of years ago. When our army is fully assembled there, we'll begin our assault on the NPCs and the last two remaining wizards."

Krael floated higher in the air and scanned the desert, expecting to see multitudes of monsters charging across the desert, rallying to his banner. He sighed in frustration; the desert was as empty as it was before.

"Have no fear, husband . . . they will come." Kora's soft voice soothed the wither king's anger.

"I only wish we had more of the distorted monsters like those that came here from the other plane of existence." Krael glared down at the ordinary mob still gathered in the village. "These mundane monsters are easily scared. They lack the cruel streak that has been burned into the souls of the warped creatures from our homeland."

"You need not worry," Kora said. "The monsters of the Far Lands will come in droves. Their numbers will make up for their lack of merciless ferocity." Kora gestured to a group of skeletons standing near a wide shadow being cast by the remnants of a wall, each afraid to stand in the cool darkness and risk destruction by Krael. "The more monsters we have, the better, even if they are from this world. They probably can't fight as well as the mutants, but they will have other uses—put them in the first wave. The NPCs will expend all their arrows and swords repelling the attacks of these mundane creatures, and if we're lucky, these new recruits will perhaps destroy half the NPCs' army before they die, leaving the rest to be easily crushed by our more-lethal comrades."

"Perhaps you're right, Kora. We must concentrate our recruiting efforts on gathering more ground forces. I'm sure the remaining two wizards will make their stand inside the Wizard's Tower. They know they can't face us in the air, even with the old woman's golems helping, so their only hope is to defeat our ground forces and then retreat. I'm sure they'll have traps set up all around the Tower, hoping to destroy our troops while they hide in that ancient structure, cowering in fright."

Kora moved higher in the air and tilted her head back, warming her faces in the bright sunlight. "But, husband, what if they do something unexpected? They do have an experienced wizard with them. That tiny wither, Kobael, told us her name . . . what was it again?"

"Mirthrandos," Krael hissed, furious at the mention of the wizard.

"Yes, that's it, Mirthrandos." Kora nodded her three skulls. "As an experienced wizard, she is a threat . . . we must be careful."

"You need not fear, wife. If the villagers cower in their underground home, we will just wait until they emerge or they starve, whichever comes first. Those NPCs are not fools. They know they must face our wither army eventually if they hope to save the Far Lands."

"So, you think they'll try to fight us in the air?" Kora asked.

Krael nodded. "They must, or we'll just exterminate all the other NPCs in the Far Lands, then save these cowards for last. Those two wizards will not hide forever; they have no choice." Krael's skulls stared off into the desert. "And now, they no longer have the Fossil Bow of Destruction, their most powerful weapon." He laughed maliciously, then turned and faced his wife. "They must come out and fight my withers with their normal, puny bows, which is what I'm hoping for."

"Really . . . you have a plan?"

Krael's skulls gave his wife three wide grins. "I have a little surprise for the wizards and their friends—something no one, not even you, wife, would ever expect."

"I'm intrigued. What's your plan?"

"I think I'd rather keep it as a surprise, wife." The wither king's eyes flashed with evil delight. "But I will say it was intended to be a living weapon, created by the NPC wizards during the Great War hundreds of years ago. When the withers betrayed the wizards and turned on them, they didn't dare make any more living weapons like us. But I recently realized that the arrogant Tharus put the ability to create these new creatures into the Crowns of Skulls."

Kora nodded. "What are these living weapons called? At least you can tell me that."

"You are very impatient, wife, but I will tell you." Krael floated closer to Kora and lowered his voice. "The creatures I will create with these Crowns will strike fear into the hearts of all villagers and likely make them beg for death." He laughed.

"Tell me more," Kora insisted.

"I'll only give you their name, and that's all." He grew silent, letting the suspense build, then spoke in a hushed voice, an evil smile on his three faces. "They're called . . . Phantoms."

"Phantoms? What are they?"

"You must wait, my dear Kora, but trust me . . . when you see these monsters and the effect they'll have on the NPCs, you will be pleased."

He glanced down at his army. The talk about his secret weapon was making Krael impatient. "Monsters, I want fifty of you, mostly the mutants, to go forth and find my enemies. Bring me back that ancient wizard's staff as a trophy."

"But, your highness, how will we find them?" a half-zombie, half-skeleton creature asked.

"Head toward the Wizard's Tower. They'll likely be on their way there, trying to remain unseen, using valleys and canyons to hide their presence. Likely, they're emptying villages as they move through the Far Lands, so the presence of children will slow their progress." Krael's eyes grew bright with evil excitement. "Make them suffer . . . Now go!"

The monsters cheered, then a group of them headed across the desert, slower creatures riding on the backs of spider-things. They followed a tall zombie with the head of a spider and a pair of stout skeleton arms, all of them hungry for destruction.

"Good hunting!" Krael's voice boomed across the desolate landscape.

The creatures growled and snarled in response, many of them holding weapons and clawed hands high in the air.

"I'm just sorry Watcher won't be there to see my creatures tear into his friends."

"You sound sad, my husband."

"I am, a little," he replied. "I didn't want to just destroy that boy-wizard . . . I wanted to make him suffer." Krael turned toward Kora. "It was my dream to destroy Watcher's friends right in front of him, making the fool witness their suffering."

"But you destroyed him; that must make you a little happy, at least?"

Krael smiled. "Of course it does. I just need to change my plans. Instead of torturing Watcher, I'll do it to the young girl-wizard with the flaming shield. Her suffering will, I think, make me happy . . . I'm looking forward to meeting her again."

"As am I, my husband," Kora said, grinning cruelly.

The two withers stared into each other's eyes, laughing as they imagined the destruction about to envelop the Far Lands.

CHAPTER 25

The NPCs moved quietly through the forest while the sun descended toward the western horizon. Few spoke; their fear of the monsters that were likely hunting them created a strained tension, stretching their courage almost to its breaking point. The iron creatures from Mira's world formed a protective ring around the company, giving the villagers a faint sense of safety, but it was barely an echo compared to the thunderstorm of dread playing through their minds.

After they'd been running for a couple of hours, the forest biome changed into that of a frozen river. The air morphed from a pleasant breeze filled with the smell of leaves and grass and flowers to one with a frigid bite, full of tiny ice crystals riding the wind and digging into exposed skin. With the flat landscape, there was no protection from the icy gusts, causing the NPCs to cluster together for warmth.

"I've never enjoyed these frozen biomes," Blaster said as he removed his dark-green armor and replaced it with white. "All these areas offer is lots of snow and ice."

"And don't forget polar bears," Mapper added. "Like the one we came across when we were looking for the witches."

"I remember." Planter nodded as she walked up a small mound of snow, her feet crunching through the thin, frozen layer of white.

"My mom saw the bear too . . . right?" Fencer's voice quivered, full of emotion. "She was . . . still alive?"

Planter nodded. "Yes, Saddler saw the bear. She thought it was beautiful." She held her shield up for Fencer to see. "And we found a shield like mine just before we saw the polar bear. It was given to your mom, to keep her safe."

"But it didn't keep her safe, did it?" Fencer sniffled as a tear tumbled down her cheek.

No one answered. There was nothing anyone could say, especially Watcher. Saddler's death had hit him hard.

Fencer moved to Planter's side, her feet almost slipping on some ice. "What happened to the shield?"

Planter glanced at Watcher, then to Cutter and Blaster . . . they all shrugged. "I'm not sure. After she was . . . well . . . after the spider . . ."

"You're trying to say, 'after she was killed?'" Unflinching, Fencer looked straight into Planter's eyes.

The young wizard nodded, her emerald eyes tearing up. "Yeah, after she was killed, it was pretty crazy. I'm not sure what happened to her shield."

"Too bad," Fencer sniffled again. "I'd like to have it; maybe it would remind me of my mom."

"Er-Lan knows where it is." The zombie scurried across a frozen river, his clawed feet digging into the ice, making a sharp scraping sound. He moved to Fencer's side and reached into his inventory, pulling out the enchanted shield, as well as a decorated pickaxe. "Er-Lan picked it up after the battle, as well as Saddler's pickaxe, and forgot the two were still in his inventory. This zombie doesn't understand the significance of the pickaxe, but it was—"

"You have my dad's pick?!" Fencer reached out and took the multicolored iron tool from Er-Lan's hand. She hugged it as if it were a long-lost sibling.

"Er-Lan did not know these were important. It was just—"

"You were hiding these things all this time?" Cutter glared at the zombie. "Why did you keep them a secret? What other secrets do you have?"

Er-Lan glanced at Cutter, then turned to Fencer and handed her the shield. The young girl, in tears, took the shield with her left hand, and it brushed against the identical shield held by Planter. Instantly, a bright flash of purple light filled the air, knocking Planter to her knees. Er-Lan moved to help his friend, but Cutter grabbed the zombie by the back of his chain mail and pulled him backward.

"You aren't touching her." Cutter glared at him. "Keep your slimy green hands to yourself."

The big NPC moved to stand between the zombie and the girls, his hand reaching for his weapon.

"Now calm down, Cutter," Mapper said. "Er-Lan is a friend, and you know that." He glanced at Er-Lan. "We're grateful the shield and pickaxe were saved. They're obviously important to Fencer."

Mapper put a hand on the big warrior's arm, pulling it to his side and away from his weapon. He then reached down and helped Planter to her feet. Everyone gasped when Planter got up; the glow from her body was much brighter than before, as if her magical power had somehow been magnified.

"What?" Planter asked, confused, but no one said anything.

Cutter glanced at Fencer, who was hugging both the shield and pickaxe while Planter glanced around.

Er-Lan stared up at Cutter, then lowered his gaze and moved away, his clawed feet crunching through the snow.

"I still think there's something going on with that zombie." Cutter glared at Er-Lan, then brought his gaze back to Watcher. "I don't trust him, and neither should you."

Watcher sighed. The conflict between Cutter and Er-Lan just caused everyone to feel more stressed. "Cutter, I would trust Er-Lan with my life. He's saved me countless times, and I have no reason to doubt his dedication."

"Well, he never saved me, and I bet he never will." The hulking warrior turned from the young wizard and trudged through the snow, an angry scowl etched into his square face.

"Yeah, I doubt he will, too, if you keep accusing him of being a traitor," Blaster called after him.

"What?!" Cutter boomed.

"Nothing . . . nothing." Blaster stepped away from the warrior, hoping to avoid being the next target of his anger.

"That's enough arguing," Watcher shouted. "All this tension is gonna tear us apart."

He slowed to a walk, then turned around and gazed at the rest of their company. They had maybe seventy NPCs in their little army, many of them elderly or very young. Fear was evident in all of their eyes; they knew the wither king was out there, hunting them, and the internal strife certainly wasn't helping.

"We need to help each other, not resort to blaming or accusing. The only way we'll survive this conflict with the withers is if we work together." He looked sternly at Cutter. "All of us are in this together. There are no traitors here, just friends and family, and that's what makes us stronger than the monsters."

"You think family is gonna help us defeat Krael and his army?" Cutter asked.

"No," Watcher replied, shocking the other NPCs. "It isn't family that will let us defeat them, it's the fact that we'll do anything to help each other." He turned from Cutter and cast his gaze across the villagers. "Together, we are strong, much stronger than the monsters. But we must remember what's important . . . and that's that no one is alone." He paused to let it sink in for a moment. "Everyone has an army at their back, ready to protect them. If we work together and watch each other's backs, then the withers will fail. Remember, if we—"

A wolf howled nearby, the sound cutting through the icy landscape.

"Monsters coming." Er-Lan's voice sounded scared. "A lot of them."

"You heard that in the howl?" Blaster asked.

Er-Lan nodded.

"Up ahead, I see some extreme hills," Mapper said, pointing with a wrinkled finger. "Maybe we can lose them in the valleys."

"Right." Watcher nodded. "Anyone too weak to run, the golems will carry you."

He glanced at Mirthrandos. The ancient wizard closed her eyes for a moment, relaying the commands to the metal giants, then opened them and nodded. The iron and obsidian golems reached down and picked up the grandparents and grandchildren in their party.

"Come on!"

Watcher turned and sprinted for the snow-covered hills up ahead. A wave of silver streaked past him as the iron wolves and their mechite riders charged ahead, making sure it was safe. Glancing over his shoulder, Watcher looked for their pursuers.

In the distance, he could see dark shapes moving across the frozen landscape. The monsters were clumped together in a large group, making it difficult to tell their number, but however many there were, he was sure it would be too many for them to fight, and they were moving fast.

It won't take long for those creatures to catch us, Watcher thought. *We need a plan . . . I need a plan.* But there was nothing in his head, no ideas, no strategies . . . nothing other than the overwhelming responsibility for keeping these people safe. He was terrified he'd fail these NPCs, and his fear of failing all these villagers and letting some of them get injured, or worse, was making it hard for him to think. Watcher knew the only thing that would help them right now was speed.

The NPCs ran as fast as they could, their feet kicking snow up into the air. Many stumbled and fell as they crossed the frozen river that wound its way across the landscape. Villagers reached down and helped the fallen to their feet, then kept going, fear keeping their legs pumping.

When they reached the extreme hills biome, Watcher charged into a narrow valley with steep hills lining the sides. Dark shadows covered the ground, the rays from the setting sun already blocked by the high stony peaks.

"You sure . . . being in a narrow valley is . . . a good idea?" Mapper asked, struggling to catch his breath as he spoke.

"It'll make a larger force easier to confront." Watcher offered the old man a bottle of water. "Confined in these valleys, the monsters won't be able to use their overwhelming numbers to surround us."

"But it can make escape for us more difficult, right?" Mapper sounded worried.

"Don't worry, Mapper, these valleys always have an exit." Watcher smiled at the old man, hoping to appear confident, though it was a lie. He was terrified.

As they ran between the steep hills, Watcher noticed many snow-covered outcroppings extending over the passes. Structures of stone and gravel stretched out from the peaks, forming a strange, patchy roof over the narrow pass, blocking some of the falling snow from reaching the ground. The overhangs were at least fifteen blocks high but appeared only in a few places. Light from the setting sun cast shades of red and orange, decorating them, making the thin layer of snow on the many cubes of gravel and stone shine as if made of gold; their height allowed them to still be kissed by the setting sun, though the ground was already masked in darkness.

Suddenly, a group of wolves returned to Watcher and the others, then barked and growled to Mirthrandos.

Skidding to a stop, Watcher glanced at Er-Lan, unsure what was wrong.

"The wolves say it is a dead end up ahead," the zombie said. "There is no exit that way."

"Then we need to go back." Watcher turned around, but he was greeted by more growls at the other end of the narrow pass. He glanced at the zombie.

"The monsters have entered the pass." Er-Lan moved to Watcher and placed a hand on his shoulder. "Many are there, blocking the exit."

Growls and snarls floated through the cold air as the monsters slowly moved through the cliff-lined pass toward the group.

"So . . . we're trapped?" Watcher glanced at the zombie, hoping for a different answer than he knew he'd get.

Er-Lan nodded, then lowered his eyes to the ground. "The wolves report there are many monsters approaching."

"How many?"

The zombie took a nervous swallow, then spoke in a hushed voice. "Far too many to fight . . . we're trapped, with no hope of escape."

Glancing up at the steep hills, Watcher looked for some way out. The hills were made of stone and gravel, with a few blocks of coal-ore here and there. Every flat surface was covered with snow as soft flakes drifted down from overhead. The sides of the hills were steep, in some places completely sheer; they'd never be able to climb their way out.

"What's the plan?" someone asked, but Watcher didn't really hear them. He was completely overwhelmed with the bitter taste of failure. He'd led them into a hopeless position, from which it seemed escape was impossible.

"What do we do?" a villager asked.

"Watcher . . . use your magic," another said.

"Watcher . . . save us."

Every terrified voice drove another icicle of guilt deeper into the young wizard's soul.

I was trying to save these people, and now I've doomed them. Fear and panic dominated Watcher's mind, making it difficult to think.

The snarling voices of the monsters were getting louder . . . they were coming.

Someone shouted out for the NPCs to build defenses, but Watcher knew they would do no good. By the mismatched sounds of the horde, he knew these were the warped monsters Krael had brought with him from the distorted lands, which were stronger than regular monsters and could do things others couldn't.

"Here they come!" Cutter shouted. "Everyone, get atop the barricade."

Villagers charged to the top of the hastily constructed defenses, hoping to hold back the flood of fangs and claws, but to Watcher . . . it seemed hopeless.

Walls wouldn't stop them, nor would arrows or swords . . . there just were not enough NPCs here to stop this mob. It was hopeless, and it was all Watcher's fault. He wanted to just give up and disappear, but he knew he didn't have long to wait for that; death was coming for them all.

This was the end.

CHAPTER 26

Distorted creatures, built from the parts of different monsters, charged at the cobblestone wall, but their stench assaulted the defenders before the mob did. The smell of decaying flesh, mixed with the musky aroma of spiders and the strange, putrid smell from the slimes, wafted across the villagers' defenses, making many of them gag. It was a terrible odor that seemed to cling to the cold, still air, the steep hills blocking any breeze.

As they reached the villagers' defenses, creepy spidery things with zombie heads or skeleton arms or huge slime-bodies tried to climb the barricade but were knocked back by swordsmen standing atop the ramparts. The warriors, led by Cutter, slashed at the creatures with all their strength, keeping the monsters down . . . but it came at a cost. Claws and teeth stabbed at the defenders, tearing into their legs and pulling them from the fortification. Warriors who fell onto the monsters' side of the wall, mercifully, didn't scream for very long.

"Watch the sides of the wall," Blaster shouted. "Some of the monsters are climbing up the steep hills."

Running toward the battle, Watcher pulled out his enchanted bow and fired at those scaling the sheer rocky faces. His arrows struck the monsters, but only slowed them down; he wished he had the Fossil Bow of Destruction right now. Firing a rapid succession of arrows, he took out a spider-enderman, then turned his aim to a spider-creeper. The monster was beginning its ignition process, trying to take out the left side of the wall, but Watcher's arrows silenced it before the monster could explode.

"We need more soldiers on the wall!" Cutter shouted.

Immediately, Watcher put away his bow and drew the Flail of Regrets. As he ran to the fortifications, the young wizard allowed his magic to fill the weapons. A bright purple glow wrapped around the spiked ball, so harsh and bright it was difficult to look at. Leaping onto the battlements, the young wizard swung the Flail with all his strength. Watcher smashed the nearest monster, the spikes tearing into the creature's HP. Squealing with pain, the half-zombie, half-enderman stared up at him with vile hatred in its cold dead eyes. Watcher swung the flail again, but this time, the monster crouched, the spiked ball missing the monster's head.

Before he could attack the creature again, the zombie-enderman jumped high into the air and landed atop the cobblestone wall. Surprised, Watcher took a step back. The creature lunged, its dark fists pummeling him in the chest. Staggering, Watcher flashed red as pain erupted through his body. He lifted the Flail, getting ready to attack, when suddenly a sparkling enchanted sword streaked through the air, hitting the monster in the side; Fencer was behind the creature. The zombie-enderman turned to defend itself, but Fencer struck it again, her curved sword taking the rest of the monster's HP. It disappeared with a pop, fear and rage painted on its dark face.

"Thanks," Watcher said. "I thought I was—"

"Duck!"

Watcher crouched just as a skeleton arrow streaked over his head. Fencer knocked the pointed shaft out of the air, then leapt over Watcher, her sword slashing through the air. She landed next to the pale, bony creature, her enchanted blade knocking the skeleton's bow from its grip. With a strong kick, the young girl knocked the skeleton to the ground; warriors below finished it off.

Mira suddenly appeared on the wall, her crooked staff swinging to the left and right, smashing attackers in their heads. When she'd made some room, she turned the staff's end toward the horde and fired a cluster of magic missiles. The shimmering projectiles disappeared amid the huge group of monsters, their sharp tips doing little to slow the horde.

Frowning, Mira glanced over her shoulder and nodded. Instantly, the ground shook as a group of iron golems lumbered toward the wall. They stepped over the barricade and attacked the monsters, their strong metal arms flinging the creatures high into the air. At the same time, wolves darted amongst the attackers. Sharp metal teeth crunched skeleton bones, zombie arms, and spider legs. They zipped through the battlefield as the golems pounded on the monsters; but there were just too many enemies. Grunting with pain, the golems flashed red as they took damage, while the wolves howled in agony.

Blaster suddenly appeared at Watcher's side, his two curved swords moving almost too fast to be seen. He attacked a monster trying to climb over the wall, then stabbed at another right behind the first. Nearby, a scream pierced the air as a villager's HP was destroyed, the poor soul disappearing from sight. More shouts of pain and fear, voices Watcher recognized, stabbed at his soul; villagers who were depending on him to keep them safe were perishing.

I'm a failure, Watcher thought. *These NPCs are dying because I couldn't—*

"Watcher, there are just too many monsters attacking us." Blaster grabbed Watcher's shoulder and shook him. "We have to do something—*you* have to do something—fast, or we're all dead."

"I know . . . I know."

"Then what are we gonna do?" Blaster jumped down from the wall and glanced at their surroundings, desperation on his face.

Watcher leaped down as well and stared at the steep valley walls, hoping for some kind of solution to pop into his head. Suddenly, a flash of green streaked past him. Er-Lan ran across the narrow pass and fell upon a giant spider, the creature sneaking up on Watcher and Blaster. The zombie stood directly in the spider's path, refusing to let the dark, fuzzy monster past. The spider stared at Er-Lan, a confused expression on its hideous face, then turned and scurried away.

"Thanks, Er-Lan," Blaster said. "You saved us."

"Fortunately, the spider chose to retreat instead of fight." The zombie quickly looked to the ground, as if he were embarrassed . . . or something else.

Cutter suddenly appeared at Watcher's side, his armor scratched and dented. "You two need to be up on the wall . . . we need help and standing down here isn't doing anything."

More cries of pain and fear filled the air, each making Watcher quiver with guilt. He tilted his head back, staring up at the dark night sky, hoping to find an answer . . . and then he saw it.

"Look up there." Watcher pointed at the overhanging blocks of stone stretching across the narrow valley. "There's hundreds of gravel blocks sitting on top of a thin layer of stone." He glanced at Blaster and smiled. "If we could strategically place a few blocks of TNT along the stone, the explosions would cause all that sandstone to come falling down on the heads of the monsters."

"What are you thinking?" Cutter glared at the young wizard. "We're down here, and the gravel is up there. What are you gonna do, just shoot yourself up there like a rocket?"

"Well . . . I haven't figured out how to—"

Blaster smiled and interrupted. "I know exactly what to do." He turned toward Cutter. "Tell the warriors I need just a few minutes; they have to hold out a little longer."

"I'll give you as much time as I can." The big warrior ran toward the battle, his loud battle cry startling both monster and villager alike.

"Do I want to know what you're planning?" Watcher asked.

"Probably not."

Turning back to the fortified wall, Blaster scanned the scene, then shouted, "Fencer, I need you over here."

The girl instantly leapt off the wall, her enchanted sword glowing in her hand. She ran to Blaster's side, a huge smile on her eager face.

"Just stand back, Watcher, and let us work." Blaster explained to Fencer what he needed, then pulled out his pickaxe and dug a single-block channel in the ground. Fencer used her father's pick and dug a second one, intersecting with Blaster's so they formed a large "+". Around the two grooves, Blaster and Fencer placed redstone dust, then positioned a block of stone at the center. Then, using six blocks of TNT, they filled the channels and poured water in the rest.

"With any luck, this should shoot me up into the air. I've positioned it so that it's right next to that ledge up there." Blaster pointed with a redstone torch. "If I don't hit it on the way up, and I don't miss it on the way down, then I should land safely up there."

"How do you know the blast won't hurt you?" Fencer asked.

Blaster shrugged. "I don't."

Fencer took a step closer. "And what happens if you hit the rock on the way up?"

He shrugged again. "I suspect that would be bad."

"This is too dangerous." Fencer turned to Watcher, eyes pleading. "He can't do this . . . it's suicide."

"I can do it," Blaster insisted.

"No." Watcher shook his head. "It's too dangerous. I won't let you do it."

"But we can't hold out much longer against these monsters." Blaster stared at his friend, his eyes pleading. "It must be done."

Watcher nodded. "I agree. That's why *I'm* gonna do it."

"You can't . . . TNT is my thing." Blaster scowled at his friend.

"And keeping people safe is my thing." Watcher placed a hand on his friend's shoulder. "Besides, I need you there for the last battle. I'm sure we'll need lots of explosive surprises to slow down the monsters. You have to be there; you're critical." He glanced at the villagers on the battle line. "The same is true for Planter, Cutter, Mira . . . everyone will have an important task in that last battle but me. You all can lead these villagers if I don't survive." He stared at Blaster, his bright blue eyes boring into the boy's soul. "You know I'm right."

Watcher moved to the center of the contraption and placed an iron helmet on his head. "Now light this thing, and let's see if it works."

Blaster pulled Fencer to the side, then drew a redstone torch from his inventory. "You sure you want to do this?"

Watcher shook his head. "I don't want to, no, but I must, for all of them," he waved his hand at the embattled villagers, then pointed at Planter, "and for her."

A look of anguished pain covered Planter's face as she held her flaming purple shield in front of the other NPCs, trying to protect as many as possible. She glanced over her shoulder at Watcher, a look of confusion and concern in her beautiful green eyes.

"EVERYONE, FALL BACK!" Watcher's amplificd voice echoed off the cold hillsides.

The thunderous volume in his voice shocked the monsters, causing them to stop attacking for an instant.

That was all the NPCs needed. The villagers jumped off the wall and retreated, running past Blaster's TNT contraption.

Watcher turned to Blaster. "Do it."

His friend sighed, then placed the redstone torch on the ground. Instantly, the TNT blocks started to blink as they prepared to explode.

"Maybe this wasn't a good idea after all," Watcher murmured to himself, then gritted his teeth as the blocks exploded, enveloping him in fire and smoke and heat.

CHAPTER 27

As the explosive blast shot Watcher into the air, the smell of gunpowder and smoke wrapped around him like a thick blanket. Soaring straight up, the young wizard looked at his feet, then leaned forward, allowing himself to fall toward his target: the rocky outcropping. He bent forward even more, trying to will himself forward a block or two.

I'm not gonna make it! he realized. The thought filled him with terror.

The monsters in the valley were moving forward now, slowly approaching his friends where they were clustered at the back of the dead-end passage. If he were to fall back onto the ground, the terrifying creatures would fall upon him, and Watcher knew he wouldn't last long then.

Reaching the apex of his climb, Watcher started to fall. Beads of nervous sweat ran down his face, even though the air was freezing. The square droplets tumbled into his eyes, stinging, but instead of wiping them away, Watcher pulled out his flail and held it ready, just in case. The outcropping came closer and closer, but it was still too far away . . . he was going to miss.

Swinging the flail with all his strength, he attacked the rocky outcropping. The spiked ball whistled as it streaked through the air, then smashed into the stone. The deadly barbs dug deep into the stone and held tight. For an instant, he just hung there, surprised he was still alive, but then the growls from the monsters down below snapped him into action.

Climbing up the metal chain onto the ledge, he dislodged the Flail and stuffed it back into his inventory. Then, pulling the TNT from his inventory, he moved carefully along the outcropping, going as fast as he could. Watcher glanced down and found the monstrous horde was just staring up at him, ignoring the other villagers . . . good. When he'd placed the last of the TNT, Watcher pulled out a redstone torch. Below, he saw Blaster and Fencer carving a wide rectangle into the snow-covered ground, then filling it with water.

If that water freezes, it won't cushion my fall. Images of him smashing into a sheet of ice filled Watcher's mind with fear, but he pushed them aside. *I've failed my friends too many times. I'm not gonna fail them here.*

Gritting his teeth, Watcher placed the redstone torch next to the TNT, then ran across the gravely surface, placing more torches atop the explosive cubes as he passed. When he reached the end of the outcropping, he jumped, aiming for the pool of water. Its edges were already beginning to freeze up, an icy blue spreading across the surface.

Suddenly, Planter was there, placing torches along the edge of the pool, melting the ice just as Watcher landed with a splash, sending water flying in all directions. At the same time, the first block of TNT exploded above . . . nothing happened. The second cube detonated and, just like the first . . . nothing happened. The blocks of gravel were still balanced precariously in the air.

"It didn't work," Watcher shouted, the taste of imminent defeat filling his entire being.

"Just wait," Blaster said, still looking up at the ledge.

The third TNT block exploded, followed by the fourth and fifth, and these finally caused the entire outcropping to become unstable, then shatter. An avalanche of gravel fell right on top of the monsters, the deadly creatures still staring up into the air, wondering what was going on. Soon, hundreds of blocks of gravel covered the horde, burying the creatures in a newly made tomb. A huge cloud of dust billowed into the air, obscuring the horde, but when it cleared, all they could see was gravel on top of more gravel . . . the monsters had been destroyed.

"It worked!" Watcher shouted in triumph.

"Of course it did," Blaster said. He glanced at the other NPCs. "I got him up there *and* I taught him everything I know about blowing things up."

"You saved us." Fencer wrapped her arms around Blaster in a warm hug.

The young boy tried to squirm out of the embrace, but Fencer's arms were strong . . . or he didn't actually fight very hard. Watcher cast him a smile, then turned to the other NPCs.

"That was stupid!" Planter glared at Watcher, her green eyes ablaze with magic power and fury. "You could have been blown up!"

"Technically, he *was* blown up." Blaster smiled. "Blown all the way up there, in fact." He pointed to the remains of the outcropping, then glanced at Planter. She cast him such a furious glare that the boy stepped back and hid behind Fencer.

"I had to do something to stop those monsters." Watcher stood tall, refusing to back down from Planter's anger. "The gravel was our only chance. If I'd failed, then all of us would be dead." He took a step closer and softened his voice. "I did the right thing, and you know it. I'm sorry it was so dangerous, but everything we do these days seems dangerous."

"That's for sure," Blaster added.

Both Watcher and Planter glared at the boy. He hid behind Fencer again.

Watcher turned to Planter. "I did what I had to do, and I'd do it again to keep you and everyone else safe."

Planter just nodded, accepting his answer, but Watcher knew she was still mad.

A howl followed by a series of barks filled the air. Watcher turned and glanced at Er-Lan, hoping to find out what it meant.

"All the monsters are gone." Mira tapped her wooden staff on the ground, causing a ball of light to form in the air, hovering above the tip of the magical artifact. "We're safe, for now, but we can't stay here for long. It's likely at least one monster survived and is running back to tell Krael."

"We need to get back to the Wizard's Tower." Cutter put his diamond sword back into his inventory. "Our only chance is to make our stand there, though I'm sure this was just the smallest piece of Krael's army. I don't know how we'll stand against them with the numbers we have."

Watcher nodded. "Then let's get going. We should be able to climb over the pile of gravel." He glanced at Blaster. "Lead on, you know the way."

Blaster nodded, then climbed over the gravelly mound, the wolves and golems following close behind.

Watcher trudged over the hill, helping the elderly at difficult spots. As he climbed, he thought about the monsters they'd just defeated.

Baltheron, those monsters seemed like they wouldn't stop until we were destroyed. He pulled out the Flail of Regrets and stared down at the weapon. *Do you know why that is?*

No doubt the wither king is using the Crowns of Skulls on them. Baltheron's deep voice was unusually soft and soothing in Watcher's mind. *Krael can use the Crowns to drive the monsters into a murderous rage, and then nothing will stop them until they've destroyed everything in sight.*

"Great." Watcher shook his head, then glanced at Mirthrandos. "How do we fight creatures with such hatred in their hearts? How can we stand against that kind of flood? This is just a little piece of Krael's army; he probably had hundreds more, just like these." He glanced at Planter. "Is this impossible? Is the defense of Minecraft hopeless . . . am I hopeless?"

Planter jumped down from the gravel mound and moved to Watcher's side. "I've learned things are truly hopeless only when you give up. You remember when the zombies invaded our village?"

Watcher nodded, then smiled, grateful Planter's anger had faded a bit. "Of course; it feels like it was just yesterday."

"I know, me too." She sighed. "Anyway, when the zombies were pounding on the door of our house, I asked my mom and dad if it was hopeless, and you know what they said to me?"

He shook his head. The memory of that terrible day played through Watcher's mind. That was when the world had turned upside down and nearly everything he loved had been destroyed. "What did they say?"

"My mom said, 'Things are hopeless only when you give in to despair and just give up. Where there is life, there is hope. All you have to do is know who you are— who you really are—then realize what you can do when you have faith. If you keep trying, you can accomplish great things, even if you're terrified."

A tear trickled down her cheek at the memory.

"Then they stood at the door and fought back when a dozen zombies broke into the house. They didn't give up; they just kept fighting while I snuck out the attic window and ran for the forest. I know I hate this magic stuff for what it's done to me, but I won't give up on our fight, and I won't give up on you. I know you can figure out a way for us to defeat the withers and these terrible monsters. All you have to do is remember who you really are, and just be Watcher."

He nodded, considering her words. *Who am I, really?* The thought bounced around in his head as images of himself as a scared kid materialized in his mind. The pictures then morphed into the boy falling on his back when trying to join the village's army, then changed to an image of a terrified kid trying to stop the monster warlords. All of these versions in his mind had involved Watcher being someone he wasn't, rather than just being himself. But he didn't have very much confidence in the old Watcher, the boy who failed at everything he tried. And now it felt as if he was going to fail again, and all NPCs would pay for that failure with their lives.

Walking out of the narrow valley, he followed the rest of their company as they moved along the edge of the biome, the glow from his body casting a circle of purple light on the dark surroundings. With his eyes to the ground, Watcher mumbled to himself, "How can I stop Krael's horde? There are too many of them, and too few of us."

Er-Lan moved to his side and placed a clawed hand on his friend's shoulder. Watcher looked up at the zombie and smiled. The presence of Er-Lan always brought him a little comfort; his friendship was always unwavering.

"There is a way to defeat these overwhelming odds," Mirthrandos said. The light from the top of the ancient wizard's staff was a welcome relief.

"What do you mean, Mira?" Watcher asked.

"Well, Tharus had a secret weapon. It was—"

"Wait!" Cutter shouted. The big warrior grabbed Er-Lan by the back of the armor and pulled him away from the two wizards. "Surely you aren't gonna discuss any secret weapons in front of a zombie."

"Cutter, I thought we talked about this." Watcher glared at the big NPC. "Er-Lan is family."

The hulking warrior shook his head. "I don't care. Talk about your strategy all you want, but not in front of the zombie. I'll make sure he's safe at the back of the formation." Cutter smiled at Er-Lan. "Besides, this monster and I have lots to talk about, don't we?"

Er-Lan just lowered his head and walked silently to the rear, Cutter following close behind.

"Why is Cutter being so mean to Er-Lan?" Planter asked, annoyed.

Watcher shrugged. "You remember when we first ran into Er-Lan?"

Planter nodded. "Sure."

"Cutter didn't trust him back then, and he made it pretty clear he hated all zombies." Watcher sighed. "Something must have triggered all this anger for it to come back now. Hopefully he'll lighten up on Er-Lan and treat him nicer soon."

"I wouldn't count on it; Cutter is pretty stubborn." Planter turned to Mira. "Now tell us about this secret weapon."

"Well, Tharus called it 'The Answer.'"

"'The Answer?'" Planter sounded confused. "The answer to what?"

"It was his answer to the monster problem during the Great War." Mira waved her staff in the air, then flicked it three times, and instantly, an image of a battlefield appeared, as if it were floating on a layer of mist. In the image, a small group of villagers stood atop a soaring tower made of quartz and colored glass. Beacons adorned the sides of the cylindrical tower, lighting it with a soft, blue glow.

On the other side of the battlefield was a huge company of monsters. They paced back and forth, many of them looking up into the sky, clearly ready to fight. Then, a silent command unleashed the horde, and the monsters charged through the foggy landscape, intent on destroying the NPCs. One of the villagers, clad in shining armor and wearing a long purple cloak, raised his hands into the air. They already glowed with a bright iridescent light, but quickly became more intense, until the wizard was enveloped with a radiant blaze. Suddenly, the tower gave off a brilliant flash of power.

The wave of magical energy flooded across the battlefield, blasting into the monsters and turning each of them to ash, but the wave didn't stay contained within the battlefield; the surge of destruction spread all across the landscape, destroying every monster it touched. Flowing through dark tunnels and lonely caves, the magical power sought out monsters underground or in the Nether or the End and destroyed them all. Every monster had been turned to ash.

The image disappeared, leaving Watcher and Planter with more questions than answers. As they pondered what they'd seen, they came to a flat section in the Extreme Hills biome, allowing them to cross the landscape without getting entangled again within the many valleys and mountains.

"That's 'The Answer?'" Planter's voice was weak with shock.

Mira nodded.

"I can't believe you'd suggest that." The shock drained from her voice, replaced with rage. "This weapon, made by Tharus, it destroys all monsters in the Far Lands, right?"

Mira shook her head. "No. Rumor had it that The Answer would not be limited to just the Far Lands. Tharus made this weapon to reach *all* monsters."

"You mean it would exterminate the monsters all across this world?"

Mira shook her head again. "Not just this world . . . all worlds."

Watcher was stunned. The level of destruction Mira described was beyond terrible. He didn't have words to express what he was feeling. Was it fear or horror or disgust toward Tharus? Or was he feeling horror and disgust toward himself because he might need to use this solution to save his friends and every NPC in all the worlds within the Pyramid of Servers?

"This is ridiculous." Planter's anger was growing. "We won't do it. Following in the footsteps of a genocidal maniac like Tharus is not an option."

"If your only choice is the survival of NPCs or the survival of monsters . . . what would you choose?"

Mira's voice was soft, and sadness echoed through her every word.

Planter shook her head. "No! There must be another way." She turned to Watcher. "Tell her, Watcher. We won't do that, no matter what. Erasing all monsters from all the worlds of Minecraft is simply not an option."

Watcher glanced at Planter, then turned his gaze to Mira. He saw truth in the ancient wizard's eyes—a sad truth that told him she knew how to use this weapon . . . and that they had no choice.

He sighed, then turned to Planter.

"No . . . I see that look in your eyes, Watcher." Planter pointed at him with an extended finger, her arms glowing bright. "We can't do this . . . it's wrong on cvcry level."

"I know, but what if we have no choice?"

"There's always a choice!" she snapped. "When it comes to violence, there's always a choice. We can't let her do this."

"You need not worry about me, child." Mira's voice was soft and soothing, but did little to quell Planter's anger. "I cannot use Tharus's weapon; only a descendant of his can." She turned to Watcher. "But you can. You're a descendant of Tharus. I knew it as soon as you put on his cape and it started to sparkle; the cape of the Wizard of War will only work with his descendants. Tharus was the Wizard of War hundreds of years ago, and today, Watcher is the same."

"You mean I'm related to Tharus?"

Mira nodded, walking around a hill of gravel, Planter and Watcher staying at her side.

An iron wolf trotted up next to Planter, Fixit riding on the animal's back. The little mechite looked up at Planter and smiled; he could likely sense the tension in her. She reached out and stroked Fixit's soft, silver hair.

"Then you're saying only Watcher can use this terrible weapon?" Planter stared at Watcher, relieved and hopeful.

Mira nodded. "That's correct."

"He won't do it . . . I won't allow it." Planter stared at Watcher, her emerald-green eyes boring into his soul.

"Planter . . . if we have no choice, then we—"

"No!"

"But if Krael is about to win, then we must—"

"Destroying every monster is *not* the answer." Planter glared at Watcher. "There must be another way." She turned back to Mira. "I won't allow this to happen."

"Child, you may have no choice."

Planter scowled. "I hate all this magic and wish it were gone."

Before either of them could answer, she ran off to the front of the company, Fixit and the wolf at her side.

Watcher glanced at Mira, uncertain what to say.

"I'll tell you what I know, but then you'll have to make your own decision." Mira sounded sad. "Just remember, if you wait too long, you might not get a chance to use Tharus's weapon, and then everyone you know will be destroyed."

"Thanks for not adding any pressure." Watcher tried to smile sarcastically, but the fear pulsing through his body made it difficult. "Okay, tell me everything."

And so Mira went through what she knew about 'The Answer,' Watcher nodding and making mental notes, but the whole time, an overwhelming feeling of dread was wrapping itself around his soul.

Watcher was now the Wizard of War . . . No, he was the Wizard of Death.

CHAPTER 28

Krael hovered within the ancient church, drifting back and forth along its length, staring up at the gigantic holes carved into the sloping roof by his flaming skulls. Sunlight streamed through the few colored-glass panes not yet shattered, splashing blues and reds and oranges on the wooden floor. Most would find it beautiful, but to the wither king's six eyes, it was hideous. Facing the glass, he fired another string of flaming skulls, destroying the last bit of beauty put here by the ancient builders, leaving behind charred holes. The king of the withers smiled.

Kora came rushing into the room, flying through the shattered roof. "I heard explosions, my husband; is everything well?"

Krael smiled, then gestured to the smoking hole in the wall. "I was just . . . redecorating."

Kora glanced at the new destruction and nodded, grinning.

The monster army had only just arrived. There had been a group of monsters from the Far Lands already waiting for him, but not as many as he hoped; for some reason, the group of monsters he'd sent out to find the NPC army had never returned. Krael knew his forces were large and powerful enough to destroy the NPCs and the two remaining wizards, but he still wanted a larger army . . . no, not larger, but *largest*; Krael's ego demanded he have the largest, strongest army ever seen in Minecraft.

"Have any more monsters arrived?" the wither king asked.

Kora shook her head. "No, my husband. But some of the monsters say there are zombie-towns and skeleton-towns farther away, but it will still take some time for those creatures to arrive."

"How many do we have now?"

"Hundreds, but I'd be more comfortable if we had more."

Krael frowned. "I agree; we need overwhelming odds, so we can snuff out the last two wizards and take over everything. Perhaps if we—"

A part-enderman, part-spider creature suddenly appeared, a mist of purple particles hugging its warped body for an instant, then fading away. It looked up at Krael with its eight spider eyes, all of them filled with fear.

"Sire, I have news of a battle," the enderman-spider said.

"What battle?" Krael demanded.

"I was with the group of monsters you sent out from the desert village." The creature took a step back, dragging one of its arms along a wooden bench, the wickedly curved claw where its hand should have been tapping nervously on the furniture. "We ran into a group of villagers in an extreme hills biome . . . it was them."

"What do you mean, *'them*?'" Krael descended lower as Kora moved behind the enderman-spider, ready to fire if the creature attacked her husband.

"The wizards . . . I saw their purple glow. It had to be them."

"And you attacked them, correct?" Kora asked.

The monster glanced nervously over his shoulder, then took another step away from the wither king and his wife, its claw digging into the wooden bench as it moved. "I felt it best to . . . remain at a safe distance so I . . . could report to you." The monster cringed, expecting to be destroyed; all monsters knew Krael's penalty for cowardice was death.

Krael considered the monster's words, then moved closer. "You did well, my friend; be at ease. Reporting this was the right thing to do. Tell me what happened."

The enderman-spider breathed a huge sigh of relief, then glanced up at his king. "The battle took place within a narrow valley. The villagers were trapped and couldn't get out. Our monsters closed in on them and fought, destroying many, but—"

"Was that old woman there?" Krael hissed.

"And the young girl with the shield?" Kora added.

The enderman-spider nodded his spider head. "Yes. I heard many of our monsters complaining about the shield, and I could hear the old woman shouting commands to her golems. She also fired magic missiles from that staff she carries; the sound is very distinctive."

"So, you saw the old hag fighting?" Kora moved closer, a suspicious expression on her three faces.

The monster shook his head. "I didn't see—only heard—but I know it was her. She did a lot of damage with that staff of hers."

Krael nodded, considering the information.

"We must learn more about that old woman before the battle." Krael glanced at his wife. "Where is that little wither who seemed to know so much about her?"

"You mean Kobael?" Kora asked.

Krael nodded his three heads. "I haven't seen him for a while."

"He must be here somewhere." The wither king glanced at a nearby group of withers and motioned for them to come near. "Brothers, we must find the little wither named Kobael. He's the smallest amongst us, so he shouldn't be hard to find."

His eyes grew bright, a warning to the monsters if

they weren't fast enough. They each floated backward a bit. "Find him quickly and bring him to me. Now go!"

The monsters flew away, some flying through the huge, broken windows of the church, while others floated through the gigantic holes in the ceiling, which had been recently created by Krael.

"Why is it that Kobael knows so much about this wizard?" Krael asked, wondering about it for the first time.

Kora shrugged. "I don't know. Maybe it was because the wizard saved him during the Great War?"

"But why would the wizard do that?" Krael glanced around, annoyed the other withers hadn't found Kobael yet. "And why would that tiny wither learn the wizard's name? What, did he hang out with her and share stories?"

"I have no idea, my husband."

"Well, I'm gonna find out. It isn't normal for a wither to know the names of their victims. And, come to think of it, if Kobael knew the name of the wizard, then he must have spoken to her. Why didn't he just destroy her?"

"I don't know, husband." Kora floated closer to her king. "Maybe, during the Great War, Kobael was—"

"He isn't here," one of the withers shouted as they floated back down through the hole in the roof. "We searched everywhere; that little wither is gone."

"Gone?! How can that be?!" Krael's eyes blazed with rage. In his fury, he fired a flaming skull at the wall, blasting a huge hole into the side of the church.

Slowly, Krael's anger subsided. He glanced at Kora, fuming. "I don't know what's going on here, but I don't like it."

Krael turned back to the enderman-spider. "Where's the rest of your company? Surely most of them survived." Krael glared at the monster, demanding an answer.

"Well . . ." The monster spoke with a weak, terrified voice. "None survived but me."

"I didn't hear you." Krael moved closer. "What did you say? Speak up!"

"I said, none survived." The enderman-spider cringed again, awaiting its destruction. "They used some kind of TNT thing. It caused an avalanche that destroyed all of the monsters."

"Hmm." Krael nodded his heads, his eyes getting brighter again as his rage grew.

"Sire, I knew you'd want this information as quickly as possible." The enderman-spider spoke quickly and nervously. "I teleported back to the desert village, but found you'd left. Searching across the landscape, I looked for you until I finally found you here."

Beads of sweat tumbled down the monster's fuzzy black face.

Krael floated higher into the air, still saying nothing. The monster took another step back, its claw still digging a deep scratch into the pew.

"You need not fear, my friend. I will not harm you, despite your obvious cowardice." Krael smiled reassuringly.

The enderman-spider relaxed a bit, letting his fuzzy arms hang down at his side.

"Kora," Krael said casually, turning to his wife, "destroy him!"

The enderman-spider turned to take a step for the exit, but he didn't have a chance. Kora's flaming skulls struck the creature in the back, enveloping the enderman-spider in their blue flames as the projectiles exploded. The creature disappeared with a pop, its glowing balls of XP tumbling into the newly formed crater.

"Well done, my wife."

Kora beamed with pride.

"But that missing little wither has me angry." Krael drifted toward his wife, his anger growing again. "There's something going on here that I don't understand."

"You should relax, husband," Kora said, making her voice as soothing as possible. "I'm sure that tiny wither is just scouting the surrounding forest, making sure the villagers are not trying a sneak attack."

"Scouting . . . ha! I'd never send a monster as pathetic as Kobael on scouting duty. He's useless, and he knows it. More likely, Kobael is a coward and flew away, afraid to help his king in the battle to come. No one ever even saw that puny wither fire a single shot in any of the battles we've had with Watcher and his fools. No, that wither is a traitor, and he will be treated as one when he is found."

Kora sighed. "Very well, as you command. What are your orders?"

Krael floated up through a huge charred gash in the roof until he hovered above the ancient church, then moved between the two steeples that stood over the main entrance. He stared down at the monsters congregating around the ancient structure, some hiding in the shade of the nearby forest.

"Fools," he hissed.

"What did you say, my husband?"

"Nothing." Krael turned toward Kora. "We'll wait here until the last of the monsters arrive." He glanced at the sun overhead. "The NPCs will likely make their stand in the Wizard's Tower. I want to attack them after the sun has set, which will give the monsters of this world a bit more courage. Maybe they'll fight a little harder before they're destroyed in the first wave."

Krael laughed. "Spread the word. Soon, the total destruction of the Far Lands will begin with the annihilation of Tharus's precious Tower and the doomed NPCs who cower within."

Kora smiled, her three heads nodding, as Krael's eyes blazed with evil delight.

CHAPTER 29

Weaving his way around oak and birch trees, Watcher ran through the familiar woods, a feeling of dread slowly rising up from within his soul. He knew what was up ahead and wasn't sure if he wanted to see it again.

Thick grass covered the forest floor, the verdant blades swishing back and forth with each step the group took. The children loved the grass. The long strands reached up to their waists, making their upper bodies appear to float through the green sea.

"We're almost there, I think." Mapper ran at the young wizard's side, a smile creasing his square, wrinkled face. "It'll be good to be home again."

Watcher nodded. "But you know what we must pass through first, right?"

The old man glanced at the young wizard, his smile fading. "Yeah . . . I know. But it's important to be reminded of the past, so we know where we're from and hopefully don't make the same mistakes again." He put a gnarled hand on Watcher's shoulder as they ran. "I always taught my students, 'Those who close their eyes to the past are—'"

"Are doomed to repeat it." Watcher gave the old man

a smile. "I remember when you taught that to me in school."

Mapper smiled. "Well, I'm glad to know at least one student was listening to me."

A majestic howl floated through the forest, followed by a series of squeaks and whistles. Watcher glanced over his shoulder at Er-Lan.

"That wolf and mechite say the village is empty." The zombie tried to give his friend a strained grin, but it just looked more like a grimace.

Watcher suspected Er-Lan felt the same unease about returning to their village. For the zombie, it probably felt like returning to the scene of a crime.

For Watcher, though, it was as if he were returning to his greatest failure. It was here, during the zombie attack, where he'd let his fear dominate his actions: he'd pretended to be unconscious, rather than try to stop the zombies, because he had no faith in himself. Back then, some bullies had thought Watcher to be a scrawny, puny nothing of a villager, someone who was worthless and weak—but worse was the fact that Watcher had accepted their judgment. He had wanted to be something more, but his lack of confidence made him fail over and over again. And now he was back in the same place, the familiar taste of ridicule and failure filling his entire being.

The company stepped out of the forest and entered the shattered remains of Watcher's village. The afternoon sun bathed the ruins with bright light, the long shadows from trees bordering the village stretching across the ground. It seemed to Watcher as if the trees were casting their shadows in salute for those who perished here. But that was just Watcher's overactive imagination looking to make sense out of the atrocities of the past.

An uneasy silence spread across the group. NPCs stared at the charred walls and collapsed homes with heavy hearts, each reminded of their own demolished communities.

Watcher scanned the crowd for Planter. She was easy to find; a bright, iridescent glow surrounded her body as her rage built at the sight of the village. Next to her stood Mira, whispering into Planter's ear, helping both her fury and the glow to subside as her anger was put into check. Watcher wanted to go to her and give her some comfort, but he couldn't even stop his own feelings of anger and guilt . . . so how could he help her?

A rocket suddenly streaked through the air, then exploded in a shower of colorful sparks.

"What was that?" Watcher pulled an enchanted bow from his inventory. Notching an arrow, he pulled back on the string and pointed it into the air, on the lookout for enemies.

An object streaked overhead, just above the tree line, too fast to identify.

"Did anyone else see that?" someone shouted in fear.

"Was it a wither?" a terrified voice asked.

"Are the withers here?"

"What do we do?"

Panic spread through the company. The NPCs looked for places to hide, but most of the structures were in ruins.

"Everyone, calm down!" Mira's voice boomed through the air. "Golems, form a perimeter. Wolves and mechites, search the forest for monsters. Everyone, pull out your bows and get ready to—"

The object streaked by again, but this time Watcher saw what it was—or, really, *who* it was.

"Everyone relax." The young wizard put down his bow and held his glowing hands up in the air. "It's not the withers or the monsters; it's a friend."

Just then, a small shape with a pair of iridescent wings swooped into the village, gliding lower and lower until it touched down onto the ground; it was Winger.

Running to her, Watcher wrapped his arms around his sister. "Winger!" Watcher was so glad to see her, he almost wept. "You made it back." He released his hug, but his sister wouldn't let him go.

"I was so afraid I'd never see you again," she whispered. "I'm so glad you're here."

Watcher felt a tear drip upon his cheek. "I told you I'd be back."

"Sure, but you know I never really believe anything you say." She laughed, then finally released the hug and wiped her eyes dry.

Winger turned and scanned the rest of the company, then gasped. "What happened to Planter? She's so much brighter than before."

"Her power has increased somehow," Watcher said in a low voice. "I'm not really sure we understand it, and everyone is afraid to ask."

"Well, I'm just glad everyone is okay." Winger cast Planter a smile.

The young girl grinned, then walked toward her, Mira a step behind.

"Everyone, gather around," Watcher shouted.

The NPCs moved closer to the young wizard, fear ebbing from their square faces. They congregated around Watcher and his sister, some still with weapons in their hands.

"What happened with the withers?" Winger asked.

"We were able to escape the cave and the withers, thanks to crazy Watcher," Blaster said.

Many of the NPCs nodded their heads, looking thankfully toward the young wizard.

Watcher stood a little taller as the respect he was feeling from the NPCs drove some of his self-doubt away. "Hopefully, Krael thinks I'm dead. It might give us a small element of surprise." He turned to his sister. "How's Dad? I'm looking forward to seeing him."

"Well . . ." She lowered her gaze to the ground.

"What is it?" Watcher reached out and raised Winger's head so he could look straight into her bright blue eyes. "What happened to our dad?"

"When I made it back to the Wizard's Tower, I told him about our need for horses." Winger swallowed nervously. "I mentioned that ancient structure we visited when we were fighting the spider warlord, like you told me to."

"You mean the Citadel of the Horse Lords? That's what you mentioned to Cleric?" Planter asked.

Winger nodded.

"I assume he headed to the Citadel?" Watcher shrugged. "What's the problem?"

"Well, he didn't think he could get there and back in time to help with the upcoming battle." Winger put a hand on Watcher's shoulder, as if ready to calm him down. "So, he decided to shorten the distance necessary to get there and get back."

"You mean . . ." An expression of fear spread across Watcher's face.

Winger nodded again, a grave expression spreading across her square face.

"What is it?" Fencer asked. "What happened? Did he go to the Citadel? I don't understand."

Watcher turned and walked away, his head drooping to the ground.

"What happened?" Fencer asked. "I thought—"

Blaster put a hand on Fencer's arm. "Cleric went through the Nether. Distances are eight times shorter through the Nether than through the Overworld or the Far Lands." The young boy turned to Winger. "Did he take everyone with him?"

"Almost. There's still people at the Tower, but not very many."

"But . . . why would he take almost everyone with him?" Fencer sounded confused.

"The dispensers at the Citadel will only give one horse per person," Blaster explained. "He had to take as many as possible."

"But if it's faster to travel through the Nether . . . why didn't we do that?" Fencer glanced at the other villagers, many of whom were averting their gaze. "I've never been to the Nether, so I don't understand. Why didn't we travel through the Nether to get here? What's there that all of you aren't telling me?"

"Monsters!" Watcher snapped as he pushed through the crowd and stared at the girl. "There's monsters . . . lots of monsters, like ghasts, and blazes, and wither skeletons, and magma cubes, and of course zombie-pig-men. You want to fight all those creatures while you're just saving some time?"

"Well . . . when you put it that way, I guess it does sound kinda dangerous."

"Kinda dangerous?!" Watcher exclaimed, the iridescent glow across his body getting brighter and brighter. "The Nether is *the* most dangerous place in all of Minecraft, and my dad went there just to reach the Citadel faster."

"I'm sure your father is gonna be alright," Planter said from behind. Her voice always had a soothing effect on Watcher, causing the bright glow of magical power hugging his chest to slowly recede and get dimmer. "We just need to trust him and hope he gets back to us in time."

Watcher nodded, trying to calm himself.

"Well, if he doesn't get back with the cavalry, I think we'll be in a lot of trouble," Blaster said, then cringed when he saw Watcher lower his head to look at the ground.

"Wow, you're a really sensitive guy." Planter glared at Blaster.

"That's one of his best qualities," Fencer said, stepping closer to Blaster.

The boy just rolled his eyes as Watcher raised his head and grinned at Blaster's discomfort.

"I'm glad you're enjoying this!" Blaster spun around and stormed away in a huff, Fencer on his heels.

"Are we ready to move?" Planter asked. "We can be back to the Wizard's Tower in an hour."

"Yeah, I'm almost ready." Watcher turned to his sister. "Can you give me one of those rockets?" She handed one to him. It was a red-and-white striped cylinder with a large, dark-red nosecone on the top. Watcher flicked it in his right hand, lighting the fuse, and in a second, the rocket shot out of his hand and streaked up into the sky. "Hmmm . . ."

"Watcher, what are you thinking?" Winger asked.

He walked around his sister and gently held her Elytra wings between two hands. "This gives me an idea." Watcher smiled.

"Really?" Winger replied. "What are you thinkin'?"

Watcher just nodded his head, lost in thought. "I haven't quite figured out all the pieces yet. Hopefully I can tell you something more when we reach the Wizard's Tower." Watcher patted his sister on her shoulder, his smile growing bigger. "Maybe we aren't as helpless as we think."

And for the first time in a long time, Watcher felt something he hadn't felt for a long, long time: hope.

CHAPTER 30

They rode through the forest in complete silence, the golems doing their best to move quietly by avoiding breaking branches with their tall bodies. The wolves and their metallic riders formed a wide circle around the large company of NPCs, moving without making a sound. The only noise Watcher could hear was the gentle rustle of the leaves in the constant east-to-west breeze and the *swish-swish* of the tall grass.

Turning his head constantly from left to right, Watcher scanned the area for threats; he knew Krael and his horde of distorted monsters were out there, somewhere, hunting them. All of the NPCs in his company knew it, too, and they all looked scared. Watcher could feel constant glances being directed toward him, each worried stare reminding him he had to figure out the final battle plan, so they wouldn't all be destroyed.

The thought of failure terrified him.

There were little children, mothers, fathers, grandparents . . . every facet of the NPC community were here in his company, and they deserved the right to live out their lives.

If I make the wrong decision, they'll all be doomed, Watcher thought. *I can't stand having this responsibility.*

They have faith in you, a deep voice boomed within his head.

Planter glanced at Watcher, hearing Baltheron's words in her head, too.

These villagers will do what you ask, Baltheron continued. *They will follow you into battle, no matter how dire the odds may appear.*

That's what I'm afraid of. A feeling of dread spread through the young wizard. *I'm afraid they'll stand and fight when they should just run away.*

No war has ever been won by running away, Taerian said, the Gauntlets of Life flashing briefly as he spoke. There was an accusatory tone to the ancient wizard's voice. *Running from a threat just makes the threat stronger.*

Watcher nodded; that was something he knew a lot about. Every time he ran from the bullies in their village, it had just seemed to make them bolder and more abusive, and with Watcher being so small and weak, he couldn't stand up to them; he'd just get a beating. Instead, Watcher had found a better solution, and that was to be where they didn't expect him and have a strategy they didn't expect, like a secret escape route, or jumping across tree branches that couldn't bear their heavier weight, or leaping from roof to roof to get away. The element of surprise had always confused the bullies.

"Change the situation to one where the bullies are weak, rather than strong." That had been his father's advice, and it had helped a lot, and at times even—

"Wait a minute."

Watcher stopped in his tracks. The rest of the company quickly formed a defensive formation, something Cutter had taught them. They drew bows and notched arrows, ready for an attack from any direction.

"What's wrong?" Mapper moved to the young wizard's side. "Do you sense the withers coming?"

Watcher shook his head. *I know what we'll do,* he

thought. *We're gonna change the situation to one where we're strong and the withers are weak.*

Somehow, Watcher could feel the minds within his possessed enchanted weapons smile. Turning, he glanced at Planter and Mira, the two wizards standing next to each other, the glow from their magical power casting a wide circle of iridescent light. They both nodded and smiled, agreeing with his decision.

"We can really do this," Watcher said softly. "We can defeat Krael and his mob of bullies." He glanced at his sister, her Elytra sparkling with the mending enchantment woven into the wings. Pulling out the Wand of Cloning, Watcher smiled. "We can do this!" he shouted triumphantly.

Many of the NPCs glanced at Watcher, confused, but also relieved.

"Shhh . . . what are you doing?" Cutter glared at the young wizard. "Are you insane? You need to keep your voice down. Monsters might hear you."

"Let 'em hear me." Watcher glanced at the sun. It was getting closer to the western horizon; they had only a few hours before nightfall.

"Who goes there?" a voice shouted suddenly from the shadows.

"Is that Builder I hear?" Watcher asked.

Horses' hooves stomped the ground as four mounted soldiers came out from behind a thick copse of birch trees.

"Watcher . . . is that you?" one soldier asked.

The young wizard nodded. "Yep."

"I'm glad you're back." Builder took off his iron helmet and wiped his brow. "There have been lots of monsters around, and they're getting aggressive, but that's not the worst part."

"Why is there always a 'worst part?'" Blaster smiled at the soldier.

"Blaster, be quiet," Planter snapped. "The serious villagers are talking now."

Fencer laughed and grinned at the embarrassed boy.

"What's the worst part?" Mapper asked.

"The zombies and skeletons don't catch fire in the sunlight anymore." Builder put his helmet back on. "They're walking around in broad daylight as if they own the place. How can they do that?"

"Hm. I felt some kind of magic ripple through the fabric of Minecraft." Mira tapped her staff on the side of a tree, and instantly, the ground rumbled as the golems approached. "I bet Krael did something to make them impervious to the rays of the sun. That can't be good."

"It doesn't matter. I'm sure Krael is gonna attack tonight . . . I can just feel it." Watcher glanced up at the soldiers on horseback. "I need you to stay with the children and elderly. Help the golems and make sure they all get back to the Wizard's Tower."

"Got it." Builder nodded.

"The rest of us, we're running to the Wizard's Tower. We have a little surprise to prepare for Krael and his friends." Watcher stood tall, brimming with confidence. "We can do this if we work together and work fast . . . but there isn't a lot of time. Stealth is no longer important. Speed is what we need."

"Then what are we waiting for?" Mapper took off, sprinting for the Wizard's Tower hidden within the forest. "Let's see if any of you can keep up with me!" the old man called out, but then he caught his foot on a tree root and tumbled to the ground. He climbed to his feet and glanced back at the company, turning red with embarrassment. "Oops."

Then he turned and sprinted again. Behind him, the NPCs laughed and followed the old man.

Cutter slapped Watcher on the back as he passed. "I hope your plan is a good one, or this will be the shortest Great War in history."

"That's my hope." Watcher started to run, moving to Cutter's side. "One way or another, the Great War ends for good tonight."

Ripples of fear spread through Watcher's mind at the thought, trying to drown his courage, but he refused to let the fear in. Tonight, Minecraft didn't need a scrawny, scared boy who was afraid to fail his companions. Tonight, Minecraft needed Watcher: the boy who refused to give up, no matter what.

He glanced at Cutter. "It's time we showed Krael who he's really messing with."

"Absolutely." The hulking warrior slapped the wizard on the back confidently. "It's time for war."

CHAPTER 31

As Watcher ran through the forest, thoughts of the upcoming battle raced through his mind. His half-formed plan played through scenario after scenario as he fought mock battles in his imagination. Each time, he imagined Krael doing something to defeat them eventually. He wanted to shout in frustration, but the young wizard knew it would only make the rest of the NPCs more nervous.

Ahead, he spotted Mapper. Sprinting, Watcher reached the old man's side, then put a hand on his shoulder and slowed to a stop. The old NPC gladly stopped to rest and leaned against a tall oak tree; clearly all this running was taking a toll on him.

"Mapper, I need you to continue to the Tower." Watcher handed the old man a flask of water, which he gladly drank. "We need lots of healing potions, as many as you can make."

Mapper turned to his friend. "Why more healing potions? I think they already brewed enough for each person to have plenty. Why do we need more?"

"They aren't for NPCs." Watcher gave his friend a mischievous grin. "They're for something special that I think you'll like . . . a lot."

Mapper nodded suspiciously. "You seem pretty pleased with yourself."

The young wizard just shrugged. "Come on, let's get to the Wizard's Tower. There is still much more to do."

Without waiting for a response, Watcher turned and continued toward their home, Mapper a step or two behind. Ahead of them, the ground shook under the thunderous footsteps of the golems as the metal giants charged through the forest, the sounds of breaking branches and crushed leaves filling the landscape. Every now and then, Watcher caught a glimpse of a silver wolf's metallic fur reflecting the light of the sinking sun, making them appear to shimmer and sparkle.

As they neared the Tower, they encountered cobblestone walls with archer towers built high into the air. The walls stretched around the Tower, the entire barricade scores of blocks in length; he doubted they had enough warriors left to man the entire thing.

My dad better get here in time. Watcher shook his head, worried.

There are many solutions to any problem, Taerian said. *We've waited a long time to finally see the real end of the—*

Taerian, that's enough! Baltheron's words felt spikey and angry in Watcher's mind; it was as if the Gauntlets of Life were about to say something they shouldn't. He wanted to ask, but he knew there wasn't time for any distractions.

As he ran, a strange tickling sensation nibbled at the back of his head. It slowly spread down his spine, as if a thousand tiny spiders were running along his spine. He glanced over his shoulder at Mirthrandos.

"You can finally feel it, right?" Mirthrandos asked.

Watcher nodded.

The ancient wizard glanced at Planter. "I bet you can also sense it as well."

The girl nodded, her long blond hair looking like a golden waterfall as the locks spilled down her back under the late afternoon sun. A concerned expression spread across her face. "What is it?"

"It's Tharus's Tower." Mira pointed at the structure as they slowed to a stop, then stepped into the clearing.

A gaping hole scarred the grass-covered ground. It was at least fifty blocks across, its edges rough, as if carved by countless blocks of TNT. Protruding up through the hole was an elaborate structure made of quartz and stained glass, with shining beacons dotting its exterior; it was the Wizard's Tower, their home.

"Why can we feel something from the Wizard's Tower?" Watcher grabbed Mira's arm and pulled her to a stop, with Planter settling at the old woman's other side. The rest of the villagers moved past them, quickly following the rocky trail leading into the ancient building. "We never felt anything before."

"You're both stronger now; the more you use your magic, the greater your power becomes." The ancient wizard put a comforting hand on Planter's arm. "Your power will grow, whether you use it or not; it just grows faster this way."

"It feels like there's something inside the tower, something hiding in the—"

Planter cut Watcher off. "You're wrong. It's not something hiding inside the tower . . . it *is* the tower. The power we're feeling is the tower itself."

"You're wise for such a young wizard." Mira smiled at her. "Planter is correct. The Wizard's Tower, as you call it, was built by Tharus himself. The entire structure is a weapon . . . it's *the* weapon."

"You mean. . . it's . . ." Watcher's voice trembled a bit.

Mira nodded. "The Tower is part of Tharus's Answer to the monster problem. Tharus planned on using it against all the monsters in Minecraft. The warlocks knew this and tried to stop him."

"They tried to destroy the tower?" Planter asked.

The old woman shook her head, her long gray hair swishing back and forth across her back. "No, the Tower cannot be destroyed, but the warlocks knew the Tower had to be above any obstacles so it could send out its destructive wave. So, to stop Tharus, they—"

"They dug underneath it and caused the Tower to fall into a massive sinkhole." Watcher stared into Mira's eyes in understanding. "The monster warlocks did it to defend themselves."

"Yes, and to defend *all* the monsters on every plane of existence, as well." The ancient wizard tapped her crooked staff on the ground, then held it in the air and moved it in a circle. Instantly, the wolves and golems spread out around the gigantic sinkhole, setting up a defensive perimeter around the Tower.

Watcher glanced nervously at the sun. It was getting closer to the horizon; they likely didn't have much time. He stared down at the sunken tower. "With the Wizard's Tower sunken into the ground, how can we use Tharus's Answer to defeat the monsters?"

"You'd have to wait until they're right at the edge of the hole, then activate it." Mirthrandos stepped to the edge of the hole and peered down, then turned back to the two young wizards.

"No . . . there must be another way." The iridescent glow around Planter's body intensified as her rage grew. "We could fall back to a better location and fight from a position of strength. Or we could—"

"Krael's withers will find us soon enough. He'll have endermen appear first, to make sure you're here, then he'll surround the place and send his ground forces into the Tower. They'll crush these fortifications in minutes." Mira pointed to the hastily constructed cobblestone walls running along one side of the sinkhole. "After they break through the walls, they'll enter the Tower, trapping everyone inside; that's when the slaughter will begin. Anyone who tries to flee will be destroyed by the withers. This is going to be a massacre. There aren't enough villagers here to make a stand against Krael and his army; Tharus's Answer is the only way."

Watcher looked at Planter. The glow around her body was receding as an expression of profound sadness spread across her face. "I hate magic and everything associated with it." Planter glared at Watcher and Mira furiously.

"You must be ready to use the Tower if necessary," Mira said. "Tharus didn't trust any of the wizards during his time. All of us were blocked from accessing the Tower's magical enchantments, but you can use it." She moved a step closer and peered down at the young boy. "You must be ready and not hesitate if the time comes. There's only going to be one chance; if you fail, we'll all die."

Watcher sighed, leaning against an oak tree. The weight of this task was overwhelming. Now, instead of just being responsible for the lives of the NPCs following him, he was responsible for *all* villagers, everywhere. He was so afraid to fail, he just wanted to curl up in a hole somewhere and hide.

Suddenly, a chill spread across Watcher's skin. It was an eerie feeling, not caused by the wind or weather, but by something he feared: a wither. Spinning around, Watcher drew Needle in one hand, the Flail of Regrets in the other, ready to strike.

"I know you're there," he yelled. "Come out and you won't be harmed. But if you fire your flaming skulls, you *will* be destroyed."

"Watcher . . . what are you talking about?" Mira was confused.

"There's a wither in that oak tree, spying on us." Watcher pointed with Needle at the thick branches.

Mira narrowed her eyes and held her staff at the ready, its end glowing bright. Planter glared at Watcher, then drew her shield, the edges sparkling with power.

Slowly, the smallest wither Watcher had ever seen emerged from the foliage. It seemed so tiny that it likely couldn't hurt a soul, but still, Watcher was ready to destroy it.

"Kobael!" Mira dropped her staff and ran to the monster.

"What are you doing?!" Watcher shouted. "Get back!"

But the ancient wizard just wrapped her arms around the monster, hugging it tight. "You're alive. I hoped you had survived the Cave of Slumber. My wish has come true. Where have you been?"

Kobael's center head smiled at Mira while the left and right skulls stared at the other two wizards in fear. "I don't like the look of those weapons."

The tiny wither started floating up into the air, clearly afraid of Watcher and Planter.

Watcher glanced at Mira. "Is this the one you saved during the Great War?"

Mira nodded.

"Are we safe?"

She nodded again.

Watcher lowered his weapons and put Needle back into his inventory, but kept the Flail of Regrets in his hand, just in case. He glanced at Planter and nodded. She lowered her shield, then stuffed it back into her inventory.

Planter stepped forward and looked up at the wither. "It's alright. If you're a friend of Mira's, then you're a friend of ours as well."

The scared expressions on the tiny creature's three faces faded away. Kobael glanced down at Mirthrandos, then smiled and moved closer.

"Kobael, I've missed you so much." Mira smiled. "I told my friends here all about how we met so long ago and—"

"There's no time to talk. I must tell you what I've learned." Kobael moved closer to Watcher. "You're the wizard Krael hates, right?"

Watcher nodded.

The tiny wither smiled. "Krael thinks he killed you. I can't wait to see the expressions on his faces when he learns he's wrong."

"You know I can't let you go back to Krael and tell him." Watcher's voice resonated with conviction. He gripped the Flail tight, just in case.

Kobael shook his three skulls. "I'm never going back to them. I'd rather live alone for the rest of my life than be around those terrible monsters."

"Well, Kobael, what did you learn about Krael?" Mirthrandos put a hand on the wither's shoulder, then pulled him close.

With each skull looking at a different wizard, Kobael spoke. "Krael isn't just planning on killing all of you. He wants to kill every villager in this entire world."

"You mean in the Far Lands?" Planter asked.

The tiny wither shook his three heads. "No, he wants to destroy *every* NPC in this plane of existence. After he destroys the NPCs in the Far Lands, he plans on moving into the Overworld, growing his army as he does. Krael wants to destroy *every* NPC in this plane of existence. And when he's done here, he plans on going to every other plane of existence in the Pyramid of Servers. Krael wants to destroy every NPC in every world all across Minecraft. And when he's exterminated the NPCs, he'll likely turn on the monsters, until only withers remain."

The wizards gasped.

"He'll destabilize the whole Pyramid of Servers." Mira's voice sounded weak as the shock of this news settled in.

"What does that mean?" Planter asked.

The ancient turned and looked at the two young wizards. "If the Pyramid of Servers collapses, then all of Minecraft will be gone . . . forever."

Planter gasped. "Oh no."

Kobael nodded.

"He must be stopped." Watcher's magic grew brighter, as did his anger at the thought of Krael's plans.

Suddenly, a *whoosh*ing sound, just barely audible over the rustling of the leaves, drew his attention back into here and now.

"They're here," Watcher whispered.

"What?" Mira leaned forward.

Another *whoosh* sounded high overhead, this one louder. Some leaves fluttered to the ground.

Mira turned and glanced up at the oak, her staff held at the ready. "Did you hear that?"

Another *whoosh,* this one followed by an evil chuckle, caused more leaves to fall to the forest floor.

"They're here," Watcher warned.

He drew his enchanted bow and notched an arrow. Another *whoosh* pierced through the darkening forest. Without waiting, Watcher turned and fired at the sound, though his target was invisible in the shadows. A chuckle was cut short, and then there was another *whoosh.*

"It's the endermen; they found us." Watcher drew another arrow and pulled it back, waiting for another shadowy creature to materialize nearby. "Krael will be here soon. We must—" Another *whoosh*ing sound drew his attention. Watcher spun and fired without even looking, allowing his hearing to guide his shot. "We must warn the others." He looked up into Mira's eyes, an expression of fear etched into his iridescent face. "The Great War is here, and it's time to fight . . . or die."

Not waiting for an answer, Watcher ran to the edge of the sinkhole and stared down into the darkness. As the NPCs followed the rough-hewn steps into the pit, Watcher imagined everything that *might* happen tonight. Images of death and destruction filled his mind as waves of terror smashed into his soul.

What if I can't do it? he asked the magical weapons in his inventory. *What if I can't stop Krael?*

Then all is lost, the ancient wizards said in unison.

For a moment, Watcher looked for a place to hide; a hole that he could just crawl into and disappear. But then Planter moved next to him, her shield blazing with purple flames. She glanced at him and nodded at him, then stared out into the forest, a look of confidence and strength on her beautiful face.

"I have to do it, somehow," Watcher said. "I have to make my little trick work, or else . . ." He didn't want to finish the sentence. A feeling of dread enveloped his mind as he thought about what might happen tonight, but, shaking his head, he pushed the feeling away. Gritting his teeth, he ran down the stairs leading into the ancient structure, hoping the impossible would happen, and they'd somehow live through the night.

CHAPTER 32

The rest of their army made it into the Wizard's Tower without any more endermen appearing; the message was likely already being whispered in Krael's ear that the NPCs were at the Tower. Hoping to avoid having anyone attack Kobael, Watcher amplified his voice and told all the NPCs that the tiny wither was a friend. Then Mira went in with Kobael and hid him within the underground passages to avoid detection by any other endermen.

Watcher was the last to enter the Tower. When he finally stepped off the stairs and entered the ancient structure, he was greeted by complete silence. The gentle tickle from the Tower was now an annoying itch spreading everywhere; the magic from the ancient structure seemed to be infusing itself into Watcher's body, its energy filling every space within him. He could feel the great power, but had no idea what it did, nor how to use it. For now, all he could do was try to push the sensation aside and focus on their battle plans.

Their army stood uneasily on the ground floor, many villagers shifting nervously from foot to foot. The expressions on their square faces was self-explanatory; everyone was terrified. They all knew Krael was out there somewhere, and Cleric still hadn't returned with the all-important cavalry, if he would be able to return at all.

Taking slow steps through the crowd, Watcher grasped hands, patted villagers on the back, and smiled reassuringly to the NPCs, trying to ease their worries, but he knew it had little effect. These people were rightfully scared; the biggest and most lethal army in all of Minecraft's history was descending upon them. They were outnumbered three-to-one or four-to-one or . . . who knew for sure? Whatever the ratio, it wasn't good.

"I know you're all scared." Watcher's voice was soft and calm. "But we're gonna weather this storm and keep Minecraft safe from these monsters. We just need to have faith and work together, then we'll—"

"I saw the endermen," someone shouted in a panic from the back of the crowd. "They materialized in the trees. When they saw we were all here, they disappeared. The monsters will be here soon."

"You're right. The monsters will be here soon. But we have a plan, and—"

Suddenly, a pulse of energy flowed out from the Tower and surged through Watcher. He'd never felt so much power in his life; it was almost too much to contain. His body gave off a bright flash of iridescent light as his legs buckled, and he fell to his knees. The other NPCs had to shield their eyes from the intense burst of energy, many turning away.

"What was that?" someone asked.

"Was it an attack by Krael?"

"Maybe it was the Crowns of Skulls?"

Panicked arguments broke out amongst the villagers, their fears amplified.

Then Watcher felt something soft rub up against him. He opened his eyes and found one of the wolves leaning against him, its fine silver fur softer than a feather. Fixit sat atop the wolf, peering at the young wizard, a worried expression on his metallic face.

Reaching out, Watcher patted the wolf on the side and smiled at Fixit, then slowly stood. "It's okay, everyone." The young wizard held his hand up into the air, silencing the crowd. "That wasn't an attack, it was just some of my magic reacting to the Tower. It's nothing to worry about."

"Nothing to worry about?" Planter glared at him. "Do you know what you're doing?"

He just shrugged and smiled at her. She returned the smile with a scowl, then moved to the back of the crowd, clearly frustrated with him.

Turning, Watcher scanned the crowd for a certain NPC, and when he spotted him, he moved to his friend's side. "Blaster, you think you could prepare some surprises for when the monsters arrive?"

"No problem." They boy smiled as he put on his black leather armor. "We just gathered all the materials. I have a few ideas that'll be fun to watch."

"The monsters will attack from the east," Watcher said. "The first wave will come when the sun has completely set, but the moon hasn't risen yet; it'll be the darkest part of the night." The room became very quiet. Turning, he found every NPC staring at him, terrified expressions on their faces. His explanation had just made this real for all of them. "So Blaster, put your traps to the east of the tower. They'll do the most damage there."

"You got it, sir. Wizard." Blaster did a graceful, sarcastic bow and gave his friend a smile, then ran up the stairs, with Fencer and eight NPCs following close behind.

You must use the Answer to defeat the monsters, Dalgaroth said in the wizards' minds. *You can destroy all of the monsters that way.*

Mira and Planter turned toward Watcher.

A strange look spread across Er-Lan's face, as if a profound sadness had just spread through his being.

But the Tower is too low. I'd have to wait until they're

right on top of us, Watcher thought. *That'll be too dangerous.*

It's the only way, Mira added with her mind.

Planter glared at the other two wizards, then turned and stepped out of the Tower for a moment, with Fixit and his wolf following close behind.

Use the cape, Taerian said in Watcher's mind.

"What? I don't understand."

While you're using the cape, no one else can hear our thoughts. Taerian's scratchy voice felt abrasive in the back of Watcher's mind, as usual.

Watcher nodded, then gathered his power and sent it into the cape. A brief tingling sensation spread across his body, and then he disappeared as the NPCs around him gasped in surprise.

Baltheron, you were here when Tharus made the Tower. Tell him.

Tell me what? Watcher asked.

Tharus stored huge amounts of energy in this tower; you just tasted the smallest bit. Some of it was meant for the Answer, but there is still enough power in the Tower to do many other things.

Like what? Watcher asked.

Baltheron's voice became a whisper as he explained all the surprises hidden within the Tower, and with each new revelation, Watcher smiled wider. When the ancient wizard was done explaining everything, Watcher pulled his magic from the wizard's cape and reappeared. Instead of a scared expression on the young wizard's face, a look of excited confidence stared back at the NPCs. Some of the villagers smiled and stood a little taller.

"You sure like disappearing in front of everyone!" Planter looked furious. "People were scared, and we thought . . . why are you smiling? We're about to face our greatest battle and you're standing there grinning like an idiot. What's going on?"

Watcher moved to her and placed a reassuring hand

on her shoulder. "It'll be alright. I have a few surprises in store for Krael and his army, starting with this."

He pulled out an iron pickaxe, then moved to the far wall of the tower, where he could tell, now that Baltheron's instructions had alerted him, that one of the quartz blocks making up the floor sparkled faintly.

"What are you doing now?" Planter stormed across the room, her footsteps pounding the ground as he swung the pick with all his strength. "There's no time to be digging. We need to get ready and—"

The block shattered, throwing shards of quartz into the air. Watcher dropped the pick and knelt, peering into the hole. An ancient chest lay hidden in the darkness, a thick layer of dust covering its top. Reaching down, Watcher opened the lid, and instantly, Planter put her hands to her ears, trying to block out sounds no one else could hear.

"What's in there?" Cutter asked, moving to the boy's side. He knelt and reached into the chest, pulling out stacks of shields, each one bright red with three dark skulls emblazoned across their centers. They sparkled and shimmered with magical power just like the ones carried by Planter and Fencer.

"I can hear them all," Planter moaned. "They're all talking to me at the same time. I can't understand what they're saying, but I hate it. I hate all this magic!" She turned and staggered away, Mapper going with her and helping her find a seat.

"Everyone on the ground gets a shield." Watcher distributed the shields to the villagers. "Don't touch them together unless the situation is truly dire. They'll protect us only once, so it must be when things seem hopeless." He walked to Planter's side. "Planter will be at the center of the wall of shields. She'll know what to do."

"What are you talking about?" Planter scowled, confused.

"Baltheron just told me you'd know what to do when you bring the shields together. We have to trust him." Watcher shrugged. "We have no other choice."

She glared at him. "I hate this."

"I know." He nodded, then turned to Cutter. "Let me explain my plan."

And he explained what he had in mind. Each step in his battle plan was described, the pieces like a choreographed dance. Watcher told them what to do, and what not to do . . . like run away. And as he went through the plan, the NPCs seemed to stand up a little taller. The strategy, though incredibly dangerous, gave him the smallest bit of hope.

"It's time." The young wizard held his fist in the air. "Strength and courage."

"Strength and courage," the NPCs replied, the mechites squeaking and the wolves howling.

Turning, Watcher charged up the stairs that led to the top of the Tower. When he reached the top, he found the forest bathed in darkness. The sun had set and the moon had not yet peeked its lunar face above the horizon; it was the darkest part of the night . . . and that meant that the battle was almost upon them.

A shiver of fear slithered down his spine, but he pushed the emotion away and looked to the east. He gathered his magic and poured it into the wizard's cape, causing him to disappear from sight.

"I'm ready for you, Krael. It's your move," his voice ringing with strength.

Just then, a majestic howl cut through the air; it was a warning from one of the wolves patrolling the forest: the wither king and his army were here.

And the Great War began . . . again.

CHAPTER 33

Watcher stared out across the dark forest, the sparkling canopy of stars overhead shining down at him as if each of the glistening pinpoints of light were eager to watch the terrible spectacle about to unfold. A chill spread across the land as the constant east-to-west breeze seemed to whisper into his head the names of those already fallen in this horrible conflict. Watcher knew the wind wasn't really saying anything; it was the guilt over failing to protect these villagers that was creating the haunting voice in his mind. He knew he couldn't save them all, and that many would lose their lives tonight, but he also knew he had to take responsibility for what was about to happen. If he couldn't save these villagers, then no one could.

Reaching under his chest plate, Watcher pulled out Mira's blocking stone and stared down at the inky-black gem. A faint sparkle of magic surrounded the artifact. Holding it higher, he raised the stone to eye level and peered into its faceted surface. There seemed to be tiny faces staring out of the ancient artifact, thousands of them, all swirling around within it like grains of sand in a windstorm.

Are those the faces of the dead? Watcher thought.

Just then, he saw the face of Fencer's mother, Saddler, come into view, her dark brown eyes filled with compassion, just as he remembered them. She tried to say something, but her words were trapped within the stone. Watcher moved the artifact closer, but still heard nothing.

"I can't block out the voices of the injured or dying," he said to himself. "Hiding from my responsibility won't help anyone. I must own this and face my fear of failure." Then he yanked on the stone hard, causing the thin chain around his neck to snap.

Instantly, the voice of Saddler whispered to him in the back of his mind. When he heard what she said, he gasped; it was her last words before she died in that terrible battle with the spiders.

"I know you can do it. Save my daughter, please . . ." she said, and then she disappeared for a second time and the stone grew dark. As always, Saddler had had complete faith in him, regardless of the odds.

Leaning over the edge of the tower, Watcher looked down at the defenders on the ground. Wolves and golems and villagers all turned and glanced up at him, somehow sensing his need, although he was invisible. Though they were scared, the fear etched plainly into each square face, the villagers and metal creatures also had faith in him. Below, Planter and Mira glanced at each other, then each raised a fist into the air as a salute to the Wizard of War. They too believed Watcher could see them through the terrible battle about to crash down upon them.

If all of them have faith in me, maybe I should have faith in myself as well, Watcher thought.

That's the smartest thing we've ever heard you say. The wizards in his weapons seemed to smile, somehow.

Watcher nodded and stood a little taller, then turned and gazed into the forest to the east, where redstone torches placed against the trunks of oaks and birches burned a dull crimson in the darkness, casting a faint glow that Watcher hoped would go unnoticed. He knew they were part of Blaster's TNT contraption, likely intended to bring a redstone signal into the treetops to trigger some kind of lethal surprise.

The sudden crunch of footsteps on the ground drew everyone's attention. Archers standing atop the cobblestone towers notched arrows and took aim, warriors standing atop the fortified walls drew their weapons, and NPCs with buckets of water stood ready on the barricade, ready to pour the liquid onto any attackers.

"Hold your fire!" a voice shouted.

Watcher's keen eyes scanned the dark forest, looking for the source of the sound. Then he saw it: a group of villagers racing across the battlefield, at times leaping into the air, as if jumping over some obstacle.

"It's us. We're coming in," one of the villagers shouted.

Watcher recognized the voice; it was Blaster. As he approached, the boy pulled off his black leather cap, revealing his head bobbing up and down as he sprinted through the darkness. A step or two behind ran Fencer, always at his side, as usual. Several other villagers ran with the pair; they had likely just finished setting the TNT traps.

With a giggle, Blaster smiled and waved at his friends. "This is the biggest TNT contraption I've ever made." The young boy was almost giddy. "I can't wait to see what it does."

"You need to calm down and concentrate." Fencer moved next to him and put a hand on his back, trying to quiet him down a little. Some of the other NPCs standing behind the fortified wall laughed, causing Blaster to turn away, embarrassed, but he didn't move away from her as quickly as he could . . . *interesting*, Watcher thought.

Spreading the last bit of redstone dust on the ground, Blaster ran the crimson trail up to the edge of the barricade, then pulled out a redstone torch and stood there, waiting. Fencer jumped onto a block of dirt and climbed over the wall, then pulled out her bow and stood atop the fortification, a look of grim determination on her square face.

"I hope Watcher was right about the monsters," Cutter said from atop the wall to Blaster, his booming voice easy to hear. "He said the monsters would attack from the east. If they come from anywhere else, we're in trouble."

Blaster glanced up at the hulking warrior as he paced back and forth on the wall. "Don't worry. He knows what he's doing." Then, lowering his voice, he said, "I hope."

"Well, if he's wrong, then we'll have to—"

Suddenly, a foul, putrid odor floated across the landscape, coming to the NPCs from the east. Everyone instantly recognized the smell.

"Zombies," Cutter hissed. "I guess Watcher was right." The big NPC glanced toward the Tower, the top of which was barely above ground level. He nodded, knowing the invisible wizard would see him. Reaching into his inventory, Cutter pulled out his diamond sword. "Everyone, get your bows ready."

The NPCs along the walls and on the archer towers notched arrows to their bows, then waited patiently for the monster to come within range. Already, snarls and growls floated out of the dark forest, though the sparkling stars overhead did little to illuminate the soon-to-be battlefield.

And then the villagers saw them: dark shapes moving through the forest, barely visible to the NPCs on the walls. Watcher was about to shout a warning when a rocket shot into the air.

"That's the first trip wire." Blaster shifted excitedly from foot to foot. "Now comes the second and third trip wires."

"What happens with those?" Fencer asked.

Blaster smiled. "Absolutely nothing, just a harmless click."

"Why did you do that?"

"The monsters will think the trip wires are just there to scare them." Blaster giggled. "They'll get overconfident and careless, and that'll be a mistake."

The monsters growled, their feet shuffling through the long blades of grass. A click sounded in the distance, followed by another as the two trip wires were triggered. The snarls grew louder as the crunch of the monsters' footsteps grew nearer.

Blaster just grinned.

Suddenly, an explosion rocked the forest as a huge ball of fire billowed into the air, followed by branches, blocks of dirt, and flailing monster bodies. The mob shouted in fury, then continued forward; now they were charging. As they charged, another trap detonated, tearing into the monster formation without mercy. Blocks of TNT ignited to the left and right of the attackers' group, driving them into a tighter formation.

Blaster glanced up at Cutter. "Make some noise."

"Everyone, yell," Cutter said, then shouted as loud as he could.

The other villagers screamed and yelled, each of them taunting the monsters, making their enemies that much angrier.

"Light the torches," Blaster shouted.

NPCs pulled torches from their inventories and placed them along the ramparts. Instantly, they came to life, flames dancing at the end of each. They cast a flickering circle of light upon the fortified walls and defenders.

"COME AND GET US!" Cutter screamed. He banged his sword against his iron chest plate, other NPCs doing the same.

This enraged their attackers, causing them to surge toward their enemies. The lead monsters stepped on pressure plates hidden in the darkness, and more explosives detonated, these at the rear of the mob, driving them forward.

"Blaster, set off the rest of the TNT," Fencer begged. "I'm nervous."

"Not yet."

The monsters could now easily see the villagers. They roared furiously, their voices filled with rage. Charging as fast as they could, the mob advanced on the NPCs, knowing the defenders were completely outnumbered.

"Blaster . . . do it!" Fencer looked scared, as did the other NPCs.

"Not yet." He smiled at her, then shouted to the other NPCs. "Hold your fire. Don't shoot any arrows . . . yet."

The monster group was now close enough that the villagers could tell it was a collection of spiders, zombies, skeletons, and slimes, all of them the standard creatures of the night. Krael was doing what Watcher had expected: holding the warped and distorted monsters for the second wave.

"I think maybe it's time for some fun," Blaster shouted. He held the redstone torch high over his head, then placed it onto the ground, a wide grin on his face.

The redstone dust on the ground instantly grew bright, its intense red signal running through the thick, grass-covered surface. Repeaters amplified the signal strength as the redstone dust split into multiple strands.

"Almost there." Blaster sounded like an expectant father, waiting for his child to be born.

Now, redstone ladders on the sides of the trees lit up, sending the signal into the treetops.

"They're getting closer," someone shouted.

"Almost there," Blaster said, his voice filled with excitement.

"But the monsters are only twenty blocks away. We need—"

A series of explosions suddenly punctuated the night as Blaster's final trap became alive. Blocks of TNT blossomed into existence, enveloping the monsters within their fiery grasp, and low-hanging tree branches burst into life as the explosive cubes hidden within their leaves detonated. Blast after blast echoed across the landscape as Blaster's masterpiece unfolded, wreaking havoc amongst the monstrous horde. The monsters were hammered from the left and right, then above. Having nowhere safe to run, they just stopped and allowed the fiery jaws of Blaster's TNT creation to devour them.

In seconds, it was over. A few monsters lay on the ground, stunned and confused, but most had disappeared completely, leaving behind glowing balls of XP that littered the cratered landscape.

"Archers . . . attack!" Cutter yelled, and a wave of pointed shafts leapt into the air, falling upon the surviving monsters. Many tried to get to their feet and run, but they didn't stand a chance. The creatures screamed in fear and pain, but before they could retreat, a second volley of arrows silenced the terrified voices and cleared the battlefield of the few remaining monsters.

The battle was a complete success . . . for now.

The villagers cheered, many banging their weapons against their shields and chest plates. As they celebrated, more growls percolated through the forest, but these sounded different. They were meaner and louder, with a clear thirst for revenge in each terrible voice.

"More monsters coming." Cutter turned to Blaster. "Any more TNT traps out there?"

The young boy shook his head. "Those monsters triggered them all."

How many are *there?* Planter thought, the words resounding in the other wizards' minds.

Watcher peered into the darkness. The moon was peeking up from the eastern horizon, casting its silvery light onto the landscape and illuminating much of their surroundings.

I see maybe a hundred of them, Watcher thought. *They're still the normal monsters from the Far Lands.*

"There's maybe a hundred of them, all regular monsters." Planter glanced at Cutter. "None of the distorted creatures yet."

"A hundred . . ." Cutter shook his head in disbelief. "It really doesn't matter what kind they are. We can't stop that many."

"We will." Planter's words had steel in them, silencing Cutter's doubt. She glanced up at Watcher, though the young wizard atop the Tower was still invisible. Watcher could see the fear in Planter's eyes; she knew what was coming.

Wait until they're right on top of you, then use Tharus's Answer. It was Mirthrandos, her words echoing both in Watcher's and Planter's brains.

Planter shook her head, her eyes pleading with Watcher to stay his hand.

There must be another way, Planter thought. *More destruction can't be the answer. Maybe we can—*

Suddenly, the monstrous horde bellowed its fury all at once, the snarling monsters clearly in a murderous rage. Moving as one, the terrible creatures charged through the blasted remains of the dark forest, the moonlight making their sharp claws and fangs easy to see. A terrified silence spread across the defenders; each of them terrified this would be one of their last moments in Minecraft.

"There's too many," someone said. "How can we stand against that horde?"

"Stick to the plan," Cutter growled.

"But there are so many of them. What if it doesn't work?"

Cutter just glared at the NPC, silencing her complaints.

Watcher wanted to be down there at Planter's side, but he knew his place was on the tower; he was the last line of defense, but he knew if he used the Answer, Planter would likely never speak to him again.

Gritting his teeth, he just stood there and watched as the horde descended upon his friends.

CHAPTER 34

The monsters charged across the pockmarked battlefield, their angry faces clearly visible in the moonlight. Snarling and growling with demonic rage, the monsters filled the forest with sounds of unbridled fury. Many of the NPCs shook with fear.

"Archers, get ready." Cutter held his sword high over his head.

The monsters likely saw the NPCs and their razor-sharp arrows, but they didn't slow. They just continued their charge, every monstrous eye filled with rage.

"FIRE!"

The sparkling faces of the stars were momentarily obscured as a wave of arrows streaked through the sky, each pointed shaft seeking monster flesh. The monsters glanced up at the descending arrows and quickened their pace, but it didn't help; the arrows fell upon the monsters, piercing their HP. Howls of pain filled the air, but their shouts of agony were mixed with even louder growls of rage as the monsters stared at their enemy and charged even faster.

The archers fired arrow after arrow, but they were barely slowing the mob's advance. Mirthrandos fired her tiny magic missiles at the approaching horde while the iron and obsidian golems charged at the monsters. A wave of silver composed of metal wolves and mechite riders shot out from the sides of the barricade and darted through the monster formation, the animals' jaws snapping at the monsters' legs while the mechites' sharp knives slashed at their bodies. Even though they were doing a lot of damage, the monsters ignored them and continued their charge; it seemed nothing was going to stop the mob.

"Our wall won't be enough to stop those monsters." Blaster glanced at Cutter as he drew his two enchanted curved swords. "Part of the horde will hit the center of the wall while the rest run to the edges and go around." He glanced at Fencer, his eyes filled with worry. "We can't hold this position."

"We can." Cutter's voice was filled with finality, as if just saying it would make it true. "We stick to the plan."

"Our plan didn't include a second attack as big as this." Blaster glared at the approaching monsters, the hum of bowstrings sounding like a hive of bees around him. "We need to do something."

The full stench of the monsters had now reached the valiant defenders; it was terrible, making many of them gag. The swish of the creatures' clawed feet through the long grass sounded like a crashing ocean wave, easily audible over the pounding of their feet; they were getting close.

"What do we do?" Blaster looked up at Cutter, fear in his eyes.

Cutter glanced at the NPCs atop the wall and those perched in the archer towers. They were continuing to shoot their arrows. Monsters were falling to the ground, but not enough of them. In seconds, the horde would be on top of them. They wouldn't last long.

Cutter turned to Planter, a look of desperation in his steel-gray eyes. "We need you."

Planter sighed and lowered her gaze to the ground. Slowly, she put away her bow and pulled out the bright-red shield, its edges glowing with iridescent magic.

"Everyone, pull out your shields," Cutter shouted, his booming voice startling Planter and almost causing her to stumble off the cobblestone wall. The big warrior moved next to her. "Don't worry, I'll be right behind you."

The young wizard just grunted, her head still downcast.

More NPCs climbed atop the cobblestone wall and moved close together, while the archers in the towers kept firing at the nearest monsters. They were still getting closer.

"We have to hurry!" someone shouted.

"What if this doesn't work?" asked another.

"It'll work," Cutter bellowed. "Just be quiet and do as you're told." The big warrior spoke softly into Planter's ear. "They're ready. We have to do this now, before it's too late."

Planter sighed and nodded. Pulling up her shield, she held it before her, the three dark skulls staring out at the approaching mob. Gathering her magic, she poured it into the shield, and instantly, the glowing rectangle reached for Planter's mind, trying to draw her consciousness out of her body. She moaned, then spoke, her weak voice barely a whisper. "Touch them together."

"What?" someone asked.

"Move together and touch your shields to the ones on your right and left. Make a wall of shields." Cutter's voice crashed against the landscape, startling both villager and monster alike. The horde slowed its advance slightly, unsure what was happening.

The NPCs moved closer together, pressing the edge of their shields against those of the villagers next to them. Finally, they were all touching. Planter breathed a sigh of relief as her shield stopped pulling on her mind and instead reached out to each shield.

A small part of Sotaria is in each shield, Mirthrandos thought in awe. *After all these years, she's coming together.*

Suddenly, the voice of the great shield maker, Sotaria, filled Planter's mind, and all of the shields flared bright, creating a wall of purple flames. The monsters skidded to a stop for a moment, afraid of the magic before them.

Use the key, my great-great-great grandchild. Sotaria's voice was soothing, like a lullaby, easing everyone's fears for a moment.

The monsters, seeing nothing happening, charged ahead, kicking aside wolves and mechites, some even attacking the stout golems' legs. One of the obsidian golems fell, disappearing amidst a storm of claws and fangs.

The monsters were only twenty blocks away.

Use the key, child, before it's too late, the ancient wizard Sotaria said, her words resonating in all of the wizards' minds.

But I don't want to kill. I don't want to be like . . . him.

Watcher knew she meant him. He sighed.

A shield does not cut. A shield does not pierce. Sotaria's voice lost its soothing tone and became serious. *A shield stops those who wish to do you harm.* Her voice grew louder now, as if the ancient wizard were looming over the battlefield. *Use the power in the shields and stop those who would hurt your comrades. Do it, before it's too late . . . use the key!*

Planter glanced over her shoulder at Watcher, an expression of profound sadness on her beautiful face. She nodded, then gritted her teeth.

The monster army was close now . . . too close. Watcher could even hear individual growls and snarls. He wanted to be down there at Planter's side, but he knew his place was here, directing the next act in this terrible play.

Planter reached into her inventory and pulled out the key she'd taken from her childhood home, then pressed it into the slot on the back of her shield. Instantly, Planter and the other shields grew brighter and brighter. The NPCs looked at her, afraid, and some moved away, but Cutter's voice boomed loud across the battlefield, keeping them in place.

"Stand your ground and trust Planter," the big warrior called to his left and right. "Her magic will protect us, but only if we stand with her, so stay where you are, keep the shields together, and have faith!"

The NPCs, despite looking terrified, stayed put, keeping their shields touching, forming a long, red wall.

"Do it now," Watcher whispered. The monsters were nearly at the wall; the stink of decaying flesh was strong in the air. "Come on, Planter, you can do it."

Planter grew brighter, the iridescent light coming from her body turning night into day. Suddenly, she screamed, her magic amplifying her voice and causing the battle cry to resonate in the minds of everyone on the battlefield. Iridescent shafts of pure energy shot out from each shield, streaking across the charred battlefield almost too quickly to see. The magic struck the monsters, the purple light enveloping each one like a lavender serpent, squeezing the monsters tight in their sparking coils. With expressions of surprise and shock on their horrific faces, the creatures stopped their charge and just stood there for a moment. Then all of them just fell to the ground.

Are they dead? Planter asked Sotaria. *ARE THEY DEAD?*

No, my child, they have not been harmed. The monsters are just asleep.

Watcher could see the stress instantly leave Planter's body. She slowly lowered her shield as the other NPCs did the same, then turned and smiled with relief at the invisible Watcher atop the Wizard's Tower.

The NPCs cheered, many of them drawing swords and jumping off the wall, intent on destroying the sleeping monsters.

"No!" Planter shouted, her magic still glowing bright across her body and amplifying her voice. "Leave them be. They aren't a threat anymore and will not be harmed."

None dared challenge the wizard; they sheathed their weapons and climbed back atop the fortified wall, still cheering.

Suddenly, an eerie chill spread across the landscape, causing tiny square goose bumps to form on the arms and necks of the defenders, Watcher included.

The young wizard instantly recognized the sensation: "Krael," he warned.

Slowly rising from amidst the trees, the king of the withers floated into the sky, cackling with an evil, hateful laugh.

"That was a nice trick, girl, but it won't do you any good against me and my army."

The NPCs looked shocked and terrified to see the glowing wither king.

"I'm sure that fool, Sotaria, didn't tell you, but that trick with the shield takes time to recharge." Krael's three skulls grinned viciously.

"The withers are here." Cutter glared up at the floating monster, then turned back to the other NPCs. "Next part of the plan . . . now!"

Immediately, fifty villagers dropped their shields and leapt off the wall, then ran to the gigantic sinkhole around the Wizard's Tower and followed the rough steps leading down into the structure.

"Ha ha ha." Krael laughed. "Look, Kora, they're running away."

Another wither rose out of the foliage and floated next to the wither king. "Yes, my husband, I see . . . they're cowards, just as you predicted."

"I'm sorry they didn't get to see my next surprise." Krael rose higher into the air, grinning, as loud, vicious growls floated out of the forest; more monsters were coming. But these creatures sounded different. There was not just a thirst for violence in their voices, there was also a desire to cause suffering, and as much of it as possible.

"I know that sound." Planter glanced at Cutter, her emerald-green eyes filled with fear.

Another wave of monsters crept slowly out of the darkness, like a deadly fog. There were nearly twice as many in this horde as there were monsters laying asleep in the thick grass. All the creatures were a mishmash of body parts: skeletons with spider heads, zombies with long enderman arms, slimes walking atop stubby creeper feet . . . every horrific combination imaginable advanced on the NPCs. The looks of vile hatred on their scarred and distorted faces were almost too painful to see. The monsters trampled shrubs and sleeping monsters alike as they moved into the cratered battlefield, stepping on their unconscious brothers and sisters with no regard for their safety.

Krael's evil laugh filled the dark sky. "Now, my brothers and sisters."

The wither army floated up from amidst the trees and branches, the moon bathing them in a mystical silver light. The glow from the three Crowns of Skulls painted the dark withers with an iridescent purple light.

"Look at the pathetic NPCs trying to defend themselves." Krael laughed. "Half of your comrades wisely ran away already. Only the foolish could hope to stand against my beautiful creatures." The monsters on the ground spread out across the battlefield, growling and snarling. "I killed your foolish leader, Watcher, so no one is coming to your aid. My withers will hold their attack. I give the gift of destruction to those monsters on the ground." Krael drifted closer to his infantry. "Monsters . . . attack!"

Instantly, the monsters charged at the defenders, their strong, disjointed bodies crashing through trees and trampling those unconscious on the ground.

"Archers . . . FIRE!" Cutter roared.

The remaining NPCs, only a couple dozen, all fired

their bows rapidly, but they all knew it wouldn't stop these monsters.

"Keep firing!" Blaster moved back and forth, encouraging the defenders, but he too knew they didn't stand a chance as the horde rushed toward them.

Suddenly, a bright sphere of light formed in front of the cobblestone wall. It grew bigger and bigger, pushing back the darkness, until it was impossible to gaze upon it. The monsters, unsure if it was some kind of trick, stopped in their tracks, their angry growls changed to nervous murmurs. Even Krael seemed confused.

When the light faded, two warriors stood there, both clad in diamond armor. One of them, a girl with curly red hair spilling down her back, held an enchanted bow. The other, a boy, held two diamond swords and had a blood-red ring sparkling on his finger. A group of letters floated above his head, spelling out the name G A M E K N I G H T 9 9 9. He glanced over his shoulder and smiled reassuringly at Cutter and Blaster, then turned back to face the mob.

The monsters just stood there, unsure what to do.

"I'm Gameknight999, and this is my friend, Hunter," the boy shouted at the monsters.

"Friend? Is that what you said?" Hunter sounded annoyed.

"Ah, let's not do this now . . . there's a battle to be fought."

She rolled her eyes. "I guess. Fine, continue with what you're saying. I know how you love your idiotic speeches."

Gameknight gave her a scowl, then continued. "We've come to end the conflict." He pointed at the monsters with his two swords. "You must stop this violence now. I will allow you to leave the battlefield without any punishment."

The monsters, at first stunned by the bold declaration, glanced around at each other, then all started to laugh.

A zombie pointed a razor-sharp claw at Gameknight999. "You're just two more villagers to destroy . . . all the better." The monsters slowly advanced toward the NPCs.

"Very well. If that's the way you want it, so be it." Gameknight smiled at Hunter, then turned back toward the approaching horde, swords ready. "Come on, monsters . . . let's dance." With a look of grim determination, he ran towards the charging creatures, the redhead behind him shooting her flaming arrows with pinpoint accuracy as she sprinted at the attackers.

Cutter glanced at Watcher and smiled, then turned toward the advancing monsters. "Come on, everyone, IT'S TIME TO FIGHT!"

The diamond-clad newcomer suddenly yelled, "FOR MINECRAFT!" and the other NPCs echoed his battle cry.

"FOR MINECRAFT!"

"FOR MINECRAFT!"

"FOR MINECRAFT!"

CHAPTER 35

The monsters, startled by the small force of villagers charging at them, stopped in their tracks, unsure what to do. Before they could figure it out, the villagers smashed into them, the newcomers fighting with lethal skill. Cutter moved to Gameknight's side, while Blaster and Fencer moved to Hunter's. The sheer ferocity of their attack had the monsters confused and afraid. But when the mob realized that these few warriors were all the villagers could muster, the horde laughed and quickly surrounded them.

"What is this trickery?" Krael screamed in fury. "Who are these newcomers? Are they wizards?" None of his withers said anything. The Crowns on the wither king's heads grew brighter and brighter as his rage built. He glared down at the NPCs, then shouted with all his might. "WITHERS . . . ATTACK!"

That was the signal. Watcher released his magical hold on Tharus's Cape and suddenly appeared atop the Wizard's Tower, his body glowing with an intense purple hue. Krael screamed in utter surprise, disbelief and rage etched into each of his three faces.

The monster, hearing their king's shout, stopped fighting and pulled back away from the small band of villagers. They all stared up at the boy with the flowing cape as his body grew brighter and brighter.

"I've learned a thing or two while you foolishly thought I was dead." Watcher smiled, then yelled, his amplified voice filling the Far Lands with cloudless thunder. "BEHOLD, THE MIGHT OF THE WIZARD'S TOWER!"

Watcher raised his hands over his head, his body now brighter than the sun. The Tower itself glowed as if wreathed in purple flames, then started to shake. Suddenly, the forest around the protruding tower exploded, tearing a deep gash into the forest floor. Chunks of wood and leaves and dirt flew into the air, many of the cubes pelting the withers floating nearby. Slowly, the tower and the ancient structure underground rose from the now-enlarged hole like an ancient sea monster rising from the depths. The glittering structure floated upward until the entire building was above ground level. Blocks of dirt appeared beneath it, filling in the hole beneath it. Settling on the ground, the ornate building stretched for hundreds of blocks, dominating the landscape. Watcher smiled at the wither king, whose face was a visage of shock.

Just then, fifty NPCs emerged from a staircase and stood atop the structure's roof below Watcher. Each wore a pair of Elytra wings, like Watcher, a red-and-white striped tube in their hands. Mira moved onto the roof with them, her crooked wooden staff glowing with magical power. Just then, Kobael floated up from behind the ornate structure and hovered just above the roof.

"There's the traitor!" Krael screamed. "That puny wither dies first. Everyone, ATTACK!"

All the withers fired a huge barrage of flaming skulls directly at Kobael.

"No!" A profound sadness filled Watcher's soul as the flaming skulls descended toward the harmless creature.

The tiny wither was terrified, too scared to move; it just hovered there, unable to act.

"Not again," Mirthrandos hissed. "NO MORE KILLING!"

Moving with lightning speed, the ancient wizard dashed across the structure and stood in front of the flaming skulls, using her body and her magic to protect the terrified monster.

"Mira . . . no!" Watcher raised his arms and channeled his magic into the Gauntlets of Life. A shaft of light streaked out into the forest and hit a cluster of oaks, and instantly, the oaks turned to stone as the life was pulled out of them and sent back to Watcher. With every ounce of his magical power, he fired bolts of purple lighting toward the monsters, causing the withers to scatter and hide beneath the leafy foliage. Then, jumping off the Tower, Watcher leaned forward, opening his Elytra. The wings snapped open and caught the wind, letting him glide off the tower and to the roof below. He knew he'd never get there in time; someone was about to die.

As the fireballs streaked toward them, Mirthrandos put her body right in front of Kobael's. The ancient wizard's iridescent glow was bright, at first, but it grew weaker as her magic absorbed the blasts from the flaming skulls. She cried out in pain as the projectiles crashed into her, but still she stood tall, refusing to sacrifice her friend. The wizard drew on every ounce of magic, making her bod grow brighter, but there were so many fireballs. With each impact, her magic was torn from her body. The enchanted glow grew weaker and weaker until finally, the purple shimmer flickered one last time, then went out.

Mirthrandos was defenseless.

More flaming skulls fell upon the ancient wizard, hammering her body and knocking her down. But she refused to give up. Mirthrandos tried to stand, but her HP was just too low. The last skull smashed into her body, making her fall back down just as Watcher reached her side.

"Mira, are you okay?" Watcher knelt and cradled her head in his arms, then pulled out a potion of healing and held it to her lips. "Here, drink."

She shook her head. "No, I've lived long enough."

"Why did you do that?" Kobael floated to her side, the young wither choked-up with emotion. "You sacrificed yourself for me . . . again."

Mirthrandos glanced up at the wither. "I couldn't let that monster destroy you, Kobael. You're my oldest friend." She turned toward Watcher. Extending a shaking, wrinkled hand, she put it against Watcher's cheek. "Krael will destroy everything if he isn't stopped. Use Tharus's Answer—it's the only way. You'll never defeat his armies."

Watcher shook his head.

"You must realize something Tharus never understood." The ancient wizard coughed, her skin growing pale. "He thought he was the most powerful wizard in the world, which he was, but . . ." She coughed again, worse this time. "But he also forgot who he really was. You can't make that mistake."

"Who he was? I don't understand."

A string of coughs ravaged her body, weakening her even more. "He was Tharus, yes, but he'd lost himself to his magic. You must be yourself. Don't make the same mista—"

And then, Mirthrandos, the oldest wizard in Minecraft, vanished, leaving behind three balls of XP and her crooked wooden staff.

A wave of grief enveloped Watcher's soul. *This isn't happening; it can't happen. She was a wizard, and—*

A vile, malicious laugh floated through the air. "Finally, that old hag is gone." Krael laughed again, causing the withers to join in, all of them chuckling cruelly.

Watcher's grief turned to rage as his body grew brighter and brighter, his magic building again. He stood up with Mira's wooden staff in his left hand, a firework rocket in his right. Any trace of fear or uncertainty was now replaced with a pure, unquenchable fury.

"Krael, it's time I taught you some respect . . . and school is now in session." He glanced at the NPCs on the rooftop. "Fliers . . . ATTACK!"

As one, he and the NPCs sprinted to the edge of the roof and jumped.

And so began the first Great War in the Sky.

CHAPTER 36

Watcher and the other NPCs streaked upward, the tiny fireworks rockets giving each of them a speed boost and allowing them to climb high into the sky. The scattered withers, surprised to see all the airborne villagers, just stared at them, stunned.

"Bows!" Watcher shouted. "Use healing arrows."

The NPCs notched the sparkling healing arrows to their bows, then fired, and fifty arrows streaked through the night sky and fell upon their targets. The undead withers screamed out in pain as the potions imbedded within the arrowheads splashed across their dark bodies; the healing potions acted like poison to the withers and any undead monsters.

"Evasive action!" Watcher banked to the left, the other NPCs flying erratically around him.

The withers, enraged, fired flaming skulls at the NPCs, and though most of the deadly projectiles just flew up into the open sky, some found their targets. Villagers screamed out in pain, some tumbling from the sky as the withers' attacks smashed wings and hammered bodies.

Watcher angled downward and sped toward a pair of withers, firing another string of healing arrows. Four shafts struck the first wither, destroying the monster. More arrows leapt from his bowstring, hitting the second monster, causing it to flash red, but his last arrow missed; that wither survived, for now. Putting away his bow, Watcher pulled out a handful of rockets and launched one at the surviving withers, using the speed boost to ascend into the night sky. Then, launching rocket after rocket, he continued to pick up speed, easily dodging the flaming skulls pursuing him.

Watcher glanced down at his friends on the ground. The monsters were moving closer to them, their angry growls easily audible even at this altitude as their shock faded. The villagers were completely outnumbered, and, at an achingly slow place, the monsters moved closer, letting the fear within the NPCs grow with every step.

"I have to get down there and help." Watcher glanced over his shoulder. His air force, led by his sister, was buzzing around the withers, using their speed to avoid the deadly flaming skulls. They fired the healing arrows, making the withers flash red as they took damage, their glowing balls of XP looking like a colorful rain.

Leaning forward, Watcher dove toward the attackers on the ground. He pulled out the Flail of Regrets with his right hand and a handful of rockets in his left. He wasn't sure he'd be able to make it in time.

The monsters were getting closer, but the two newcomers, Gameknight999 and Hunter, didn't wait for their attack; they charged at the nearest creatures. Gameknight's two diamond swords became a whirlwind of destruction, cleaving through HP and destroying one monster after another, and the redhead's arrows pierced the creatures with pinpoint accuracy, adding to the carnage. Cutter, Blaster, and Fencer fought with them, their blades wreaking havoc. The rest of the villagers fought along the left and right sides, with a few watching the rear, but it was hopeless; it was just a question of time before the monsters overran them. They were doomed.

Suddenly, a green figure streaked out of the base of the Wizard's Tower; it was Er-Lan. The zombie ran through the monsters' formation, the warped and distorted creatures ignoring him, assuming he was on their side.

As Er-Lan moved, a huge spidery creature with the head of a zombie and the arms of an enderman attacked Cutter. Its dark fists smashed into the big NPC's iron armor, causing him to flash red. He turned to face the monster, but another creature dove at him, slashing at Cutter with long, sharp claws. But then Er-Lan dove into the battle. The zombie smashed into the monsters, using his body as a battering ram. The young zombie knocked the monsters away, then turned and faced Cutter, smiling.

"You came to finish me off yourself?" the big warrior boomed angrily.

Er-Lan just turned away from Cutter and faced the attacking monsters, arms outstretched. Suddenly, the young zombie gave off a bright iridescent flash. Bands of purple light wrapped around his body, then flowed to his arms and legs; like a giant glowing snake, it wrapped around his body. A fierce, amplified growl boomed from Er-Lan, echoing across the landscape and making the monsters pause for just an instant.

Kneeling, Er-Lan plunged his clawed fingers into the ground, then screamed as loud as he could. A wave of purple energy spread out from the zombie, making the blades of grass under the monsters' feet sparkle and dance as if electrified. The strands then stretched upward, wrapping around the legs of the attackers. The warped creatures stared down at the long grass, confused at first, then realized they were becoming entangled. Slashing at the grass, they tried to cut through the strands, but the grass just grew faster. Many of the monsters tried to flee, but with their legs captured, all they could do was fall down.

More grass grew up from bare patches of dirt,

capturing every monster on the battlefield, but leaving all the NPCs alone.

The villagers, realizing they'd just been pulled from the jaws of death, all cheered.

"What have you done to my army?" Krael bellowed.

The king of the withers fired a barrage of skulls at a group of flying NPCs, striking two and causing them to plummet to the ground, smoking. He then turned to the east and fired a single, flaming skull toward the rising moon, where it exploded over the forest.

Suddenly, the growls of more monsters percolated out of the trees; the fireball had been a signal.

"Behold, here is the rest of my army." With a sneer, Krael laughed. "Prepare to meet your doom."

A huge group of monsters, larger than all the rest combined, emerged from the dark forest and charged at the NPCs. The ground shook as their clawed feet pounded the forest floor, charging at their enemy.

Planter glanced up hopelessly at Watcher as he streaked overhead.

What do we do? she thought, her sad words resonating in Watcher's mind.

I don't know. Despair filled his mind. *We've lost, and all of us are going to die.*

The sadness in Planter's thoughts was almost too much to bear. *Maybe a few of us can escape,* Planter thought. *If we—*

Wait for it. Baltheron's voice suddenly boomed through the two wizards' minds.

"What?" Watcher said aloud.

Wait for it. The voice from within the Flail of Regrets was filled with confidence.

But if we wait, we'll be destroyed. Planter glanced up at Watcher, confused and afraid.

The young wizard was about to say something when a large rectangle suddenly popped into existence near the battlefield, its interior filled with a sparkling purple field. And then the most beautiful thing happened:

Cleric, riding on a pristine white horse, came charging out of the portal, and behind him came a constant stream of mounted warriors, each wielding an enchanted sword in their right hand and holding a shield in their left.

The cavalry charged toward the battle, slashing at monsters still struggling to stand. All the NPCs fell upon the monsters captured by Er-Lan's grass, their swords, axes, and arrows taking HP from the distorted creatures until only glowing balls of XP remained.

"Dad . . . you made it!" Watcher shouted triumphantly from overhead.

Cleric glanced up at his son and smiled, then turned his horse toward the approaching mob, ready to keep fighting.

Gameknight leapt up onto a riderless horse, then pulled Hunter up behind him. He glanced at Cleric. "It's time for some fun."

The old man seemed confused by the stranger's presence, but he still shrugged and kicked his horse into a gallop. "Attack, everyone!"

"No, you have to yell *For Minecraft!*" Gameknight corrected him.

Cleric seemed more confused. He gave the warrior a conciliatory smile and nodded. "OK, then . . . FOR MINECRAFT!"

"FOR MINECRAFT!" the cavalry shouted, charging at the incoming monsters.

Watcher launched another string of rockets, picking up speed, then climbed high into the sky again.

"NO!" Krael screamed. "My monsters were supposed to destroy those pathetic villagers. Now they have cavalry." He shouted in an absolute rage, his cries of fury making the very landscape quake in fear.

Krael floated higher into the air, firing his skulls at any winged villager within range and staring at Watcher, the monster's six eyes filled with rage. "Wizard, it's time I revealed my last surprise."

"Fliers, gain altitude, now!" Watcher shouted, suspecting some kind of trap.

The NPCs banked in graceful arcs, firing rockets to gain speed as they climbed high in the sky, veering left and right to dodge flaming skulls. They flew into a huge bank of clouds drifting across the landscape and disappeared into the mist.

Watcher, though, dove for the Wizard's Tower, pulling up just in time to land atop its soaring heights. He pulled out a shield, then turned and glared at Krael.

The wither king grew brighter and brighter as the magic from the three Crowns of Skulls enveloped his ashen body with a harsh, angry hue. It soon became too intense to look at; Watcher averted his eyes.

"Meet the last living weapons created by the NPC wizards hundreds of years ago." Krael's scratchy voice was filled with vicious delight.

Suddenly, a bright flash of light filled the sky, momentarily blotting out the stars and changing night to day. Watcher looked away, protecting his eyes, and before he could turn back, a horrid scream, followed by another and another, echoed across the forest. Glancing back to Krael, the young wizard saw something he'd never seen before. A new kind of creature, one with wide wings and a narrow head, streaked through the sky, their green eyes darting to the left and right, taking in their environment as they scanned the area, likely looking for targets. From beneath, the monsters' wings were colored a dark blue, thick brown skin protected their undersides. But as they turned in great sweeping arcs, the tops of their bodies became visible. White, exposed bones stretched across their wings as if they were part skeletons, with the same blue skin stretching between the bones.

"Behold, the last living weapons, which the wizards were too afraid to summon." Krael's voice grew louder, amplified by his magical artifacts. "These are phantoms, and they only obey my commands." The wither king's three skulls stared straight at Watcher. "Phantoms . . . ATTACK!"

The terrible creatures all banked in the air and dove

down at the cavalry, their outstretched wings lined with sharp barbs. With hideous screams, they crashed into the NPCs, causing each target to flash red as they took damage. At the same time, the approaching mob on the ground charged at the horsemen and horsewomen. Just then, more withers rose out of the forest, each with a wicked smile on their three skulls.

"Withers . . . destroy the NPC fliers, but save the wizard for last." Krael laughed. "I still want him to watch the destruction of everything he holds dear."

The withers cheered, then fired a constant stream of flaming skulls into the clouds.

Shouts of pain and fear came from the villagers as the phantoms swooped down and crashed into them, leaving a faint trail of smoke from each wingtip. The winged NPCs shouted more cries of terror as some of them fell from the sky.

This is a disaster, Watcher thought. *It's hopeless.*

Use Tharus's Answer, the wizards within his magical weapons said as one.

"No," someone said from behind.

Watcher turned and found Planter climbing onto the top of the Tower, her breath ragged with fatigue.

"You can't just destroy an entire race of creatures for the benefit of another." She placed a hand on his shoulder and looked deep into his eyes.

Far below, a golem made a loud cracking sound as a phantom flew into it, the terrifying creature's wings carving through the metal giant as if it were made of butter. The metallic creature groaned once, then fell to the ground and shattered, scattering blocks of iron across the battlefield.

Metallic wolves howled in pain as the phantoms tore into them, too, the mechites on their backs dying on a single pass. It was a massacre; no NPC would survive these attacks.

"I have to do something." Watcher glanced at Planter. "I'm sorry, but if I don't—"

"If you kill every monster in Minecraft, I'll never speak to you again." She scowled. "There must be another way. Don't just take the easy solution; look for the right one instead."

Watcher shook his head. The sounds of agony from the dying stabbed at his soul, his grief nearly overwhelming.

"I have to do something." His voice was weak and filled with despair.

You have no choice. Baltheron's voice was filled with the sound of resignation and confidence. Watcher felt as if he had to comply, as if the command were taking over his very will. *Do it . . . now. DO IT!*

The young wizard sighed; he knew he had no choice. Planter yelled something at him, but Watcher couldn't hear her; somehow, Baltheron and the other wizards were blocking out the sounds.

Destroy all of the monsters . . . everywhere, the magical artifacts in his inventory said. They sounded hungry, somehow, as if they'd been waiting for this moment for hundreds of years.

With grief and despair in his heart, Watcher glanced once more at Planter, knowing this would be the final end of their relationship. Using every last drop of his magic, he allowed his powers to flow into the Tower, unlocking the nearly infinite reservoir of magical energy it contained. He could feel the Answer in there, waiting to be unleashed upon all monsters throughout the Pyramid of Servers. It would kill all of them, including his friend Er-Lan and his new friend Kobael, but Baltheron, Dalgaroth and Taerian were whispering in his mind that it was worth it, telling him he had no choice.

With another sad sigh, Watcher took hold of all the incredible power within the Tower and started to release it, starting the genocide that would spread across all the worlds of Minecraft.

CHAPTER 37

But before Watcher released the energy that would destroy every monster on every world in Minecraft, the young wizard paused.

What are you doing? Baltheron shouted in his mind. *It can finally be done. Destroy them!*

Watcher, you can't stop, Taerian bellowed, the Gauntlets of Life growing warm on his wrists. *We've waited for hundreds of years . . . do it!*

Quick, destroy them all before it's too late! Dalgaroth screamed, his screechy voice making Watcher's head hurt. *No monster deserves to live; all of them must be exterminated!*

But Watcher held on to all that power and waited.

"Something's not right." Watcher glanced over his shoulder at Planter. She was shielding her eyes, the glow from all the power within him now was nearly blinding. "All of you are so eager for destruction. It's as if you want this to happen more than anything."

Stop asking questions! Destroy the monsters . . . do it NOW! The three wizards sounded frantic in Watcher's mind.

But then Watcher felt something else hidden within the Wizard's Tower: Tharus's Answer woven into the magical building was not just a weapon designed to blast out in all directions; the Tower could be aimed.

Watcher focused on every wither and phantom, causing those terrible creatures to pull back from the fighting and glare toward the young wizard. Then, using the smallest bit of his power, he targeted the warped and distorted monsters on the ground, causing those creatures to cease fighting and stare up at the Tower in fright, too.

The three wizards screamed in his head, trying to force him to destroy the monsters, but Watcher refused. He used the smallest trickle of the magic pulsing through his body to silence the wizards; the three ancient voices became barely a whisper.

"Watcher . . . are you listening to me?" Planter was shouting at him. "I've been telling you—"

"Wait," he said softly, the power coursing through his veins magnifying the sound until it was like thunder. Watcher glanced over his shoulder. Planter was still shielding her eyes, unable to look directly at him, which was good; he didn't want to see the look on her face right now.

Gathering his power, he reached out into the very fabric of Minecraft. The lines of code connecting every plane of existence were now visible to him. Watcher could see every world; he could feel every block and sense every living creature, both monster and NPC. He realized that if he hadn't stopped using the Tower and instead targeted only the worst monsters, Tharus's Answer would have killed everyone and everything.

And then he knew what to do.

Pulling in more magical energy, Watcher cut a small slice into the very fabric of Minecraft. In the sky, a huge gash formed in the heavens. Light streamed in through the wound, the square face of a distant sun visible through the tear. A wind picked up, not in its normal east-to-west direction but directed at the terrible slash in the sky. The wind blew harder and harder until it started dragging the withers and phantoms through the menacing hole. Then, Watcher used still more power, wrapping his magic around the creatures on the ground. The warped and distorted monsters were dragged into the air, tumbling out of control as they were pulled into the rift, their screams of terror barely audible within the maelstrom.

"Watcher . . . what are you doing?"

The young wizard ignored his friend; he had to concentrate.

Krael fought desperately against the wind, trying to avoid being pulled into the tear with the rest of the monsters. Before the wither king could be drawn into it, Watcher sealed the gateway, leaving Krael alone where he was, still floating over the forest.

The wither king glared down at Watcher in shock and fury. "You took my wife from me. . . . Kora . . . she's gone."

A sorrowful, unquenchable rage filled the wither, his crowns glowing brighter as he readied another attack, but suddenly, the winged NPCs dove out of the clouds and surrounded the wither king, their healing arrows pointed at the monster, drawn and ready to fire.

"You're defeated." Watcher pointed victoriously at Krael. "Your reign of violence is over. The Great War is over. It's time for peace."

"No . . . never!" The monster was nearly insane with fury. "The Great War will never end, not while I still draw breath. You've already taken everything I care about, wizard, and now you've taken my Kora, too. I have no more reason to live save to destroy you."

NPCs on the ground rode beneath the wither with bows ready in their hands. They notched arrows and aimed up at the monster, but the young wizard raised a hand, stopping their attack.

Watcher glared at the wither king. "Violence is the first solution of the weak-minded, and that's you. A true leader would think about his followers first and himself last. But you, Krael, you're nothing but a power-hungry monster who wants to see everything burn just because you can, and you were stopped not by me, but by all of us."

Krael screamed in frustration. He turned in a circle, glowering at the NPCs flying above him, then brought his venomous gaze back to Watcher. "You took the love of my life from me, wizard. At the very least, I can do the same to you."

Suddenly, the wither king drew upon the energy in the crowns, then fired the most powerful flaming skull he'd ever created right at Planter. Instantly, all of the NPCs released their arrows, but Watcher was faster; a shaft of energy burst from his chest, striking the flaming skull and destroying it in an instant. At the same time, another beam of power shot out of Watcher and enveloped the wither, squeezing him tight until the monster and his three skulls disappeared. The NPCs' arrows passed through the empty air and landed on the ground.

Finally, Watcher released all the power and collapsed to the ground.

"Watcher, you killed them all," Planter shouted in disbelief.

Blaster and Fencer came running to the top of the tower, their swords still in their hands.

"I can't believe you destroyed all of the monsters." Planter glared at him. "You're worse than the wizards or Krael. You're a—"

Watcher raised a hand, then pointed at the ground, where Er-Lan struggled to his feet, his body still glowing with magic. Near the zombie, a dark shape floated in the air; it was Kobael.

"I didn't kill any of them." The young wizard stood and faced Planter. "Tharus's Answer would have killed not just monsters, but everything living in Minecraft, including plant life and animals . . . and NPCs."

"So instead you used it to kill just the monsters?" Blaster asked in awe.

Watcher shook his head. "I didn't kill any. That slice in the sky was a gateway to a new Minecraft world. I sent Krael's army there. There are no NPCs in that world, just monsters. I gave them what they wanted: a world just for monsters."

"But what happened to Krael?" Fencer asked, confused.

Watcher shook his head. "Krael was sent somewhere special."

"Where?" she asked.

The wizard smiled. "I sent him to the Void, where he can do no harm."

"But what about the Crowns? Can he use them to get back?"

"I'm not done yet. I'm about to make it so he can never use the Crowns again." Watcher turned toward Planter. "I know how much you hate all this magic. This much power cannot be given to anyone . . . not even me or you."

"So?" Anger simmered within Planter's emerald-green eyes.

"So, I have one last thing to do. It will end the Great War, forever this time." Watcher reached into his inventory and tossed Needle and the Flail of Regrets onto the ground. Removing the Gauntlets of Life from his wrists, he tossed them into the pile as well, then motioned to Planter. "Put the shield there."

She looked at Watcher, confused, but pulled out the red shield and added it to the mound of weapons. The pile of enchanted items shimmered with magical power.

"I think everyone should stand back." Watcher glanced at Planter. "I'm not sure what'll happen to us, but I must do this. All this magic must be destroyed. Powerful weapons like these here," he gestured to the pile, "can only cause more violence. I'm gonna stop it."

Gathering his power, Watcher connected to the massive reserve of magical energy in the Tower again, then found his targets. Some of them were nearby, while others lay hidden far away in the Far Lands, yet to be discovered. He wrapped his power around every magical thing created during the Great War, holding them all in his mind. Closing his eyes, he gritted his teeth and let every drop of enchanted power flow from the Tower and hit the targets he'd chosen.

Pain exploded through Watcher's body, as if he were on fire, but from the inside. The waves of agony surged through him, causing Watcher to fall to his knees, but he refused to release his magic. The energy from the Tower was tearing into him and Planter, but also the magical weapons before him.

The Tower shook suddenly, as if it had been struck by a giant's hammer, and the glow enveloping the structure seemed to flicker, then grow brighter as Watcher drove more power into the attack.

Suddenly, a loud crack filled the air; as if a bolt of lightning had just flashed next to his ear. The hair on Watcher's arms stood up on end, goose bumps following quickly.

And then, as quickly as it started, the pain stopped.

Watcher collapsed, falling into a heap at Blaster's feet.

"Planter, are you alright?" Fencer's nearby voice sounded frantic.

"Watcher . . . are you dead?" Blaster knelt at his side and shook him gently.

Turning his head, Watcher slowly opened his eyes. The first thing to greet him was Blaster's smiling face.

"He lives!" Blaster glanced at Fencer. "How's Planter?"

"She's alive as well." Fencer helped Planter to her feet, Blaster doing the same for Watcher.

"What happened?" Planter asked.

Watcher looked down at the battlefield. Every monster was now gone—even the sleeping ones had woken up and wandered off, free from Krael's evil magical influence. The NPCs were helping the wounded, giving out potions of healing as they headed back into the ancient structure.

"I don't see any monsters." Planter turned toward Watcher and glared at him. "Did you kill them all? Even though I told you not to, you did it anyway. I can't believe you—"

"Not all are dead," a high-pitched voice said, and Kobael floated up from behind Planter, still looking scared. "I can hear other monsters in the forest, but not the distorted ones in Krael's army, just normal zombies and spiders."

"So, you mean . . ." Planter turned back to Watcher, awareness growing on her face.

Suddenly, Er-Lan climbed onto the top of the ladder, a relieved expression on his scarred face. He moved to Watcher and wrapped his green arms around the boy, squeezing him tight.

"Watcher took it away." The zombie turned toward Planter, tears of joy streaming down his scarred face. Er-Lan smiled. "He took it all away."

Planter glanced at Er-Lan, then turned back to Watcher, confused. "What is he talking about?"

Before Watcher could answer, Cutter stepped off the ladder leading to the roof of the Tower and pointed at Er-Lan. "You see, I knew he was a warlock." Cutter turned to Blaster. "Did you see what he did on the battlefield?"

"Sure—I saw him save you, then save all of us." Blaster put an arm around Er-Lan and smiled at him. "Thanks, Er-Lan."

"Yes, but I was right! Er-Lan *was* a warlock." Cutter pointed his diamond sword at the zombie for a moment, but then tossed it off the tower. "And that warlock saved us." Cutter moved a step closer to the zombie, then reached out and put a hand on the zombie's shoulder. "Though I'm usually right, I'm not afraid to say when I'm wrong. Er-Lan . . . thank you."

The zombie smiled and nodded his scarred head. "Er-Lan is no longer a warlock, though."

"That's right," Watcher said. "There are no more

wizards, no more warlocks, no more magical swords or possessed shields . . . it's all gone."

"I don't understand." The big warrior glanced at Planter and Blaster, hoping for an explanation.

Suddenly, a smile spread across Planter's face as she realized what had happened. Looking down at her blue armor, she noticed that any kind of glow from it was gone. Grabbing the chest plate, she pulled it off her body and threw it off the tower joyfully. Quickly, she tore the rest of the armor off and tossed the rest of it to the ground far below, thrilled to be able to remove it, finally.

Then she stepped closer to Watcher and reached out, taking his hands. They both stared down at their arms.

"It's really gone?" Planter stared into Watcher's blue eyes.

The boy nodded. "All this magic has caused enough trouble, so I used the Tower and got rid of it . . . all of it."

Blaster reached down and picked up Needle. "But what about these?"

"The wizards in them are gone." Watcher nodded his head. "I realized when I connected to the Tower that the wizards in those weapons truly just wanted me to destroy all the monsters. I think their purpose in sending their minds into those weapons wasn't actually to help us in case the Great War broke out again; they just wanted—"

"They wanted to continue the Great War," Planter said in understanding.

Watcher nodded. "They wanted me to use the power in the Wizard's Tower to destroy all the monsters everywhere. Those wizards didn't really want peace . . . they wanted victory at any cost. I wasn't gonna allow that."

"Then what happened to the monsters?" Blaster asked.

"I used Tharus's Answer to create an answer of my own." Watcher grinned. "I created a world in the Pyramid of Servers and sent all the withers and phantoms and distorted monsters there. They'll finally have what they sought: a world of their own."

"But what about the NPCs there?" Fencer asked.

Watcher shook his head. "There are no villagers, just monsters. They can live however they want, without any NPCs bothering them."

Planter smiled, then reached out and grabbed Watcher's hand happily. "You did good."

"Well, I did what Mira told me just before she died. She said I . . ." A tear trickled from his eye. "I shouldn't try to be something I'm not . . . I needed to be me. So rather than trying to destroy, I tried to create."

Watcher stopped and raised his hand in the air, fingers spread wide as he thought about everything the ancient wizard had taught him, and how much he'd miss her. The wolves on the forest floor seemed to sense his thoughts and gave off the saddest howls he'd ever heard. Glancing over the side of the tower, he found the surviving golems raising their iron hands in the air, the mechites doing the same. Watcher spotted Fixit far below and tried to smile, but before he could, more tears streamed down his face. He clinched his fist tight, squeezing all the grief and sorrow for those who fell during this war, their faces playing through his mind.

Slowly, he lowered his hand, knowing everyone was lost in their sad thoughts.

"I'm gonna miss Mira. I think—"

"What's going on up here?" a cheerful voice said, coming up the ladder protruding from the hole in the tower's roof.

"You're such an idiot," another voice said.

Gameknight stepped off the ladder, then turned and offered a hand to Hunter.

"I don't need your help," Hunter snapped. "I'm a capable, strong girl."

"Well . . . I just thought . . ."

"No, you *didn't* think, as usual." She smiled jokingly at him and punched him in the shoulder, then took off her diamond helmet and set it on the ground, her long, curly red hair sparkling in the silvery light of the sun. "Obviously, they were having a solemn moment."

"Oh." Gameknight's cheeks turned a soft shade of red. "Sorry."

Watcher stepped forward. "That's alright." He extended a hand to Gameknight999. "I'm Watcher. Thank you for helping us out."

"Yeah . . . you're pretty good with those two swords." Cutter patted Gameknight on the back, almost knocking him over with his strength, but Hunter reached out and grabbed the back of his armor, keeping him from falling to the ground. "Oops."

"Where are you two from?" Blaster asked. "You just sort of appeared out of nowhere."

"Well, we've been in a lot of places and collected a lot of enchanted things." Gameknight held out his hand for them to see that on one finger sat a sparkling ring, a blood-red stone at the center glistening under the starlight. "I knew something was wrong when the monsters in the Overworld stopped burning in the sunlight."

"*We* knew," Hunter corrected with a scowl.

"Yes, yes, of course." Gameknight looked at the redhead and smiled. "We knew something was wrong, and we traced the disturbance back to here." He held up his hand. "This is a teleportation ring a demon gave to me long ago. It allowed us to come here and help."

"A demon?!" Blaster drew one of his curved swords but then looked down at the blade in surprise; it no longer sparkled with magical power.

"Don't worry; Kahn is in a different dimension, helping a small demon rule their kingdom." Gameknight lowered his hand. "This ring came from outside of Minecraft, sort of . . . from a mod."

"A mod?" Watcher glanced at Planter in surprise. "You think it still works now that magic is gone?"

"Maybe." Planter shrugged. "If it came from outside Minecraft, maybe it wasn't affected by the Tower." She turned to Gameknight999. "Hey, what was that 'let's dance' thing?"

Hunter rolled her eyes. "He likes having something to say to the monsters right before he fights."

"But doesn't that just make the monsters angrier?" Fencer asked, confused.

"EXACTLY! That's what I've been telling him for a long time, but he thinks it gives him an edge." Hunter smiled at the young girl, then moved a little closer to her and said, "I think he just likes showing off."

"Well, I can't imagine anyone else ever doing that." Planter turned to Watcher and laughed, teasing him.

Hunter turned back to Gameknight. "It seems everything here is okay now; I think it's time we went back home." She reached out and took his hand, and Gameknight put an arm around her waist. He stared into her eyes for a moment, then smiled the most satisfied smile Watcher had ever seen.

"You're right, my dear. It's time to go home." Gameknight raised his hand in front of his chest.

"Do we need to step back or anything?" Blaster asked. "I think I can speak for everyone here when I say that we don't really like magic too much."

"True," Fencer said, then moved to Blaster's side, away from Gameknight and Hunter.

Blaster looked at Fencer, then finally smiled and put an arm around her, pulling her close to him.

"That's nice," Fencer said. Blaster just nodded, a huge, unabashed smile on his face.

Planter glanced at Watcher and smiled.

"You're all ok there; just don't touch us when it happens." Gameknight glanced at Watcher. "Unless you want to go with us and see more of Minecraft. It would be dangerous—there's a lot of problems out there that need fixing."

Watcher gazed at Planter, then shook his head.

"Thanks, but everything I need is here, as long as I'm still welcome."

Planter shook her head, then moved to Watcher and wrapped her arms around him, hugging him tight. "You're such an idiot."

"I think all boys are idiots when it comes to their feelings," Hunter said.

The other girls nodded in agreement.

"Okay, here we go." Gameknight pulled Hunter in tight. "Just remember, everyone: life is an adventure and you need to live it to its fullest, but only if you're true about who you are. You can try to lie to others and be who you aren't, but you can't lie to yourself."

"Wow, that's really profound," Watcher said, impressed. "Did you write that?"

"Ha, tell 'em." Hunter elbowed Gameknight in the ribs.

"No, I didn't write it." He looked embarrassed. "I saw it on a cat poster once."

Hunter laughed, and the rest of the NPCs joined in.

"See you in the future," Gameknight said mysteriously. Then he pressed the bright red stone on the ring and the two were enveloped in a ball of light. When the glow faded, they were gone.

"Watcher . . . you coming down, or are you gonna live up there?" a voice called from below.

Looking over the edge of the Tower, Watcher spotted his dad and sister on the ground, the rest of the villagers gathered around them.

"We'll be down in a minute," he shouted.

"So . . . what do we do now?" Blaster asked, looking around.

"We live." Watcher patted his friend on the shoulder proudly, then glanced at Planter. "We plant crops. We raise animals and bake bread and build homes." He looked at each of his friends. "We just live . . . in peace."

"And don't forget about school," a voice said from the ladder. Everyone turned and found Mapper's head sticking up from the hole in the top of the Tower, his bald head almost glowing in the moonlight. "We have a lot of school work to catch up on." Mapper smiled excitedly. "The zombie warlord interrupted the school year, but now we have lots of time to catch up on all that homework."

The kids all groaned.

"I'm thinking that monster world actually sounds pretty attractive right about now," Blaster said with a grin.

"Thanks for volunteering, Blaster." Mapper climbed up another rung on the ladder. "You'll do the first book report."

Blaster sighed as the others laughed.

Fencer put a comforting arm around him. "It'll be okay . . . I'll help you. Now come on, it's time to get off this tower and go home."

They all filed down the ladder, leaving Watcher and Planter alone atop the Wizard's Tower.

"So . . . are we okay?" Watcher wasn't looking forward to hearing the answer, but he had to know.

"Well, you gave the monsters what they wanted, you saved all those villagers down there, and you got rid of all that magical stuff." She moved closer and kissed him on the cheek.

Instantly, Watcher blushed.

"So we're more than okay." Turning, Planter stepped to the ladder and climbed down. Before disappearing through the hole, she gave Watcher one more beautiful smile, then slid down.

"I guess everything is okay, then." He glanced at the ground, then looked around. "But is anyone gonna help me with all these weapons and armor? Anyone?"

"They're your toys . . . you clean 'em up!" Planter's laugh floated out the hole in the tower.

The sound of her happy voice lightened his heart. Watcher moved to the edge of the tower and looked down, making sure no one was below, then kicked the weapons and armor off the Tower. The Gauntlets of Life, Needle, and the Flail of Regrets all shattered when they hit, as if they were made of glass.

To the east, the sky blushed a colorful, rosy red as the sun peeked its bright, square face above the horizon. Its light painted the landscape with a warm crimson, causing the oak and birch trees to glow, as if they were lit from within. It was as if Minecraft was greeting Watcher with this spectacle to thank him for what he and his friends had done.

"I think today is gonna be a great day," he said, climbing down the ladder to join his friends, "at last."

AUTHOR'S NOTE

My son and I have built every redstone contraption that has appeared in every book I've written—from the massive TNT trap at the end of *Invasion of the Overworld*, to the TNT minecarts and popping TNT traps at the end of *Destruction of the Overworld*, to the TNT launcher in Chapter 27 of *The Wither Invasion*.

This last contraption was so unique, I decided to put a video on Youtube so you could all see it . . . here it is: https://youtu.be/pIrE-CRE2Vg

AVAILABLE NOW FROM MARK CHEVERTON AND SKY PONY PRESS

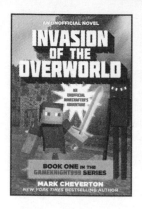  

THE GAMEKNIGHT999 SERIES
The world of Minecraft comes to life in this thrilling adventure!

Gameknight999 loved Minecraft, and above all else, he loved to grief—to intentionally ruin the gaming experience for other users.

But when one of his father's inventions teleports him into the game, Gameknight is forced to live out a real-life adventure inside a digital world. What will happen if he's killed? Will he respawn? Die in real life? Stuck in the game, Gameknight discovers Minecraft's best-kept secret, something not even the game's programmers realize: the creatures within the game are alive! He will have to stay one step ahead of the sharp claws of zombies and pointed fangs of spiders, but he'll also have to learn to make friends and work as a team if he has any chance of surviving the Minecraft war his arrival has started.

With deadly endermen, ghasts, and dragons, this action-packed trilogy introduces the heroic Gameknight999 and has proven to be a runaway publishing smash, showing that the Gameknight999 series is the perfect companion for Minecraft fans of all ages.

Invasion of the Overworld (Book One):
$9.99 paperback • 978-1-63220-711-1

Battle for the Nether (Book Two):
$9.99 paperback • 978-1-63220-712-8

Confronting the Dragon (Book Three):
$9.99 paperback • 978-1-63450-046-3

AVAILABLE NOW FROM MARK CHEVERTON AND SKY PONY PRESS

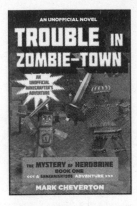

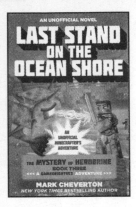

THE MYSTERY OF HEROBRINE SERIES
Gameknight999 must save his friends from an evil virus intent on destroying all of Minecraft!

Gameknight999 was sucked into the world of Minecraft when one of his father's inventions went haywire. Trapped inside the game, the former griefer learned the error of his ways, transforming into a heroic warrior and defeating powerful endermen, ghasts, and dragons to save the world of Minecraft and his NPC friends who live in it.

Gameknight swore he'd never go inside Minecraft again. But that was before Herobrine, a malicious virus infecting the very fabric of the game, threatened to destroy the entire Overworld and escape into the real world. To outsmart an enemy much more powerful than any he's ever faced, the User-that-is-not-a-user will need to go back into the game, where real danger lies around every corner. From zombie villages and jungle temples to a secret hidden at the bottom of a deep ocean, the action-packed adventures of Gameknight999 and his friends (and, now, family) continue in this thrilling follow-up series for Minecraft fans of all ages.

Trouble in Zombie-town (Book One):
$9.99 paperback • 978-1-63450-094-4

The Jungle Temple Oracle (Book Two):
$9.99 paperback • 978-1-63450-096-8

Last Stand on the Ocean Shore (Book Three):
$9.99 paperback • 978-1-63450-098-2

AVAILABLE NOW FROM MARK CHEVERTON AND SKY PONY PRESS

THE BIRTH OF HEROBRINE SERIES
Can Gameknight999 survive a journey one hundred years into Minecraft's past?

A freak thunderstorm strikes just as Gameknight999 is activating his father's Digitizer to reenter Minecraft. Sparks flash across his vision as he is sucked into the game . . . and when the smoke clears he's arrived safely. But it doesn't take long to realize that things in the Overworld are very different.

The User-that-is-not-a-user realizes he's been accidentally sent a hundred years into the past, back to the time of the historic Great Zombie Invasion. None of his friends have even been born yet. But that might be the least of Gameknight999's worries, because traveling back in time also means that the evil virus Herobrine, the scourge of Minecraft, is still alive . . .

AVAILABLE NOW FROM MARK CHEVERTON AND SKY PONY PRESS

THE MYSTERY OF ENTITY303 SERIES
Minecraft mods are covering the tracks of a mysterious new villain!

Gameknight999 reenters Minecraft to find it completely changed, and his old friends acting differently. The changes are not for the better.

Outside of Crafter's village, a strange user named Entity303 is spotted with Weaver, a young NPC Gameknight knows from Minecraft's past. He realizes that Weaver has somehow been kidnapped, and returning him to the correct time is the only way to fix things.

What's worse: Entity303 has created a strange and bizarre modded version of Minecraft, full of unusual creatures and biomes. Racing through the Twilight Forest and MystCraft, and finally into the far reaches of outer space, Gameknight will face his toughest challenge yet in a Minecraft both alien and dangerous.

Terrors of the Forest (Book One):
$9.99 paperback • 978-1-5107-1886-9

Monsters in the Mist (Book Two):
$9.99 paperback • 978-1-5107-1887-6

Mission to the Moon (Book Three):
$9.99 paperback • 978-1-5107-1888-3

AVAILABLE NOW FROM MARK CHEVERTON AND SKY PONY PRESS

THE RISE OF THE WARLORDS SERIES
A brand-new Minecraft fiction series from Mark Cheverton explores the mysterious borders of the Overworld!

The Far Lands is a hidden, mystical area located at the very edge of Minecraft's outer borders, unknown to normal users. There, the life of a young boy named Watcher is suddenly turned upside down when his village is destroyed by a vile warlord.

That single event sets off a chain of unexpected events, as Watcher and a handful of his friends vow to save their friends and bring the warlords responsible to justice. But along the way, they'll uncover a terrifying secret about the monsters in the Far Lands, one that could change Minecraft forever.

Zombies Attack! (Book One):
$9.99 paperback • 978-1-5107-2737-3

Bones of Doom (Book Two):
$9.99 paperback • 978-1-5107-2738-0

Into the Spiders' Lair (Book Three):
$9.99 paperback • 978-1-5107-2739-7

AVAILABLE NOW FROM MARK CHEVERTON AND SKY PONY PRESS

The Wither King
WITHER WAR BOOK ONE
A dangerous wither king threatens the Far Lands!

Life is peaceful and calm in the Far Lands, a mysterious area on the edge of the Overworld in Minecraft. The monster warlords have been destroyed and the NPC villages are flourishing. But an old warning still echoes in the young NPC wizard Watcher's mind: "Krael, the wither king, will bring back his army, as the monster warlocks predicted, and take their revenge on all of the Far Lands."

Watcher is right to be suspicious. His old foe Krael, the King of the Withers and wearer of two of the three Crowns of Skulls, is planning to unleash a vast army of withers imprisoned in the ancient Cave of Slumber. With the help of the Broken Eight—powerful and ancient zombie warriors rescued by the wither king to do his bidding—Krael seeks to release the withers from their slumber and wreak havoc on the Far Lands. And the only thing in his path is a skinny little wizard named Watcher.

$9.99 paperback • 978-1-51073-488-3